Let the Church
Say Amen

ALSO BY ReShonda Tate Billingsley

Let the Church Say Amen
My Brother's Keeper
Four Degrees of Heat
(with Brenda L. Thomas, Crystal Lacey Winslow
& Rochelle Alers)

Published by Pocket Books

Let the Church
Say Amen

~

ReShonda Tate Billingsley

POCKET BOOKS

New York London Toronto Sydney New Delhi

POCKET BOOKS, a Division of Simon & Schuster, Inc.
1230 Avenue of the Americas, New York, NY 10020

Copyright © 2004 by ReShonda Tate Billingsley

Originally published as a trade paperback in 2004 by Pocket Books

ISBN 978-1-4767-0887-4
ISBN 978-1-4165-8556-5 (ebook)

This Pocket Books paperback printing September 2012

POCKET and colophon are registered trademarks of Simon & Schuster, Inc.

Cover design by Krisitne V. Mills
Cover photograph by Michel Legrou

Manufactured in the United States of America

For information regarding special discounts for bulk purchases, please contact Simon & Schuster Special Sales at 1-800-456-6798 or business@simonandschuster.com

To Morgan
(my inspiration to keep writing)

ACKNOWLEDGMENTS

I am so blessed to be able to utilize my passion—writing. But I wouldn't be where I am today without the love and support of so many wonderful people.

First and foremost, my husband, Miron, who not only pushes me to pursue my dreams but who has never wavered in his support of those dreams. Thank you and I'm grateful to have you, Morgan, and Mya in my life.

To my mother, Nancy Blacknell, who has shared my joy and sorrow as I ventured into this publishing world. And don't worry—people know this is fiction . . . and not our family.

To my little sister, soror, and friend, Tanisha Tate—words cannot even begin to express how grateful I am to you for being everything from my personal assistant to my proofreader. Thank you for pushing my books like they were your own.

Of course, as always, much love to my sorors who cheered me on, supported me every step of the way, and spread the word to all of their friends and family: Jaimi Canady, Kim

Patterson-Wright, Raquelle Wooten, Clemelia Humphrey Richardson, Kristi King, Trina McReynolds, Sabrina McReynolds, Beverly Davis, Leslie Mouton, Stephanie Jenkins, and all the rest of the lovely ladies of Delta Xi.

Pat Tucker Wilson, my new literary/writing/reporting buddy. I can count on you to keep it real. Thanks for being such a great friend and supporting me in every way. See you on the bestsellers list!

Much love to the ministers who let me pick their brains: Rev. Mark Edwards (Zion Baptist Church) and A. Byron Coleman (Fifth Street Baptist Church). Also thanks to Rev. Robert Childress (Covenant Glenn United Methodist Church) and Kirby Jon Caldwell (Windsor Village United Methodist Church), who provided inspiration for my story without even knowing they were doing it.

I have to give much love to the best coworkers in the world at KRIV-TV, Fox 26 News, especially my own boss/author Kathy Williams (who has an awesome children's book; check it out at daddybooks.com); Linda Drummond; Misty Starks; Damali Keith; José Grinan; Isiah Carey; Joe McGinty; Bernadette Brown; Lashauna Sewell; LaQuanta Dixon; Erin Anthony; Sinan Sadar; Keith Rollins; Stan Kowalski; Lisa Whitlock; John Donnelly; Christina Garza; and Michelle Casas. (I know I didn't name everyone, but please don't hold it against me, I only have so much space).

Thanks to all the photogs at KRIV who understood that I just wanted to write and not carry on conversations as we traveled back and forth to our stories: Rodney Pearson, Torrey Walker, Matt Matejka, Xavier Kirts, David Lanier, Ray Williams, Dick Hogg, Chris Desmond, Todd Smith, and Harry Hulsey.

Thanks also to: Waleed Salim, Della Jones, Tulisa Hicks, Brenda Goodwin, Birdell Smith, Lawanda (LaSha) Smith, Sonny Messiah, Lucille Pervis, Stephanie Banks Packer, Russell Pierce, Keisha Tate, the Houston Association of Black Journalists (under the direction of our fabulously supportive president, Anthony Ogbo), and the men of Omega Psi Phi Fraternity, Inc., who continue to buy my books even though they'll probably never read them (yeah, Joe and Gerald, I'm talking about you).

And I would be remiss if I wrapped this up without giving major thanks to the bookstores, booksellers, and book clubs who have shown me so much love. They include, but definitely are not limited to: Tee C. Royal (RAWSISTAZ), Yasmin Coleman (APOOO), Angie Pickett Henderson (Readincolor), The Shrine of the Black Madonna (Houston), Pyramid Books (Little Rock), and Black Images (Dallas). There are far too many book clubs to name, but I have to give a special shoutout to the members of the Brentwood Baptist Church Book Club; you ladies set the standard for how a lively, entertaining, and spirited book club meeting should go.

Finally, I have to thank you, the readers, who continue to support my work, send words of encouragement, and let me know what you liked (and in some cases didn't like). You are the reason I do what I do.

Hope you all enjoy this one as much as I enjoyed writing it. Be blessed.

1

THE CHOIR WAS cutting up.

Reverend Simon Jackson enthusiastically clapped as they sang "Stomp" by Kirk Franklin.

Loretta Jackson beamed as she watched her husband swing jubilantly to the music. She knew Simon wasn't too keen on these newfound gospel hip-hoppers, as he called them, but the choir had the church on its feet. Even he had to admit they sounded good.

The choir began winding down and Simon stood and approached the podium. He was radiating with pride as he looked out at his members. And as she did every Sunday just before his sermon, Loretta gave him a reassuring smile. It made her happy to see her husband doing what he loved best, being pastor of Zion Hill, one of the best churches in Houston, as he always proclaimed.

"Let the church say amen!" Simon yelled.

"Amen!" the congregation replied in unison.

"Let's give our outstanding choir another round of applause because they sure spread God's message today."

Simon led the applause as the choir members settled in their seats. Loretta was sitting in her usual front row seat. Good music always rejuvenated Simon, so she knew they were in for a rousing sermon.

Loretta opened her Bible as she glanced around. She sighed deeply because Rachel hadn't yet made it to church and she knew Simon would take notice.

"Now, if you will, turn your Bibles to Proverbs twenty-eight, thirteen. I know everyone has their Bible, right?" Simon sang.

Several people chuckled.

"Of course we do, Pastor," an elderly woman named Ida Hicks shouted. Simon nodded at Sister Hicks, who was sitting in the front pew as well. Sister Hicks was decked out from head to toe in white, from her huge hat that looked like wings coming off the side of her head to her white stockings and scuffed-up white pumps.

Loretta tried to stifle a smile, because Simon often complained about Sister Hicks, saying she was like the student in class who always had the answer to everything. Loretta had to admit Sister Hicks drove everyone at the church crazy, but she was the original pastor's widow, so people still gave her respect.

"Well, wonderful. Has everyone found the verse?" Simon said as his gaze made its way to the back of the church. Loretta gently turned to see what he was looking at. She shook her head. Their nineteen-year-old daughter, Rachel, was trying to sneak in late—again. That meant there would be a big argument right before Sunday dinner. Simon was just about fed up with Rachel. She'd stay out partying all Saturday night, and then couldn't drag herself out of bed to make it to church on

Sunday morning. Simon always complained that if it weren't for Loretta keeping Rachel's two kids every weekend, his grandchildren probably wouldn't make it to church, either.

Loretta tried not to let Rachel's entrance sour her mood, but she couldn't help but exhale in frustration. Not only was Rachel late, but she had the audacity to come into church with sunglasses on. Simon was going to blow a gasket. Not that it would do any good. Even though Rachel was raised in the church, getting her there before the benediction was almost impossible.

Loretta snapped back to the sermon, which Simon had begun as he tried to mask the scowl on his face. "All right, I want to talk about how what's done in the dark will come to light."

"I know that's right! You preach, Pastor!" Sister Hicks exclaimed.

Simon looked at Sister Hicks and forced a smile. Loretta knew exactly what her husband was thinking. He wanted Sister Hicks to shut up and let him preach. They went through this same routine every Sunday. Loretta had thought Simon would have been used to it by now, but he still complained about it after every service.

"As I was saying, many of us do things we think nobody else knows about. But God knows!" Simon bellowed.

Loretta hoped Rachel was listening, because Lord knew she had done more than her share of dirty deeds. Simon near 'bout had a heart attack when Rachel turned up pregnant at fifteen. Then she went out and had another child three years later. Simon would barely speak to her the entire time she was pregnant. Not only was he thoroughly embarrassed, but he was extremely disappointed in their daughter. But more than anything, Loretta knew Simon was hurt by his daughter's actions, feeling that he had failed her. Although that's something he'd never, ever admit.

Loretta tried to get thoughts of her family drama out of her mind and focus all her attention on her husband. He was getting worked up now; beads of sweat were trickling across his brow. She admired his strong physique. For fifty-five years old, he was stunningly handsome with a commanding presence, like he belonged in that pulpit, born to lead people down the path of righteousness.

Simon continued with his sermon, urging his congregation to lead meaningful and fulfilling Christian lives. For twenty-five minutes he continued to speak the word, putting emphasis where needed, shouting when the urge came over him and delivering a rousing sermon. Loretta could always tell how well he preached by the number of people who got the spirit during his sermon. Usually, it was only ten or fifteen people, not counting Sister Hicks, who always got the Holy Ghost every Sunday. (In private Simon had once said that he thought it was all an act, but Loretta had told him, who was he to judge.)

As the organist began playing, Simon extended his arms as if opening the doors of the church, and invited people to join him near the pulpit. He smiled down at Loretta again. She gave him the standard "you did good" nod as she began swaying to the sounds of the music.

Loretta could feel the powerful love of her husband as he glanced around the room, his gaze always coming back to her. Simon always called her the saving grace in his family because she helped him keep it all together when it seemed like he just couldn't take any more. And in between the problems with their oldest son, David, and the drama surrounding Rachel, it seemed Loretta was having to do a lot more saving these days.

But she didn't complain. She loved her husband and her kids and would do anything for them.

So far, no one had made their way to the front of the church.

"The doors of the church are still open. Don't be afraid. Come now. Let the Lord be your guide," Simon said.

Sometimes it took a while for anyone to come up, so Simon would usually keep his arms outstretched as the music continued to play.

Loretta stole another look at Rachel. *I know she is not asleep!* But that wasn't true. She quickly turned her attention back to Simon, hoping he wouldn't notice. Of course as luck would have it, he noticed it about the same time he was wrapping things up.

Simon took a deep breath, trying not to let his disgust show to the entire congregation, but Loretta could see it clear as day. Although she would never give up on any of her kids, Loretta knew Simon was about ready to write Rachel off, just as he'd done David. Loretta sighed. If only they could hold on two more weeks. That's when Jonathan, the one child who had made Simon proud, would return home. Simon was already so excited, it's all he'd talked about the last month. Simon was always a little more tolerant of Rachel and David whenever Jonathan was around. Loretta hated how Simon differentiated between the kids. But she knew his relationship with Rachel and David was something he'd have to work through in his own due time. But that didn't mean she'd stop trying to pull her family back together. Heck, she *couldn't* stop trying even if she wanted to. She believed with all her heart that she'd been blessed with a wonderful family, despite their shortcomings and she'd do whatever it took to hold them together.

2

"DADDY, PLEASE DON'T START. My head hurts."

Rachel rubbed her temples and plopped down in a chair at the table nestled in the bay area of her parents' large kitchen.

"You're just shameful!" Simon was already sitting there reading the newspaper and waiting for Loretta to finish cooking dinner. He glanced up and glared at his daughter.

"I got there in time enough to hear your sermon. Dang, it ain't like I ain't heard it all before," Rachel snapped.

Simon threw down his paper. "Lord have mercy! Not only do I have a jezebel for a daughter, but she's a disrespectful, smart-talking jezebel at that."

Simon turned to his wife, who was removing a pan of macaroni and cheese from the oven. "Do you hear how your ungrateful daughter is talking to me?"

Loretta didn't look up from what she was doing. This, too, was a routine argument. Simon demanding respect and Rachel unwilling to give it to him. Rachel knew her mother would've rather stayed out of it, but she also knew Simon expected her mom to back him up.

"Honey, don't talk to your father that way. He is the head of this household and you will treat him with reverence," Loretta said as she cut up more onions for the roast, which was simmering in the oven.

Rachel cut her eyes at her mother. Sometimes she made Rachel want to throw up. For nineteen years, Rachel had watched her tend to her father's every whim. She couldn't recall them ever really arguing. Her mother was the most passive woman she knew, a trait Rachel definitely didn't inherit. She shook her head at her mother. If she didn't love her so much, she'd probably hate her for the horrible example she was setting for women everywhere.

"Did you hear your mother? Revere me! That means don't show up in my church at twelve twenty when service starts at eleven." Simon shook his finger at his daughter.

"You only want me there for appearances anyway," Rachel mumbled under her breath.

Simon pushed his chair back from the table. "What did you say? Don't think you're too old for me to smack you upside your head."

Loretta finally broke from her cooking. "Honey, don't get yourself worked up." She walked over and kissed Simon on the head and shot Rachel a chastising look. She then went back to cooking. Simon glared at his daughter.

"Okay. Okay. I'm sorry. I got hung up," Rachel said.

"Hung over is more like it. You were out drinking, weren't you? I should have you arrested for underage drinking." Simon stood up from the table.

"Daddy, I told you a million times, I don't drink."

"Yeah, and I'm the pope."

As Simon walked away from the table, his grandchildren raced into the kitchen, followed by Loretta's black Yorkshire terrier, Brandy. A smile crossed Simon's face and he ruffled his grandson's hair. He looked back at his daughter and said, "You think about what kind of example you're setting for these kids." He turned toward his wife. "I'm going to lie down until dinner is ready. Can you get the dog out of the kitchen, please?"

Loretta smiled and nodded. Simon threw his daughter one last scornful look, then headed out of the kitchen.

Rachel rolled her eyes, but didn't interject as he left.

"Mama, we're hungry," four-year-old Jordan said to Rachel.

"Go tell your grandma."

Rachel left for the den in the back of the house, where she sank into her father's plush recliner. She had partied all night long and her head was pounding. She wasn't in the mood for a bunch of noise from her children; she had to figure out who that tramp was Bobby was talking to last night. On her way home from partying, she had driven by his apartment and saw him standing outside talking to some woman. Although she tried, she couldn't tell who the woman was.

Bobby was Jordan's father, but not Nia's, Rachel's seventeen-month-old daughter. Rachel had gotten pregnant with her while Bobby was overseas with the army. Still, Bobby was the love of Rachel's life; she was certain of their destiny together. She had tried to plot a way to get to Saudi Arabia to have sex with Bobby and pass the baby off as his. That didn't happen and when Bobby came home to find her seven months pregnant, he was crushed. It didn't help that Nia's father was Bobby's best friend, Tony. Bobby had said he wanted to marry her. Now, he didn't want to have anything to do with her.

Rachel, however, was not willing to let go of Bobby, and no two-bit tramp was going to keep her from him.

Rachel contemplated getting up to go turn off the light so she could really relax, but she was too comfortable and decided she was so tired, a little light wouldn't matter.

She grabbed the remote, leaned back and flipped on the television. She couldn't believe her parents still didn't have cable. Her father claimed it was just another avenue for the devil to do his work, so he refused to get it.

Although she could barely afford the rent on her two-bedroom apartment, she was glad to be out of her parents' house. She had gone crazy while she lived here. Her dad's strict rules made her life miserable. Then they didn't have a computer or cable and she had to be off the telephone by nine.

Rachel was grateful when she moved out. Life was so much better. Granted, she still didn't have a computer or cable, she simply couldn't afford it. But overall, she wouldn't trade her freedom for the world.

Rachel thought about how tight things were for her financially. It probably would've been best for her to stay with her parents, but she'd rather struggle all day and night than go through that again. She really should have gone after Bobby for child support, that would've eased some of her financial woes. But she had been reluctant to do that, so sure they would get back together. Both he and Tony, who had moved to Chicago, were giving her money, but just enough to buy groceries and get her hair done every week.

Rachel had just begun to doze off when she heard the patio door slide open behind her.

Rachel turned as her oldest brother eased in.

"David, what are you doing?" She noticed that his hair was disheveled and his eyes were bloodshot.

"Shhhh . . . I'm invisible."

Rachel shook her head and kicked back in the recliner,

shifting to get comfortable. "You're a crackhead, that's what you are." She couldn't tell if he was high or not. It seemed like he stayed high, despite three trips to rehab. She didn't feel like being bothered with him anyway, so she just closed her eyes again, trying to get back to sleep. A crashing sound and her mother's scream made her jump up.

Rachel raced into the kitchen and saw that her mother had dropped a plate on the floor.

"David! Stop sneaking around here," Loretta said. "You 'bout scared me to death."

"I was just messing with you, Ma." David kept rubbing his arm as he talked. "Hey, sweet pea." He walked over to Nia, who was sitting on the floor, and kissed her on the cheek. She gurgled with laughter. "And hey to you, little man," he added, playfully punching Jordan in the head. "You got a job yet?"

Jordan, who was coloring a picture at the kitchen table, looked up, wide-eyed and innocent. "I'm too little to have a job."

"No, you ain't. I hear they're hiring down at the bus station. You could haul luggage."

"Unh-unh," Jordan responded.

"You need to take your own self down to the bus station and get a job," Rachel said.

After college David worked off and on for the state until he was injured again while trying to hang lights for a Christmas function. He'd milked the state for everything he could, and was still collecting disability.

David ignored his sister and turned back to his mother, who was picking up the broken pieces from the floor. "Where's Dad?"

"Your father is asleep."

"Good, 'cuz I didn't come to see him." David leaned down

and kissed his mother. "I came to see you. How are you doing?"

"I'm fine." She stood up, walked over, and dumped the broken pieces in the trash.

David looked nervously around. "Well, look here, Ma, I need to borrow some money. It's just a loan."

Rachel leaned up against the wall and crossed her arms. "People pay back loans. That would be impossible for you to do seeing as how you don't have a job!"

David shot his sister an angry look. "Shut up! Just 'cuz you got a little pissant job at the mall, you think you know everything."

He turned back to his mother. "For real, Ma, I'm enrolling in some classes down at the community college and I need some help paying my tuition. I have to at least put a deposit down for them to hold my classes."

Rachel laughed. "You must think she's stupid."

"I said, shut up. Ain't nobody talking to you."

Rachel looked at her brother with disgust. His once firm skin sagged from his bones. His smooth, milk-chocolate complexion was now covered with dark splotches. Drugs had sucked any semblance of beauty out of him.

"Mama, you know he ain't goin' do nothing but use the money to get high."

Loretta looked skeptically at David. "I know you ain't back messing around with those drugs."

"Ma, don't listen to her. I told you I don't mess with that stuff anymore. I'm clean. You can call my parole officer. He'll tell you."

Rachel curled up her lips at her brother's bold-faced lie. He'd done three years in prison for possession of crack cocaine. You would think after that, he would've gone straight.

Loretta looked at her son like she was trying to gauge whether he was being truthful. "I'm going to trust you on this, David, simply because I want you to know I have faith in you." She picked up her purse from the kitchen counter.

"Cross my heart and hope to die." David ran his finger in a T across his chest.

Rachel couldn't tell if her mother really believed that story or if she was just trying to lay a guilt trip on her brother.

Loretta rifled through her purse, then pulled out some money. "Okay, baby. Here's a hundred dollars. It's all the cash I have. You go pay for your classes. I'm proud of you. I know you have it in you to get your life together."

David kissed his mother again. He grabbed the hundred-dollar bill and stuffed it in his pocket. "Thank you, thank you, thank you!"

"Ughhhh!" Rachel turned and stormed out of the kitchen, back to the den. Her brother had been doing drugs since a torn ACL ended his promising NFL career. He hadn't gotten past his second year of college before he became hooked on heroin. Now, he was doing either crack or some kind of cocaine. Rachel didn't know which, but they were all the same to her. He had never stayed clean for long after his rehab stays. Their mother was too blind to see that.

"Bye, Ma," David called out as he walked back into the den and toward the patio door. "And, oh yeah, don't tell Daddy. I want to surprise him about me going back to school."

Loretta followed David out of the kitchen to the patio door. "Now, David, you know I don't like keeping things from your father. As head of household he deserves to know these things."

Rachel wanted to slap her mother. *Enough with this head of household crap.* Her mother went way too far with that. Rachel couldn't understand it. It's not like her mother was some indigent housewife who didn't have a dime to her name or any skills. On the contrary, she was a college graduate who had been teaching second grade for over twenty-five years. She made a decent salary and was set to retire next year, so it wasn't like she couldn't make it on her own if she left Simon. For Loretta, however, leaving was never an option.

Rachel watched as her brother snuggled up to their mother like he was a ten year old.

"But, Mama, God says surprises are good."

"Where does God say that?"

"I don't know. First Leviticus, seventh verse or something. I don't know. Just please, do me this one favor?"

Loretta hesitated. "Okay, baby, I won't say anything. I'll let you tell him. He's going to be so excited about you going back to school. I knew you would make us proud."

David kissed his mother one last time and walked out the door. Loretta stopped him. "David?"

"Yeah, Ma?"

"I trust you, okay?"

Rachel could have sworn she saw a glimmer of guilt flicker across her brother's face, but it passed so quickly she couldn't be sure.

Rachel scrunched up her nose, disgusted. This whole scene was absolutely sickening. How could her mother be so spineless when it came to Simon and so dumb when it came to David?

Rachel pondered it briefly as she dropped back in the recliner and made herself comfortable enough to sleep again.

3

SIMON GRINNED WIDELY at the newspaper article. His church was being featured for a new children's center they had just established in the neighborhood.

This was the twenty-sixth time in fourteen years Zion Hill had been profiled in the local newspapers. Each article hung in a frame around the conference room, his office, and the fellowship hall. Simon was extremely proud of his role in the church's growth. Zion Hill had less than fifty members when he first became pastor. Now, there were over nine hundred. The church could've had more, but it couldn't compete with the new mega, ten-thousand-member churches springing up all over town. Simon wasn't quite sure he wanted Zion Hill to become that large. He enjoyed knowing the faces of those sitting in the pews to hear his sermons.

Simon had been an associate pastor at another church before moving to Zion Hill. He was thrilled about getting his own church, and determined to make it a success. He was fulfilling a lifelong dream. As a child, he used to pretend he was preaching before a congregation. He had always dreamt of the day when he'd have a real, live congregation—one that could make its mark on the community.

Zion Hill was his baby. He had literally given birth to it and watched it grow. Now, he devoted every waking moment to ensuring its success. His children had often complained about all the time he put into the church, but Simon knew his devotion to Zion Hill was the Lord's will, and prayed that his children would understand.

"Knock, knock." Delilah Alexander, the church secretary, poked her head into Simon's office. "Pastor Jackson, are you busy?"

Simon smiled. Delilah was a stunningly voluptuous woman who left many a man swooning. Simon, however, was enamored with her because of her efficiency. He had been through several secretaries over the years and Delilah was by far the best. The only problem he had was that she seemed smitten with him and was forever making innuendos. Flirting was a line Simon never, ever crossed. Loretta was a good woman and he had been faithful to her since the day they said "I do" thirty-four years ago.

"Yes, Delilah, what can I do for you?"

Delilah shifted nervously. "I was wondering if we could talk?"

"Sure, come on in and have a seat."

Simon pointed to a chair in front of his desk. Delilah sat down and seductively crossed her legs.

Simon tried to contain his smile. If he had a dollar for every time some woman came on to him, he'd be a rich man.

He knew part of it was physical. Women were always telling him how handsome he was. At six feet two inches, he was still in great shape. His short, cropped Afro and beard were peppered with gray. Loretta was always telling him that his beard was the icing on the cake of his mocha complexion.

He also knew a lot of women were intrigued by his faithfulness. Some wondered what he saw in Loretta. She was plain but had a gentle look about her that he found absolutely intriguing. She was a little on the heavy side and very quiet. As one woman had so boldly told him once, "She's not the type of woman I'd expect to see you with." However, he was in love with his wife. He had met Loretta at Langston University in Oklahoma. They were both out-of-state students attending on academic scholarships. Loretta was from a small town in Arkansas and Simon was from Texas. They began dating at the end of their freshman year and stayed together until they married senior year. After graduation, they returned to Simon's hometown of Houston, where he began his career in the church.

Loretta was a good, God-fearing wife, and Simon was a good, God-fearing man. He took his vows seriously. He knew a number of preachers who slept around but he promised he would never be one of them, no matter how many women threw themselves at him. He almost slipped up with a woman he met at a Baptist conference a few years after he first married. In fact, he had planned to meet the woman the last evening of the conference. That was the same day Loretta told him she was pregnant with their first child. Simon took that as a sign from the Lord. He called the woman, cancelled, apologized, and had never come close to cheating again.

"Yes, Sister Alexander, what can I do for you?"

"It's my boyfriend. May I?" Delilah motioned toward the Kleenex on his desk. Simon nodded and she pulled two tissues out the box and started dabbing at her eyes. "I thought we were going to get married, but I just found out he's cheating on me. I went to Radio Shack, bought one of those devices that let you record incoming calls. I heard him on the phone talking to this woman I thought was my friend. They were making plans to meet again. It seems this has been going on for nearly a year now." Delilah started to cry softly. Simon knew this was the point when he should get up and hug her, but something told him that's what Delilah was counting on. She leaned forward, exposing her cleavage. "Why can't everybody be like you, Pastor?"

Simon sat up straight in his seat. He wanted to make sure he put on his serious face so that Delilah wouldn't get any ideas. "I'm sorry you're hurting, Delilah. I know it's hard, but you need to tell yourself you deserve better anyway. This was God's way of showing you that."

Delilah sniffed and lowered her eyes. "Pastor . . . I know you're a married man . . ."

Simon held up his hand and cut her off. "And *I* know *you* know how much I honor my wife and respect my vows." Simon always felt the need to reiterate that to the women in the church.

Delilah didn't look up. "I know you honor your wife. It's just . . . well . . . I just . . . hope one day I can find a man who feels the same way about me."

"Be patient. God has your soul mate out there. He's just waiting for you to get *yourself* ready before he brings him to you."

"You think so?" Delilah sniffed.

"I know so." Simon smiled. "Now, about this fool boyfriend of yours. What's his name?"

"Roderick."

"Roderick. Well, do you want me to get some of my boys to rough him up?" Simon joked.

Delilah laughed and dabbed the rest of the tears from her face. "You are too funny, Pastor."

Simon cracked his knuckles. "You sure? You just say the words. I ain't always been a Christian."

Delilah got up; the tears were finally drying up. "I'm sure." She looked at Simon with a smile. "Can I hug you?"

Simon felt like he had gotten his point across so he figured there'd be no harm in hugging her. "Of course." He got up and walked around his desk. Delilah took him in her arms and squeezed him tightly. She acted like she never wanted to let him go.

"Funny and faithful," she whispered.

Simon pulled back. "What did you say?"

"I said thank you. Thank you for restoring my faith in men."

Simon's expression became serious. "Don't put your faith in men, Delilah. Put your faith in God and everything else will work out."

Delilah hugged him again, then turned to walk out of the office.

"Oh, and Delilah?"

"Yes," she replied, turning back around.

"Stay away from Radio Shack. When you go looking for trouble, nine times out of ten, you'll find it." Simon smiled.

"Duly noted," Delilah replied, before turning and walking back to her desk.

Simon breathed a sigh of relief. He loved talking with people and helping them work out their problems. If he hadn't pursued the ministry, he probably would've become a full-time counselor. He was pretty good at it, too. Except when it came to Rachel and David. Jonathan listened to Simon's advice, but those other two? No amount of counseling in the world would get through to them.

Simon quickly shook off thoughts of his children; they just got his blood pressure up. He returned to his desk to do what he liked best—reading about the success of his church.

4

"LORETTA!" SIMON YELLED. "The lawn man is here. Don't you have some cash on you so I can pay him?"

Simon stood at the front door, eager to get back to writing his sermon for next Sunday. When he was on a roll, he hated to be interrupted.

Loretta walked into the living room. "Did you say something, honey?"

"Yeah, can you pay the lawn man? We owe him for this week and last week."

Loretta nervously rubbed her hands on her apron.

"Woman, you done gone deaf? Can you pay the man? I just gave you a hundred dollars yesterday."

Thinking that his wife would handle the situation, Simon turned to make his way back to his desk. He noticed, however, that she hadn't moved.

"Loretta? Oh, forget it; where's your purse? I'll get the money myself."

Simon stormed into the kitchen, where he spotted her

purse lying on the counter next to the phone. Loretta followed him into the room and stopped him from picking it up.

"It's not there," she said quietly.

Simon turned toward her. "What?"

Loretta cast her eyes down. "It's not there."

"What do you mean, it's not there? Where is it?" Simon stared at his wife, waiting for an answer. "Loretta, where's the money?"

Loretta hesitated, then quickly spoke. "I gave it to David." She spun around and scuttled out of the kitchen.

"You did what?" Simon shouted after her. He followed her back into the living room. "I know you didn't say what I just thought you said."

Loretta busied herself with arranging the magazines on the coffee table. "David is going back to school to take some classes and he needed money for tuition. He wanted to surprise you and tell you himself." She didn't look up as she spoke.

Simon looked at his wife in amazement. They had had this conversation countless times. David was not to get a dime from them. After he stole forty dollars from the church offering, Simon had all but written him off. That had to be the most embarrassing moment of his whole career.

"Excuse me, Reverend Jackson, maybe I should come back tomorrow." The lawn man's voice snapped Simon out of his daze.

"Uh, yeah, Juan. I'm sorry. Can I write you a check?"

Juan hesitated before answering. "Actually, Reverend Jackson, I'll just come back tomorrow for the cash. I haven't opened up a checking account yet and it's just easier if I get cash."

Simon nodded. "Well, stop by tomorrow after one, okay?"

"Yes, sir, after one. See you then."

Simon watched as Juan made his way down the steps of their front porch. He stood at the door trying to gather his composure. He and Loretta seldom fought. She was a good, obedient wife. Except when it came to the kids. That's the only time they ever argued. No matter what any of them did, they were still angels in her eyes. Rachel came home with not one, but two babies, and Loretta still treated her like a little girl. And David. He disgraced them at the church, stole from relatives, and had been to jail. But still, it was like she couldn't see it. In all his years on this earth, Simon had never felt compelled to strike a woman. But at that very moment, he felt like knocking some sense into his wife's head.

Simon inhaled slowly, trying to dissolve his anger. "Loretta, you were wrong. We agreed we weren't going to give that boy anything else . . ."

"But—"

"Anything!" Simon stomped his foot as he spun around to face his wife. "I'm going to get my money back, although I'm sure he probably done smoked it up or shot it up by now."

Simon left Loretta standing in the living room as he walked down the hall and into the den to get his shoes. The family pictures adorning the hallway reminded him of happier times, back when his children were still small and causing him little grief.

Simon glanced around the immaculate den. Loretta had done wonders decorating their home. Several full-grown ivies sat in plant holders across the den. The burgundy curtains matched the sofa, loveseat, and recliner that she had picked out all by herself. African art hung from each wall, just enough to add a touch of class and not overdo it.

A great homemaker. A wonderful wife. And a mother who couldn't see the forest for the trees when it came to her children.

Simon spotted his shoes sitting neatly in a corner. He snatched them up, slipped them on, then made his way back to the living room. Loretta was standing quietly by the window. She turned when she heard Simon enter. Her eyes looked apologetic.

Simon couldn't bear to look at her right now. She must've sensed his anger because she didn't say a word as he grabbed his car keys and headed out the front door.

Simon grumbled to himself the entire drive to his son's run-down apartment. David was staying with some woman who lived in public housing near one of the local universities. Simon had been there only once before, when he was trying to retrieve his sister-in-law's TV that David had stolen. Of course, it was gone by the time Simon arrived, much like he figured this money would be. But Simon still had to go. He had to give David a piece of his mind about using Loretta.

Simon navigated his 1993 burgundy Mark VII into the dilapidated housing area. Trash was scattered throughout the complex. Boards covered many of the apartment windows, and graffiti was scrawled across almost every building. Children were playing among broken beer bottles and God only knows what else. Being there saddened him very much. Not because of David, but because hard-working families had no choice but to live there.

David had a choice. He could've made something of himself. So what if he couldn't be a professional football player? He was still good enough to coach high school somewhere. He was a standout player in high school, an All-American. Any of the high schools in town would've been proud to have him. But no, after his injury, he decided to drop out of college and turn to drugs.

Drugs were the worst thing that ever happened to their community. It had devastated Simon to watch his oldest son spiral downhill. Every time David shot up, or smoked something, he lost a piece of himself. David had never been the model son, like Jonathan, but Simon had hoped he would make something of himself. That was a dream Simon had long ago given up.

Simon looked around for building seven. If he remembered correctly, the woman, whose name he didn't even know, lived in apartment 709. He eventually found it, swung into an empty parking space, and threw the car in park.

Simon noticed three men hanging outside the building eyeing his car. He shot them a stern look. Any other time he probably would've stopped and tried to spread the word of God to them, but today he was on a mission.

Rap music blared from the other side of the door. That devil, gangsta music didn't do anything but add to society's problems, Simon thought. He banged on the door. It took several minutes before a red-eyed David opened it.

Simon's mouth fell open. David was shirtless. A pair of baggy jean shorts hung from his thin frame, exposing his navy blue underwear. There were dark spots all over his arms and his face looked hollow and empty.

"Dad. What's up?" David grinned widely, his eyes still half closed.

Simon felt a twinge of sorrow for his son. It quickly waned, however, when he peered inside and noticed the syringe lying on the coffee table.

"So is this how you prepare for your classes?"

Simon pushed his way past his son and into the apartment. The smell of incense clogged his nose. A woman was sitting on the tattered sofa watching *Jerry Springer.* Her stringy hair was matted to her head. She, too, was frail, with dazed eyes. She looked up as Simon barged in.

"What's up, Pops?" She giggled before turning back to her program. It was obvious she was just as high as David.

"Dang, Mama told you about me going back to school?" David shut the door. "I told her I wanted to tell you." He continued grinning. Simon felt himself getting sick as he looked at his son's brown teeth.

"Boy, don't you lie to me. You might fool your mama with that nonsense, but I know you ain't in nobody's school!"

"See, there you go again, not having any faith in me." David laughed as he plopped down on the sofa next to the woman. "And why you being so rude? Tawny here spoke to you and you just ignored her."

Simon looked at the woman who was staring at the TV, but not actually watching. "David, I didn't come here to engage in conversation with you or your lady friend. I told you a hundred times, you are not to ask me or your mother for one brown penny."

"But I needed the money. Don't you want me to finish school so I can be a big hotshot like Jonathan?" David leaned back, crossed his ankles, and lifted his legs up on the coffee table.

"David, I want a lot of things for you. But as I've told you before, I've washed my hands of you and turned you over to the Lord."

"Oh, yeah, that's right. I keep forgetting. The Lord is goin' come down here and turn me around. You hear that, Tawny?" He nudged her. She tried to lift her head away from the TV, but it seemed like it was too huge an effort. She finally just muttered something and turned her focus back to the screen.

"The Lord is my savior!" David jumped up and started dancing around the living room like he had the Holy Ghost, as he sang, "My rock, my rock, my sword and shield. He's my wheel in the middle of the field. I know he'll never, ever let me down!"

"Stop it! Stop it right now!" Simon hissed. "Don't you dare mock the Lord in my presence!"

David stopped dancing, but the smile never left his face. He leaned in toward his father. "Sorry, good reverend. Look here. Tell your God that I don't need nothing from Him but a couple of dollars in my pocket so I can take care of myself. I don't need no saving or nothing else."

Simon glared at his son. He wondered what had he done wrong in his life to deserve a child like this. He had always tried to live a good, clean Christian life. Even as a young man, he was honest, respectful, barely ever told a lie. So why was he being punished this way?

It must be a test, Simon finally deduced. *God is testing me and my strength.* Simon composed himself. "Where is the money your mother gave you?"

David pointed toward Tawny. "Sorry, Dad, looks like school's gonna have to wait another semester. Tawny here has a bad little habit and she just took my money to feed it. Don't worry, I done already straightened her out and she says it won't happen again." He wobbled as he stood there, trying to fake an apologetic look.

Simon felt like it would be useless to argue. David was hard to talk to when he wasn't high. Anything Simon said now would be in vain. He leaned in toward his son. "You listen to me and you listen good! You stay away from my house. You stay away from Loretta, from all of us. The devil is working through you and there is no place for you in our lives. When you have cleaned yourself up and turned your life over to God, then and only then should you darken our doorstep again!"

Simon turned and stomped out of the apartment. He

heard David mutter, but he didn't even try to make out what he said.

Simon took a deep breath as he eased back into the car. He started it up, but closed his eyes before backing out. "Lord, I'm leaning on you like never before," he prayed. "Save my son. Please, Lord, save my son."

5

RACHEL SLAMMED the phone down. She had been calling Bobby every ten minutes for the last three hours and he still wasn't answering. It was three o'clock in the morning. *All the clubs close at two, so where else could he be?*

Rachel decided to call her best friend, Twyla. Twyla's boyfriend was Bobby's cousin. Maybe he knew where Bobby was.

She dialed Twyla's number. A sleepy female voice answered after the third ring. "Yeah?"

"Twyla, it's Rachel. Are you asleep?"

"What else would I be doing at four in the morning in the middle of the week?" Twyla grumbled.

"It's only three and Thursday isn't the middle of the week. Look, is James there with you?"

"Rachel, it's late. Call me tomorrow."

"Twyla!" Rachel screamed. "This is important! Is James there?"

Twyla's voice perked up. "Yeah, girl. Calm down. What's wrong?"

"I need to know where Bobby is!" Rachel was getting frantic. The thought of Bobby with another woman was driving her to the brink of insanity. Bobby meant everything in the world to her and even though he hadn't given her the time of day for the last year, she knew that eventually her love would prevail.

"Rachel, how many times have I told you, leave that man alone. He already told you he don't want you," Twyla snapped.

"Look, I didn't ask for your advice, okay?" Rachel was pacing back and forth in her living room. Everything around her reminded her of Bobby, especially the sofa. They'd bought it for Bobby's apartment back when Jordan was first born. Back when Bobby swore he was going to marry her. Back before Tony.

"Don't get smart with me," Twyla responded. She now sounded fully awake. "I will hang up this phone on you."

Rachel took a deep breath. "Okay, okay; I'm sorry. It's just, I need to find him . . . it's . . . it's Jordan. He's sick."

"Yeah, right."

"No, seriously. I need to get Bobby's insurance information so I can take Jordan to the emergency room. Do you know where he is?"

"What's wrong with Jordan?"

Rachel was trying her best to contain her irritation. Twyla was short-tempered and the wrong words could leave Rachel talking to a dial tone. "I don't know," Rachel said. "His, um, his breathing is funny."

Twyla let out a long sigh. "Hold on."

Rachel heard some rustling and James mumbling something in the background. It seemed like an eternity, but Twyla finally came back to the phone.

"I had to go into the living room. James would have had a fit if he knew I was telling you this."

"Telling me what? What do you know?" Rachel was borderline hysterical now. She caught herself before she woke up the kids. She lowered her voice. "Where is that no-good dog?"

"Rachel, what makes him a dog? The fact that he doesn't want you?"

"Just answer the damn question."

"Fine. He's over Shante's."

"Shante? Shante who?"

"Shante Wilson."

"Where do I know that name from?"

"The Shante that goes to your church. I think her parents' names are Cleotis and Lethora Wilson, something like that." Twyla yawned loudly, making sure Rachel knew she was interrupting her sleep.

Rachel was shocked. "You have got to be kidding me? Yeah, they go to Zion Hill, but I haven't seen Shante in ages. How does Bobby know her?"

"I don't know. Damn, why you asking all these questions?"

"Look, I'm just trying to find out what's going on!"

"Rachel, let it go. It's not like he's cheating on you."

Rachel felt furious. First Bobby told her that he wasn't dating anyone and then he goes out with somebody she knows! "Thanks, Twyla, I gotta go."

"Rachel, don't do anything stupid."

"Yeah, whatever. I'll talk to you later."

"Rachel?"

"What?"

"Jordan's not really sick, is he?"

Rachel didn't respond.

"Rachel?"

"What, Twyla? I gotta go."

"I don't have no bail money."

"Yeah, yeah, yeah. I'll see you later." Rachel threw the phone across the room and fell to the floor. "That bastard!" she screamed. "How could he do this to me?" Rachel buried her head in her hands and began sobbing. A tiny touch on her shoulder caused her to raise her head.

"Mommy, why are you crying?" Jordan asked.

Rachel reached up and pulled her son into her embrace. He looked so much like Bobby it wasn't even funny. The same little cleft chin and sandy brown hair. Their eyes were even the same gray color. "Oh, sweetie. Daddy made Mommy cry again," Rachel said as she held Jordan to her chest.

Jordan snuggled up close to his mother. "Daddy is always making you cry. I hate him!"

Rachel sat sniffling and rocking Jordan back and forth. She jumped up after a few minutes, releasing Jordan, then racing to the hall closet where she pulled out a phone book. She flipped to the W section, then ran her fingers along the list of names under Wilson. "Come on!" She raced into the back bedroom and scooped Nia up in a blanket. She slipped into her house shoes as she headed toward the door.

"Where are we going, Mommy?" Jordan asked.

"Just come on."

"But, Mommy, I have my pj's on."

"Boy, it don't matter, just come on."

Nia was still sleeping as Rachel snapped her into her car seat. Jordan scooted in the backseat next to his sister. Rachel climbed in the driver's side of her Ford Escort, started it up, and backed out of the driveway.

Twenty minutes later, she was pulling up to Shante's

condo on 51st Street. There had been two Shante Wilsons in the phone book, but one of them was in Pearland, a suburb of Houston. Luckily, Rachel remembered hearing Shante's parents talk about some property they owned not too far from the church. That had to be the place where Shante was staying.

Rachel threw the car in park and looked in the backseat. Jordan was knocked out. She reached back and grabbed him by the shoulder. "Honey," she said, shaking him. "Pumpkin, Mama needs you to wake up."

"Huh???" Jordan pulled his head up and rubbed his eyes. "Mommy, I'm sleepy."

"I know, baby. I'll take you home to sleep in a minute. But we have to go see Daddy."

"But he made you cry."

"I know, but we still need to go see him so he can apologize to me. You want him to apologize, don't you?" Jordan nodded. "Well then, do this for Mommy. You see that door with the big two and the five on the front." Rachel pointed to the condo just in front of them. "I need you to go up and keep ringing the doorbell until somebody answers."

Jordan looked confused. "But, Mommy, I don't wanna."

"Look, Jordan, Mommy needs you to do this, okay? Just go up there and ask for your daddy. I'll take you to get ice cream tomorrow if you do it, okay?"

Jordan looked at his mother. "Can I get chocolate with sprinkles?"

"Two scoops."

Jordan smiled at the prospect of ice cream. "Okay." He opened the back door and climbed out the car.

"Mommy's right here waiting on you." Rachel rolled down the window so she could hear. They were right in front of

Shante's door. Luckily, her condo didn't sit too far from the curb.

Jordan grinned with a determined look and walked toward the condo. Rachel watched as he stood on his tiptoes and rang the doorbell.

After a few minutes, a tall, heavyset woman wearing nothing but a T-shirt opened the door. Rachel frowned at the sight of Shante. That's who Bobby was talking to the other night.

Shante looked at Jordan with surprise. "Yes?"

"Is my daddy here?" Jordan stood with his back straight. Rachel smiled. *Make me proud, son!*

"Excuse me?" Shante said. She peered at Jordan. "What are you doing out here at this time of night?"

"Is my daddy here?" Jordan repeated.

"Who is your daddy?" Shante quickly looked around outside. Rachel ducked down in the car.

"Bobby Edward Clark, the third," Jordan pronounced.

Shante noticed Rachel's car.

"Hold on." She closed the door and went back inside. A few minutes later, the door swung open.

"Daddy!" Jordan cried as he stretched out his arms for his father to pick him up.

Bobby snatched his son up in his arms. "Jordan, what are you doing here?"

"Mommy brought me." Jordan pointed toward the car. Rachel cursed silently as she heard Bobby's voice. She hadn't really thought this thing through, but it made no sense to hide now. She eased back up into the seat. Bobby looked her way and started stomping toward her.

"You crazy . . ."

Rachel cut him off. "Now, now. We don't curse in front of the children."

"Rachel, what the hell are you doing? Why do you have this boy out here at this time of night?"

"He wanted his daddy."

"Dammit, Rachel, I told you to stop this."

Rachel got out and leaned against the car. "I thought you told me you weren't seeing anyone?"

"No, you said that."

"Well, you didn't correct me."

Bobby took a deep breath, then opened the back door, placed Jordan inside and closed it. "Rachel, what difference does it make who I'm seeing? We are not together."

"A lie's a lie."

"Look, I didn't correct you because I wanted to see my son, and I know had I told you Shan and I were seeing each other, you wouldn't have let me see him."

"Shan? Oh, now you're calling her by a nickname?" Rachel felt tears forming. Bobby used to call her Ra.

"Rachel, go home and take my son home, before I have your crazy ass arrested."

Bobby turned and walked back toward the condo, but Rachel wasn't giving up the fight. "You don't walk away from me when I'm talking to you." Rachel grabbed Bobby by the arm and snatched him toward her.

Bobby reached back, ready to slap Rachel. He caught himself with his hand midair. "Oooohh, girl. You goin' make me hurt you," he said through gritted teeth.

Rachel wasn't backing down. She pushed herself up in Bobby's face. "Hit me then, you sorry bastard. You bad. Come on, I dare you." She wasn't worried, Bobby had never been a violent man. He was arrogant, thought he was God's gift to women, but that was the extent of his faults.

Shante threw the door open. "Bobby, come on inside," she said sternly.

Bobby glared at Rachel, then laughed and shook his head. "You are one crazy bitch."

"You weren't saying that when you were screwing me last night!" Rachel screamed. She knew she was reaching now. After Nia was born, she and Bobby tried to make it work, but Bobby was so hung up on Nia not being his child that they didn't do anything but argue. Still, she had managed to squirm her way into his bed on more than one occasion. She knew he had a weakness when it came to her. Or at least he used to. They hadn't slept together in several months, but Rachel really wanted to hurt Shante.

"You hear that, Shante? We had sex last night!"

Shante sauntered over to where the two of them were standing and threw a pitying look at Rachel. "He was here all night, babe. Try another lie."

Rachel couldn't stand Shante looking all smug and confident. She couldn't believe Bobby chose this woman over her. She was a good size twenty and she wasn't even cute. Her auburn hair was pinned up with a few strands dangling loosely around her face. The little T-shirt just barely covered her goods, leaving her big old thighs exposed.

Rachel stared at the T-shirt. "Wait a minute, is that the shirt I brought you from Florida?" She looked at Bobby.

Bobby just hung his head, like he knew trouble was brewing.

"Awww hell, naw!" Before anyone could blink, Rachel was clawing at Shante like a tomcat fighting for its last meal. Shante screamed and fell down. Too surprised to fight back, she only covered her head as Rachel swung wildly.

"Rachel!" Bobby screamed as he tried to pull her off Shante. Rachel had Shante's hair firmly locked between her fingers as she banged her head against the ground while screaming obscenities. Jordan was jumping up and down in the car screaming and banging on the window.

Bobby finally managed to pull Rachel away enough for Shante to scamper back inside the apartment. Bobby had Rachel in a body lock, trying to calm her down, but she broke loose and ran to her car. She knew Shante had probably gone to call the cops and the last thing she needed was to be arrested. "You messed up!" she screamed at Bobby as she struggled to open the car door. "Take a good look at your son, because this is your last time seeing him!" Rachel jumped in just as the tears came pouring down her cheeks. She glanced at Jordan in the backseat. He was whimpering and looking out of the back window at his father, who stood dumbfounded in Shante's yard.

6

JONATHAN JACKSON STOOD at the front door of the place he'd called home all his life. He had mixed emotions about going inside. On the one hand, he really wanted to see his mother. But on the other, he just didn't know if he was ready to deal with his father yet.

After a few more minutes, Jonathan decided there was no sense putting off the inevitable. He gently placed his key into the lock, turned it, and walked inside.

"Well, looky here." Simon jumped up from his recliner and quickly walked down the hall toward his son as soon as he saw him standing in the front door. "My boy! Loretta, get out here! I got a surprise for you!"

"Yes, dear." Loretta came out of the kitchen. She was holding a wooden spoon in her hand. "I really need to get dinner finished. I . . ." She stopped talking when she saw Jonathan standing in the doorway, his father's arm proudly wrapped around him.

"Hi, Mama."

"Thank you, Jesus!" Loretta proclaimed. She raced over and took her son into her arms. "Jonathan! Oh, I've missed you so much, son! Why didn't you call and let us know what time you were getting in? I would've picked you up from the airport."

Jonathan set his bags down, leaned in, and kissed his mother. "I wanted to surprise you. Besides," he leaned back out the front door and waved, "Kevin dropped me off." Simon looked out at the young man sitting in the black Mustang GT parked outside. He'd been Jonathan's best friend since junior high school. Kevin waved, then sped off.

"Come on in here and sit down," Simon said, closing the door.

"You sure do look good. Atlanta has been good to you," Loretta said.

"Yes, Mama. The city is really great." Jonathan had graduated from Morehouse College the past spring with a divinity degree, but he still had to finish a class for his minor in sociology. Now that he had completely finished, he decided to return home until he figured out what he was going to do.

"My boy, the college graduate." Simon beamed. The whole family, with the exception of David, had driven down to Atlanta when Jonathan got his degree. Simon and Rachel had argued the entire trip, but Simon had never been happier as he watched Jonathan walk across the stage.

"So, have you given any thought to seminary school?" Simon asked.

Jonathan walked away from his father to study the new pictures of Nia and Jordan sitting on the fireplace mantel.

"Yeah, I thought about it. And I'd really like to go. You know I would love to follow in your footsteps, Dad."

Simon didn't give him time to finish. He walked over, grabbed Jonathan, and pulled him into a tight embrace.

Jonathan knew now was the time to draw back and give his father the "but" part, only he couldn't bring himself to do it. He knew how much Simon was counting on him. Maybe there was some way he could make his father happy and become a preacher. He just hadn't figured out how he would do that.

Simon pulled Jonathan into the den. "Just leave those bags; we'll get them later. I want to catch up with you!" He was filled with enthusiasm. "Loretta, can you please get us something to drink, some lemonade or tea or something?"

Loretta, who was following behind them beaming, nodded. "Yes, dear. Lemonade it is. I'll be right back."

"Maybe you can preach next Sunday, get you some practice," Simon said.

Jonathan laughed nervously. "Whoa, Dad; slow down. I just got here. I think I'll take back my old position of choir director. That is, if it's still open. I know when we talked a few weeks ago, you told me you hadn't found anyone for it. So maybe I can start there before you throw me into the pulpit."

Simon didn't respond. He was too busy smiling.

"Why do you keep staring at me?" Jonathan asked.

"I'm just so proud of you, son," Simon responded. "Tell me, did you finish your class okay? Have you found your future Mrs. Jackson?"

Jonathan knew he would be bombarded with questions the minute he walked in the door. He loved his father to death, but sometimes he could be so overbearing. The plane ride from Atlanta had been exhausting. He would've given anything just to go lie down right now, but he knew that would be next to impossible.

"The class went fine, and now I'm officially finished with school. And no, I haven't met my wife yet."

"Boy, you mean to tell me all those lovely women at Spelman, and you ain't found one worthy of being called Mrs. Jackson?" Simon asked.

Loretta returned and handed them each a glass of lemonade. "Simon Jackson, would you leave that boy alone? He just got in the door and you are trying to make him a preacher *and* a husband," she said, laughing.

Jonathan smiled at his mother. Saved by good old mom. He definitely didn't want to get into a conversation about his love life with his father.

"Sweetie, are you hungry?" Loretta asked. "I made your favorite, smothered pork chops and rice, with a side of my green beans and potatoes, just the way you like it."

"Ummm, I am hungry, Mama," Jonathan said. "But I'm sorry, I don't eat pork anymore."

"You what?" Simon said. "Boy, you were raised on the pig."

"I know. I just don't eat it anymore. It makes me sick now if I try."

"So, you a Muslim?" Simon asked, concerned.

"No, Dad, I'm not a Muslim. I just don't eat pork."

A worried look crossed Loretta's face. "Oh, baby, I wish I'd known. Now, what are you goin' eat? I can try and fix you up a steak or something right quick."

Jonathan got up, walked over and kissed his mother on the cheek. "No, Mother, no need to do all that. I can just eat the vegetables and be fine."

"Are you sure?" Loretta asked.

Jonathan smiled lovingly at his mother. She had always pampered him. "I'm sure. But first, I'd like to change out of these clothes and into something more comfortable." Jonathan had on a pair of gray slacks, a long-sleeved, crisp white dress shirt, and a tie. He didn't know why he'd worn a tie on the plane; habit, he guessed. He'd been wearing them since he was in high school. He even walked around campus regularly in a shirt and tie.

"Okay, baby," Loretta responded. "You go get changed and I'll get your plate ready."

"Thanks, Mama. By the way, where are Rachel and David?"

At the mention of David's name, Simon turned up his nose and mumbled. From his reaction, Jonathan knew things weren't much better between his father and brother. The last time he was home, six months ago, they'd committed David to rehab for his drug problem. His father was so angry then that he didn't join the rest of the family to check David in. It was an ordeal and Jonathan had been anxious to get back to school. David's stay in rehab was the reason he missed Jonathan's graduation.

"I suppose they're at home," Loretta said. "Rachel will probably be by later. And David . . ." Loretta looked at her husband.

Simon huffed and said, "David isn't welcome here."

Jonathan debated whether to ask for the latest on his brother, but decided against it. He knew it would start a whole other conversation, or even an argument, and he had already spent the last week arguing with the love of his life, Tracy. He definitely wasn't in the mood to go down that road again.

"Well, I'm going to get changed. I'll be back down shortly."

Simon dropped David from his mind, and he smiled. "Everything is just as you left it, son," he said.

Jonathan managed to return his smile. His father had such a look of admiration on his face. He hated to think that eventually, that look might change forever.

7

RACHEL SAT in the front passenger seat of her mother's blue minivan. Her bottom lip was poked out like she was a pouting six-year-old.

Her mother continued swaying her head to the sounds of Mahalia Jackson on the tape player. Either she was oblivious to Rachel's frustrations, or she just chose to ignore her.

Rachel shifted in her seat and let out a loud, long sigh.

Loretta smiled.

"What's so funny?" Rachel asked.

"You." Loretta went back to singing and swaying.

"Why am I funny?"

"Because you always want somebody to do something for you, but you never want to do anything for anyone else."

Rachel rolled her eyes. "That's not true."

"Whatever you say, sweetheart," Loretta answered in a light-hearted tone. "That's why you're sitting over there now acting like a child."

"No, I'm not," Rachel protested. "I just don't understand

why I have to go with you to visit the sick and shut-in. Half those folks don't even like me. The other half don't even know me."

"Well, if you put it that way, I don't understand why I have to babysit every weekend."

Rachel sucked her teeth. She hated that her parents constantly threw babysitting in her face. It's not like they didn't enjoy spending time with their grandkids. They just wanted to blackmail her.

"It's good for you to get out and give back. The Lord has given you so much."

"Oh, gimme a break."

"No need pouting about it. We're here now." Loretta pulled into the driveway of Mattie Broadman, a longtime member of Zion Hill.

Mrs. Mattie was eighty years old and chronically sick, and her only daughter lived three hours away. Rachel couldn't understand why they didn't just put her in a nursing home. Loretta explained to her that Mrs. Mattie made both family and friends promise to let her live out her last days at home. Her husband, Cecil, had been abused in a nursing home, so Mrs. Mattie swore she'd kill herself before she went to one.

"I still don't understand what good it does for us to be here. She's mean and hateful every time we come by," Rachel said as she stepped out of the van.

Mrs. Mattie had been Rachel's Sunday school teacher, and the meanest woman she'd ever met. She seemed to get meaner the older she got.

Loretta motioned for her daughter to get moving up the walkway. "I told you it does you good and despite the way she acts, it does Mrs. Mattie good as well. It lets her know her Zion Hill family cares about her."

"But I don't care about her."

"Rachel," Loretta snapped and turned toward her daughter, "that's your problem. You don't care about anyone but yourself. And Bobby." Loretta's expression turned serious. "Have you ever thought that maybe that's why God isn't delivering you the blessings you want? Because you're so selfish. Lord only knows how I raised such a selfish child." Loretta shook her head, turned around and rang Mrs. Mattie's doorbell.

A few minutes later, a scratchy voice yelled from the other side. "Who's there?"

"Mrs. Mattie, it's Loretta and Rachel. We came to visit and we brought you tea cakes." Loretta held a bag up to the peephole.

Mrs. Mattie mumbled something they couldn't make out, then started unfastening what sounded like fifty different locks on her front door.

The door swung open. It seemed to Rachel that Mrs. Mattie had aged since the last time they were there a month ago. Her beige duster hung from her small, frail frame, and her completely white hair hung to her shoulders. It was so thin, you could see right through it. She looked Loretta and Rachel up and down, a scowl plastered across her face. "Well, don't just stand there; you letting the flies in."

Rachel turned up her nose as she stepped inside the house. A stale, mothball smell permeated the air. *It looked like the flies were already in,* Rachel thought as she made her way down the foyer of Mrs. Mattie's Victorian-style home.

The two-story brick house may have been at one time a truly beautiful place, but the house had been neglected since Mr. Broadman passed away four years ago. The ceiling in the front room was sagging and looked like it would cave in at any minute. A thick layer of dust seemed to cover every piece of furniture in the house. The walls were a dingy yellow and the swinging door from the dining room into the kitchen hung on its hinges.

Loretta leaned in and gave Mrs. Mattie a hug. "How are you feeling today?" she asked.

"I'm alive. I guess that counts for something." Mrs. Mattie stared at Rachel as if she expected a hug from her, too. Loretta turned toward her daughter and slightly thrust her head toward Mrs. Mattie. Rachel didn't understand and threw her mother a confused look before realizing what she was asking. Rachel silently cursed, took a deep breath, leaned in, and hugged Mrs. Mattie. The woman didn't return her hug.

"Well, long as you here, you might as well make yourself useful and go wash the dishes in the kitchen sink," Mrs. Mattie said to Rachel.

Rachel looked at the elderly woman like she had lost her mind.

"How's the grandkids?" Mrs. Mattie asked, ignoring Rachel's icy stare.

"They're doing fine. Jordan is getting so big," Loretta responded.

Mrs. Mattie turned back to Rachel, who hadn't moved. "What are you waiting for, gal?"

Rachel looked to her mother in protest.

"Just go do it, Rachel," Loretta pleaded. Rachel couldn't be sure, but she could've sworn there was a smirk on Mrs. Mattie's face.

Fine, Rachel told herself. At least she wouldn't have to sit in this dusty front room and pretend like she was interested in Mrs. Mattie's conversation.

Rachel huffed, then turned and walked into the kitchen. It

looked bad. The countertops were clean, but what looked like three months worth of dishes were piled in the sink. A ceramic chicken cookie jar with a broken beak was turned over on its side. A teakettle sat on the gas stove. It looked like tea had boiled over and never been cleaned up.

I know she don't expect me to clean all this up. Rachel looked back toward the front room, contemplating whether she should tell her mother cleaning this kitchen was out of the question.

Mrs. Mattie and Loretta walked into the kitchen.

"Have a seat at the table," Mrs. Mattie said, pointing to the rickety kitchen table that was being supported by a phone book on one end. "I'll make us some coffee to have with these tea cakes."

She turned her attention to Rachel, who was leaning against one of the counters, pouting. "Gal, rinse out that teakettle and boil us some hot water."

Again, Rachel wanted to protest, but her mother's sharp look stopped her. Rachel huffed, snatched the teakettle, and emptied out the brown liquid that had probably been sitting in there for weeks. It was bad enough she had to play Hazel the maid, but then they were bringing their conversation into the kitchen, where she would be forced to listen.

Mrs. Mattie sat down across from Loretta at the table. "What about Pastor Jackson? How's he?"

"He's doing fine. He's at the church right now," Loretta replied.

"Lord, every time I talk to you that man is at the church. Doesn't that bother you?"

Rachel filled the kettle, placed it on the stove, then turned the fire on as she leaned back. She wanted to hear her mother's response to Mrs. Mattie's question.

"No, I'm okay with it."

Rachel let out a long sigh. *How could anybody be okay with never seeing their husband?* she wondered as she poured dish-washing liquid and began running hot water in the sink.

"Now, Loretta. You must not forget that I was married for fifty-one years to a minister. And I never did get used to the time he spent in the church." Mrs. Mattie leaned in and lowered her voice. "Maybe if he had spent more time at home, you wouldn't be dealing with such a fast one over there."

Loretta snickered. Rachel wanted to turn around and throw a plate at Mrs. Mattie. Despite the fact that Mrs. Mattie lowered her voice, Rachel had the strangest feeling Mrs. Mattie could care less whether Rachel heard her or not.

"Simon is there enough for our family," Loretta said.

"Hmph, no, he's not," Rachel muttered as she scrubbed what seemed like two-month-old beans from a plastic bowl.

"Uh, excuse me," Mrs. Mattie interjected. "This is grown folks' business."

I am grown, Rachel wanted to say. But for the life of her she just couldn't bring herself to say anything smart to Mrs. Mattie.

"As I was saying," Mrs. Mattie continued, "kids need both of their parents full time, especially boys. Speaking of boys, how are them boys?"

"Jonathan is home now," Loretta replied.

"Oh, that's wonderful. That's a sweet boy if I ever seen one. You all must be so proud of him."

Rachel wanted to gag. If she never heard another pro-Jonathan comment in her life, it would be too soon.

"As for David," Loretta kept talking, "he's still going through some things. You know the devil is at work on him."

"Umm-hmm," Mrs. Mattie tsked. "And from what I hear, the devil is winning."

Loretta's voice softened. "I'm staying prayerful."

"Well, I guess that's all you can do. Just make sure at the top of your prayer list, you put that one there," Mrs. Mattie said, pointing at Rachel. Rachel was getting just about fed up. Here she was, elbow deep in nasty dishwater and this woman was talking about her.

"You're a better woman than me," Mrs. Mattie continued. "I had to put my foot down and tell Cecil he was goin' have to spend more time with us and less with that church."

Rachel stifled a sarcastic laugh. That would be the day. Her mother putting her foot down, yeah, right.

"Oh, I could never do that. I believe in letting Simon be the head of the household."

Mrs. Mattie shook her head sympathetically. "Chile, it's one thing to let your husband lead and another for you to follow him blindly."

Finally, Rachel thought, Mrs. Mattie said something that made some sense.

"I would never say Simon is leading us blindly."

"Take it from me, I've been there. All you have to do is look at your children. I know Simon, been knowing him since he was knee-high to a pup. Knew his daddy, too. The difference is the elder Reverend Jackson knew how to say no. He knew how to delegate to others so it didn't take away from his family. You see out of eight of that Jackson clan, near 'bout all of 'em doing well. I don't know why Simon is so gung-ho on the church. He lets everybody tell him what they need him to do, then them folks go home to their family."

Loretta sighed. "Mrs. Mattie, I stopped long ago trying to figure out what was the driving force behind Simon's desire to make Zion Hill the best church in the country, which is his ultimate goal. Personally, I believe it has something to do with the fact that his father lost his church when Simon was a teenager."

Mrs. Mattie nodded, recalling the story. "I know that hit Reverend Jackson hard. He loved that church. My sister went there and I remember her telling me the members had voted to get rid of Reverend Jackson because they said the church wasn't prospering under him. His health deteriorated after that, he was so distraught."

"I know," Loretta continued. "And when he finally died of heart failure on the day of Simon's high school graduation, Simon was devastated. I believe my husband is now trying to accomplish what his father could not. But Simon would never admit to that. He won't even talk about his father and the church. Always just changes the subject."

Rachel listened on in awe as she moved a plate into the other side of the sink to await rinsing. She had never known that about her father. She knew her grandfather was a minister, but she had no idea he had lost his church.

Loretta tried to shake off the melancholy look that had crept up on her face. "Whatever the reason, my husband is happiest when he's giving his all to Zion Hill. I know that the kids have a hard time accepting that, but I'm hopeful at some point we can find a happy medium."

At some point? Rachel wanted to scream. They were all freaking grown now. What difference did it make now whether he came around? Anything her father tried to give them now was too little, too late as far as she was concerned.

Mrs. Mattie took Loretta's hand.

"You can try to kid yourself all you want about it not making a difference, but it's hurting your family. And I know you well enough to know it's hurting you, too. I just think you're too stubborn to admit it, because you gotta be a good and supportive first lady." Mrs. Mattie released her hold, her expression turning deadly serious. "You better get your husband straight before your children are too far gone, if they ain't already."

8

"SEE, IT FITS PERFECTLY. Just like when you left!"

Loretta beamed at Jonathan, who was wearing a navy blue and yellow choir robe. It was the same one he had had five years ago. She had kept it stored nicely in a box in the closet, awaiting his return home.

"It's a choir robe, Ma. I'd have to gain a lot of weight for me to outgrow it," Jonathan said, joking.

Simon called from downstairs that he was about to leave, so Jonathan and his mother quickly gathered up their things and raced downstairs.

"You nervous, Son?" Simon asked once they were nearing the church.

Jonathan stared at the large brick building that had been their second home for as long as he could remember. He could tell whoever built Zion Hill had put a lot of love into it. Each window was intricately adorned with a myriad of colors. The tall, white cross that sat on the front lawn loomed high above the structure, giving an appearance that it guarded all those who entered.

"No, Dad. I'm right at home, working for the Lord." Jonathan felt horrible making a comment like that, but he knew it was what his father wanted to hear.

Simon gushed with pride. "That's my son!"

They pulled into the pastor's parking spot in the back of the church, then headed inside. Jonathan separated from his parents to rehearse his solo in the choir room.

He was softly singing when he felt someone watching him. He turned around and released a gentle smile at Angela Brooks, his high school sweetheart.

"Hello, Angela," he said. Angela was a tall, elegant, caramel-colored beauty who could've very well pursued a career in modeling. She was wearing a burgundy, calf-length peasant dress that looked stunning on her.

"Hi. I heard you were back in town. How long have you been here?" Angela asked.

"Just got back recently."

"Oh, and you couldn't call anyone?" Angela crossed her arms and pretended to pout.

Jonathan put his music notes down on the table and walked toward her. "I didn't think you'd want to hear from me."

Angela's smile faded. "You thought right."

Jonathan looked to see if she was joking. He surmised that she wasn't. She looked as lovely as the last day he'd seen her. Although now, her long locks had been replaced by a short feathered and flipped haircut. It was beautiful on her, accenting her almond-shaped, hazel eyes.

"You cut your hair off?"

"I needed a change."

Jonathan could see the pain in her eyes. "Look, Angela, I'm sorry."

Angela stopped him before he could continue. "Hey, don't apologize to me. I get dumped by the loves of my life all the time. I'm used to it."

Jonathan didn't know what to say. He knew this day would come. He and Angela had not ended their relationship on good terms. "I didn't dump you."

"Oh no, what do you call it?"

"We just kind of grew apart, that's all."

Angela looked at him like she wanted to give him some choice words right there in the church. "No, *you* grew apart. *You* changed. I remember how difficult it was to get you to even kiss me after you came back from school two years ago. You seldom called and when we did see each other, you were distant. And after you went back your junior year, you wouldn't even make love to me."

"I told you I just wanted to stop fornicating." Jonathan was having a hard time looking Angela in the eyes. She was right. He had become distant from her. He kept trying to get the nerve to break things off with her, but he always backed out. He didn't want to do it over the phone, and when he saw her over the Christmas holidays, he just couldn't bring himself to do it.

Angela rolled her eyes in frustration. "Oh, Jonathan. Save that, please. I know that's what you told me. But I also know you. You may be a preacher's son, but you liked having sex with me, premarital or not."

She was right about that, too. He used to love being with her. Angela had to be the best lover he ever had, and he'd been with his share of girls since losing his virginity at fifteen to his best friend's twenty-three-year-old sister. The funny part was, everyone thought he was so sweet and innocent, including his father, but Jonathan had been around. He just knew how to keep his trysts secret. Even when he and Angela were together, he had all kinds of women on the side. That all changed, though, when he met Tracy.

"Angela, where is this conversation going?" Jonathan asked, wanting to remove himself from her glare.

"Nowhere, Jonathan. I'm not mad at you, I respect your decision. I just wish you had been man enough to tell me you'd found someone else."

Jonathan froze. *What did she know?* He had taken the coward's way out: sending her a brief "Dear Jane" letter, telling her that he wanted to concentrate on graduating and that they should go their separate ways. He totally avoided her calls and never returned her tear-filled, then anger-filled, messages. She had called him everything but a child of God. Finally, after about a month she just stopped calling. Fortunately for him, he hadn't run into her on his trips home from school. This was their first time talking in over a year and a half.

"Wh . . . what do you mean, someone else," Jonathan stammered.

Angela laughed at his nervousness. "You never have been good at lying. I know you went down to Morehouse and found you another woman, a college girl and all. But I'm okay with that." Angela nodded like she had prepared for this moment many times.

Jonathan's nervousness eased and his eyes softened. He reached out and took her hand. "Angela, I didn't leave you for anyone else. Okay? That much I promise you." He wasn't totally lying. He hadn't broken up with her because of Tracy per se. But rather because he was confused about what he wanted.

Angela looked at him like she desperately wanted to believe him. Finally, she spoke. "Whatever you say, Jonathan. I just wanted to say hello." She turned to leave, then stopped and looked back over her shoulder. "And, oh yeah, good luck with your song today."

Jonathan nodded his head to say thank you and watched Angela walk into the sanctuary. He hated hurting her; she had been really good to him. But he had changed when he went to college. He thought that he was in love with Angela while they were together, but Tracy had shown him what true love really was. Tracy had introduced him to feelings he never knew existed. Feelings that had changed him completely.

"Oh, Tracy," Jonathan said softly to himself. "I really miss you."

"Boy, are you in here talking to yourself?" Jonathan hadn't noticed his father come in the other door to the choir room.

Jonathan laughed nervously. "No, Dad, I was just practicing."

"You don't need no practice." Simon slapped him on the back. "You got natural-born, God-given talent. I just saw Angela leave. She's looking beautiful as usual. It sure would make me proud to see you two get together." Simon winked. "Well, let's get going; service is about to start."

Simon led his son out to the pulpit just as the processional music began playing. Jonathan took his seat next to his father. Only associate pastors were supposed to sit in the pulpit, but Simon had been adamant about Jonathan sitting with him.

The service flowed along smoothly. As one of the members finished giving the church announcements, Jonathan moved to the mic at the west end of the choir stand. The pianist started playing and Jonathan, removing the mic from the stand, began rocking back and forth to the music. The words to "Precious Lord" were emblazoned in his heart, it was his mother's favorite song. He had learned it by the time he was five years old, so he could've sung it without the music.

Surprisingly, he felt totally at home. Singing had always been his passion. He had been singing in the choir since he was a little boy. He even sang with an R&B band in Atlanta. His father would have had a heart attack if he knew that. It would have also hurt him to know that Jonathan very seldom attended church at school and wasn't active in a choir there.

Jonathan didn't realize how much he missed gospel music until he started getting into his song. He bellowed out his solo, his voice getting louder and stronger as he went along. When he was finished with his part, he turned to the choir and had them join in. It was absolutely amazing. When the choir was finished, there wasn't a dry eye in the house.

Simon was the first one on his feet, applauding like crazy. Jonathan stretched his arms skyward. The spirit had really moved through him today. That was surprising because he didn't think it was possible anymore.

He looked out at the crowd adorning him with love, and joy filled his heart. The only thing that would make this moment more complete would be having Tracy by his side. But that was a pipe dream. As much as he felt at home at Zion Hill, the church would never welcome Tracy. The members were old school and they'd never understand how he could possibly be in love with another man.

9

Rachel glared at the clock over the choir stand. 1:45. It sounded like her father was nowhere near winding down. He had signaled for the organist to cut the music, usually a sign that he had no intentions of wrapping up his sermon anytime soon.

"And the Lord giveth and He taketh away!" Simon bellowed.

Rachel had no idea what her father was talking about. She usually didn't pay much attention to his sermons. Hadn't in years. It seemed like he was always preaching directly to her and she had had enough of that growing up. Heck, the only reason she even bothered coming to church was because her father had vowed they'd stop watching her kids if she didn't. And their babysitting was the only thing keeping her sane. She loved her children, but she was still young and wanted to party. But now, sitting there watching the hands on the clock inch closer to two, she was starting to wonder if it was all worth it.

"I know someone here today is fighting the word of God," Simon continued.

Thank you, Jesus. He was finally opening the doors of the church. That meant Rachel could get home, or rather to her parents' house, eat, then crash. Last night's party had worn her out. She was already going to have to hear it because she missed Jonathan's solo. She had eased in just as the crowd was applauding, and like always, her father had noticed. Rachel actually tried to make it in time to catch her brother, but as usual, she just couldn't drag herself out of bed.

Rachel stood with the rest of the congregation. She tapped her foot impatiently as she waited for people to head to the front. She hated this part of church almost as much as she did the sermon itself. Just when you thought the last person had stepped out, here comes another person. That, in itself, always made her father go on another ten minutes.

Rachel plopped down in her seat after Simon motioned for everyone to sit back down. The church secretary, Delilah, leaned over and whispered something in Simon's ear. When that huge smile crossed his face, Rachel knew they weren't about to be dismissed anytime soon.

"Brothers and Sisters," Simon began. "We have five new people who come to join us today by Christian experience. Let the church say Amen!"

"Amen!" the crowd replied.

Rachel let out a long, obvious sigh as Simon went down the line, asking each person his name, former church, why he or she wanted to turn his life over to God, their third grade teacher's name, the works.

Rachel glanced around the church. *Am I the only person who is irritated and ready to go?* She was amazed at how all the people were sitting so attentively, but that was the thing about Zion

Hill, they had loyal and faithful members. Simon could probably preach right through to six o'clock and they wouldn't care. Many of them regarded Simon right up there with God himself. She didn't particularly care for any of the members. They were always throwing nasty looks at her like she was a disgrace to a man so regal as Reverend Simon Jackson. While she was growing up, she couldn't do anything without someone running back to tell her father. Between those memories and the amount of attention her father bestowed upon the church, she had no love for Zion Hill.

Rachel heard her father asking for prayer for the five new members. *Finally*. She almost fell off her pew when Simon said, "Before we go, Sister Hicks would like to share a testimony with us this afternoon."

Rachel couldn't help it. She let out a loud, obnoxious cough, one that caused several people to shoot her chastising looks.

"I don't believe this," Rachel muttered, ignoring the stares. Why they continued to let this woman testify was beyond her. Sister Hicks had a testimony every week.

"First, giving honor to God, Pastor Jackson, First Lady, family and friends," Sister Hicks began.

Rachel could no longer contain her irritation. She didn't care that anyone could see her huffing and puffing. This was unbelievable.

"I'm here today to tell you God is an awesome God!"

"We know that, you told us last week," Rachel mumbled. The little boy sitting next to Rachel laughed. His mother didn't think it was so funny. She shot them both wicked looks.

Sister Hicks kept talking, tears welling up in her eyes. "Them doctors told me this cancer was goin' eat me alive. They gave me six months to live."

"Cancer? Is that all? Last week it was hypertension. The week before that glaucoma. Next week, it'll probably be her big toe," Rachel said to no one in particular.

"Well, my six months was up yesterday and devil be gone! I'm still here!! And feeling better than ever!" Sister Hicks proclaimed.

"Well whoopty, freaking doo." Rachel was on a roll now. By this time, the little boy was cracking up at Rachel's comments. His mother popped him on the leg and leaned toward Rachel, her big-brimmed hat poking the little boy in the face.

"Rachel, Reverend Jackson would not be pleased. You need to have some respect and consideration." The woman turned her nose up in disgust, leaned back in the pew, then turned her attention back to the front.

Rachel just glared at the woman. She wanted to flash her middle finger and tell her to consider *that*. But even though her father considered her a heathen, she didn't want to go that far in the house of the Lord.

The organist had started back up and Sister Hicks was dancing around and shouting. The sight actually made Rachel laugh. Sister Hicks had to be pushing ninety.

The entire congregation stood up and was clapping and shouting along with Sister Hicks. Rachel stopped laughing long enough to make a run for it.

She eased past the little boy and his mother, making sure to step on the woman's toe. The woman yelped. Rachel faked a "sorry" look and continued on out of the pew. Her father would just have to be mad.

As Rachel got to the door, she heard her name.

"You're leaving now, Rachel?"

It was Lester's voice. Rachel debated whether to pretend

she didn't hear him and keep going, but she had already stopped.

"Hello, Lester," she said, turning around. "Yes, I'm leaving. I don't feel too well."

"Oh, I'm sorry to hear that. Is there anything I can do?"

Rachel stared at the young man who had been pursuing her since she was thirteen years old. He was one of the nicest people she had ever met in her life, but that was about the only good trait God gave him. He had to be nice because he was too dang ugly. "No, Lester. I'm just going to go lie down."

"Okay, but umm, Rachel, have you given any thought to my dinner invitation? I sure would be honored to take you and the kids out to eat. We can go wherever you'd like."

She knew he really wanted her to say yes, but Rachel just couldn't bring herself to do it. Lester was twenty-two years old and still had acne like he was fifteen. The bad part was he was light-skinned, the color of warm butter, and his pimples were bright red. His hair was both straight and nappy, like it started out wanting to be "good hair," but then changed its mind. And on top of that it was red!

Lester worked at State Farm Insurance Company, so he had a good job with benefits, but Rachel could find no benefits in going out with him. She couldn't just flat out trash him though, because he'd helped her pay her rent one time. And there was no telling when she would need him again.

"Oh yeah, dinner," Rachel responded. "Well, you know, me and Bobby, we . . ."

"I talked to Bobby." Lester cut her off. "I hope you don't mind. I asked him what his intentions were with you."

Rachel cocked her head. "You did what?"

"Rachel, don't be mad. I just wanted to make sure I didn't step on his toes."

"How dare you talk to Bobby about me?" Rachel hissed. She didn't even know Lester knew Bobby like that.

"Rachel, please. I just can't stand the way he treats you. I saw him at the barbershop and overheard him talking very disrespectfully about you and couldn't stand it, so I said something."

Rachel stood with her hands on her hips. Leave it to Lester to come to her defense, despite the way she treated him. She almost smiled at the thought, but realized she had an excuse now to get rid of him. "Lester, I don't appreciate you talking to my boyfriend."

"Your ex-boyfriend," Lester responded.

"Whatever. Just don't ever talk to Bobby again. I'm going home! Good-bye!" Rachel turned and dramatically threw open the foyer doors, wanting Lester to think she was madder than she actually was. However, she was more concerned with Bobby bad-mouthing her. That was going to have to stop. But just how she'd make that happen, she didn't quite know.

10

THE CHURCH MEMBERS were filing out at their usual, slow pace. David sat on the stoop at the corner store across the street. He watched his father meet and greet members. Of course, Loretta was poised by his side. And Jonathan was positioned firmly right next to her. The prodigal son. David laughed as he imagined how proud his father must be to have Jonathan standing there with him, greeting the good folks of Zion Hill.

David had seen Rachel high-tail it out of there before the service was even completely over. He thought about calling out to her, but she was moving so fast he didn't have time to get near her.

David took a long drag on his cigarette, letting the smoke sit in his mouth before exhaling. Everyone who came out was hugging Jonathan, patting him on the back. No doubt, David imagined, telling him what a great son he was.

David couldn't help but be bitter at his brother's status in their family. Everyone from relatives to members of the church were always talking about how "great" Jonathan was. How

Loretta and Simon should be so "proud." Then they'd look at David with disdain, shaking their heads, lamenting that they didn't know where Loretta and Simon "had gone wrong" as far as he was concerned.

Their disdain he could deal with. It's the hurt he saw in his father's eyes every time Simon looked at him, that cut to the core of his heart. No one understood just how much he needed, how much he wanted, his father's acceptance. Sure Loretta tried to make up where Simon fell short. And David loved her dearly for trying, but there was nothing like having his father's love. And it had been a long time since David felt any semblance of love from his father.

"Ohhh, baby, we hit pay dirt!" David glanced up at Tawny standing over him. She was dancing around excitedly. "That woman in there didn't even notice me bump into her." Tawny held up a black wallet. "And I moved so fast, she definitely didn't feel me take this. And look, baby." Tawny opened the wallet and pulled out two one-hundred-dollar bills. "Ol' girl was loaded! You were so right about them church folks carrying cash."

Tawny was so excited, but David wasn't sharing in her enthusiasm. It had been his idea to hit the soul food restaurant down the street from Zion Hill. He knew that several members went there after church for dinner. The place was usually packed and David thought Tawny, an experienced pickpocket, could easily score them some money.

"I can't believe we ain't come here before this!" Tawny proclaimed.

David just grunted and turned his attention back to his family, who was saying good-bye to the last of the church members.

"What's up? Why you look so down? We got two hundred

dollars. We can get real high tonight," Tawny said, seductively rubbing the money across David's face.

David didn't know what it was but he no longer had any interest in getting high. He had no interest in anything. He just wanted to be by himself.

He stood up, tossed his cigarette down, and started walking toward the church.

"Where are you going?" Tawny yelled.

David thought about just ignoring her. But Tawny wasn't one to be ignored. She would follow him and act a fool and that was the last thing David wanted.

"Look, baby," he said, turning to Tawny. "I got some business I need to handle. Why don't you go take the money and buy yourself something nice and I'll meet you back at the apartment."

"I had planned on buying something nice, something real nice," she said, waving the money.

"No. No rocks, okay?" David was getting flustered. He didn't realize the affect sitting there watching his family would have on him. He really was getting tired of his life, but every time he tried to move one step forward, Tawny pulled him two steps back.

"What? You don't want to get high?"

David realized it would be useless to try and reason with her. Tawny was a bona fide addict and she wasn't trying to hear anything about giving it up.

"Naw, baby. It's just, my brother is back in town. And, I think, maybe I can hit him up for even more money." David would say anything to get Tawny to leave.

The thought of even more money brightened Tawny's expression. "Damn, that would be right on time," Tawny exclaimed.

"Okay, so you go on and I'll catch up with you this evening."

Tawny smiled, then reached over and hugged David, sticking her tongue in his ear. Any other time, that would've seriously turned him on. But right now, it only repulsed him.

"Later, baby. Don't be too long, okay. I don't want to have to smoke up all the stuff on my own," Tawny said.

She giggled and walked off. David imagined that at one time, Tawny was probably very pretty. She had turned to drugs after dating a drug dealer named Raymond. Raymond almost killed her once he discovered she was sneaking his stash. But by that point, she was well beyond hooked.

David and Tawny had hooked up after he noticed her picking someone's pocket at the bus stop. He had just started using heroin every now and then to escape the pain in his life—the disappointment from losing his football career before it even really got started. Once he got with Tawny, heroin was upgraded, or downgraded rather, to crack cocaine. And his usage had gone from every-now-and-then to almost daily. The worst he had ever sunk was when he went to his father's church with the sole purpose of getting money off the collection plate. His father had banned him from the church after that. And he hadn't set foot in Zion Hill since.

But today, something had come over him. David didn't know if it was seeing his brother, or just seeing the family being a family. Either way, he longed to be a part of that again.

He made his way to the steps of the church just as the last person was filing out. Loretta spotted him first.

"David!" She called out, extending her arms to embrace him.

David reached in and hugged his mother. As usual, it felt so good being in her arms. He wished he could go back to being a little boy, when Loretta used to hold him, rocking him and singing his favorite songs. She kissed him on the cheek and pulled back. "Were you in the service?"

"No, I didn't quite make it to the service," he said. "But I was in the area and wanted to say hello."

Jonathan had moved in closer and was standing behind Loretta. "What's up, big brother?"

"Nothing much, little brother." David reached out to shake Jonathan's hand. He hadn't seen Jon since the last time his family tried to put him in rehab. He knew Jon was disappointed in him as well.

Jonathan took David's hand, then pulled him into an embrace. "Man, you better give me a hug." David smiled and patted his brother's back as they hugged. He pulled back and stared at his father, who was standing at the top of the steps.

"Hey," David said.

"David." Simon looked like he was sizing up his son. "I hope you're not here to cause any problems."

"Simon, don't be like that," Loretta snapped. "We haven't seen David in almost two months."

Simon crossed his arms. David couldn't make out the look on his face.

"Did you come to the house of the Lord to be cleansed?"

Suddenly, David didn't feel like coming over here was such a great idea. "I just wanted to say hi, that's all. I didn't want to cause any trouble."

David looked helplessly at Loretta, who had tears forming in her eyes. She reached out and rubbed his chin.

"Baby, you don't look so good. Come home and eat dinner with us. I made your favorite, oxtails and rice and green bean casserole. When's the last time you had a decent meal?" Loretta said.

David glanced back at his father. "I'm straight, Ma. I know Daddy doesn't want me around and I want to respect his wishes."

Loretta kept her gaze on David, adjusting his shirt that was drooping off one shoulder. "You know how your father is. It'll be okay. It's just dinner. You have to eat. Plus, you can catch up with your brother. Ain't that right, Simon?" Loretta finally turned to her husband, pleading with him to give in.

"That's okay, Ma," David interjected once Simon didn't respond. "I have stuff to do anyway." David found himself fighting back tears. What he wouldn't give just to sit down and have dinner with his family.

"Please, David."

"You heard the boy. He got stuff to do," Simon sternly said.

Loretta shook her head as the tears started falling. "Look at what you're doing, Simon. He's reaching out. He's trying and you just keep shutting him out."

David reached up and squeezed his mother's hands. "It's okay, Mama, don't cry. Daddy's right. I need to get myself together before I come back into your life." David was trying hard to ward off the tears. "I gotta go." He kissed Loretta on the forehead, then turned to Jonathan. "I'll see you around, okay?"

Jonathan nodded, his eyes misting as well.

David stared at Simon one last time. "Bye."

Simon didn't respond and David turned to walk away. "David?" Simon called out just as he made it to the sidewalk. Simon uncrossed his arms and walked over to his son. His look had softened and was actually etched with concern. "I hope you understand . . . I just . . . I just want better for you, that's all. It hurts your mother . . ." Simon lowered his head. "It hurts me, to see you like this." Simon took a deep breath. "Whenever you want some help. Whenever you really want to let those drugs go, you call me, okay?"

David felt the tears trickling down his cheek. He could not believe what he was hearing. He wished he could just let the drugs go, just like that. He thought about even saying he would just so his father could accept him again. But he had been down that road before and he knew if he wanted to make things right, really right, he would have to seriously make some changes.

"Thank you, Dad," David responded. "You don't know how much that means." David gently wiped his eyes, nodded at his family, then turned and walked away from the church, a huge smile plastered across his face. "Maybe I really can let this stuff go," he mumbled to himself.

David knew that wouldn't be easy, but now, more than ever, he knew he wanted to at least try.

11

RACHEL IGNORED the homeless man begging her for spare change. This neighborhood was going to the dogs. She remembered when she was growing up, the Fondren area was a nice place to live. The football player Warren Moon and the gospel singer Yolanda Adams used to make their homes there. But the proliferation of apartment buildings over the years had completely brought the area down. The corner store she was at had burglar bars all over the windows and the owner, Rashid, wouldn't even open the doors after ten. You had to buy whatever you wanted through a small drawer.

Rachel pushed her quarters into the pay phone and punched in Bobby's phone number. She was still fuming about having to use the corner pay phone in the first place. Apparently, Bobby had blocked both her and her parents' numbers because every time she tried to call him from either place, she got a message saying "calls not accepted." She also knew he had Caller ID on his phone, which was another reason he wasn't answering.

She tried paging him and putting in 9-1-1, but even that hadn't worked. What if something happened to Jordan? How was she supposed to get in touch with him then? She figured the only way he would answer was if he didn't recognize the number.

Sure enough, he picked up.

"Hello."

Rachel took a deep breath to calm down. "Hi."

Bobby paused. "Rachel, what do you want?"

"Don't get all nasty with me. I just called to see how you were doing. I heard about Eric."

Twyla had told Rachel about Bobby's best friend, Eric, killing himself. She didn't really think black men committed suicide, but Eric sure enough did. Twyla said something about him and his girlfriend having a fight, things getting out of hand, and him shooting himself. Although she'd never wish anyone dead, she really didn't care that much. Eric never liked her, so she definitely wasn't sad about his death, but she needed a conversation piece with Bobby. "How are you holding up?"

"I'm okay. Thanks for asking. Now what do you really want?"

"I was just checking on you, that's all."

"Yeah, right."

"I was. Anyway, don't you want to know how your son is doing? You haven't even called to check on him."

"Rachel, I can't deal with you today."

Rachel leaned against the phone booth and started twirling the metal phone cord. "Jordan asked about you."

Bobby let out an exasperated sigh. "How is he?"

"He misses his daddy," Rachel purred.

"I miss him, too."

Rachel could tell she was getting to him. If Bobby had a soft spot for anyone, it was for his son.

"He asked me would you come see him."

Bobby hesitated again. "Can you drop him off at my mother's?"

Rachel bit down on her lip. She had to keep her cool. "I can't. My car broke down," she said, lying. "I can't make it over there. You can come over to my place, though."

"I don't know."

"Bobby, you can come see your son. I promise I won't bite you."

"Rachel, I don't want no drama."

"You won't have any. I promise," Rachel said in the most sincere voice she could muster.

"All right. I'll see you in about thirty minutes. Bye."

Rachel said good-bye and placed the phone back on the hook. She was smiling uncontrollably. She glanced at her watch and figured out how long it would take her to change and get cute. Luckily, she had just left the beauty shop, so her hair was looking good. She just needed to change into something sexy. She was determined to seduce Bobby and get him back into her life.

Rachel raced home. The kids were still asleep. David was asleep on the sofa as well. He'd been there since yesterday, when his girlfriend kicked him out of the apartment. Rachel almost didn't let him stay with her, but the bottom line was he was still her brother.

Rachel hated leaving her children with David, but she thought it would be okay since she was just running to use the phone. Now, however, with Bobby coming over, David had to go.

"Hey!" Rachel shook her brother trying to wake him up. "David! Wake up. You gots to go."

"Huh? Wha . . . what's going on?" David wiped his face trying to wake up.

Rachel turned her nose up at her brother's putrid smell. His white Nike T-shirt was now a dingy yellow and splattered with food stains. It looked like he hadn't changed clothes in a week. His hair was in desperate need of cutting. No wonder Tawny put him out. But then, judging from the one time Rachel had met her, she didn't look much better.

Rachel didn't feel like fighting her brother either way, so she thought quickly. "Uh, I just talked with your girlfriend's cousin. She told me Tawny has already moved somebody else in y'alls' apartment."

"What?" David jumped up. "You lying!"

"For real. You better get over there and handle your business."

"That's why she put me out." David muttered. "She claimed it was because I was broke and she was tired of buying all the um . . ." David caught himself and looked at Rachel, ". . . of buying everything," he continued. "And all this time it was just so she could move somebody else in!"

"You better go check it out," Rachel said as she started straightening up the sofa. David lived on the other side of town, so he'd be gone awhile. If she got lucky with Bobby, she just wouldn't answer the door when he got back.

David jumped up and slipped on his gym shoes. He grabbed the keys to his rickety old truck and raced out of the apartment without saying good-bye.

Rachel closed and locked the door, looked in on the kids in the back bedroom they shared, then walked into her bathroom. She popped in her favorite CD, turned the shower on, jumped in and lathered down with Peaches-n-Cream shower gel. A few minutes later, she was standing in her walk-in closet, trying to find something to wear. She decided on a red Tommy Hilfiger skirt and a black sleeveless sweater that showed off her ample bosom. Rachel sprayed on Bobby's favorite perfume, Trésor, then went to switch the Tupac CD for something romantic.

More than an hour passed and Rachel was starting to get irritated; that's when she heard a car pull up out front. She excitedly raced to the window and looked out. She didn't recognize the black Ford Expedition, but saw that it was definitely Bobby behind the wheel. *Since when did he get a new truck?* Rachel closed the blind she had been peeking out of and moved toward the door. She gave Bobby time to knock.

"Who is it?" she seductively called.

"It's me."

Rachel leaned against the door and smiled. "Me who?"

"Stop playing games and open the door."

Rachel put the chain on the door and cracked it open.

"Bobby, oh, I didn't know if you were still coming, it being so late and all."

"Well, I'm here now. Where's Jordan?"

Rachel scanned his body. He looked so good in a tan shirt that fit snugly on his muscle-filled chest and crisply starched blue jeans. Her eyes made their way down to the key chain in his hand. "You got a new car?"

Bobby huffed. "Just go get Jordan."

Rachel straightened up and smiled. "Why can't you answer my question? You think I'm going to try to put you on child support just because you seem to be rolling in dough?"

"I am not rolling in dough. If you must know, the truck belongs to a friend."

The smile left Rachel's face. "A friend? Who?"

"Rachel, just go get Jordan." Bobby had a look across his face like he regretted coming to Rachel's in the first place.

Rachel stood on her toes and looked down at the truck. The license plate on the front said "Miss S."

Her eyebrows narrowed and she felt her blood starting to boil. "I know you did not come over in *her* truck."

"Rachel. Don't do this. I just want to see Jordan."

"Is that Shante's truck?" Rachel screamed through the cracked door. Bobby didn't respond. "Answer me!" she yelled.

"Rachel, my car is in the shop. I didn't have any other way over here. Now please . . ."

Rachel didn't let him finish. She slammed the door in his face.

Bobby started pounding on the door. "Rachel! Jordan! Jordan, it's Daddy."

"Go to hell!" Rachel shouted through the closed door.

"I thought you said I could see Jordan," Bobby said in a calm voice.

"I changed my mind; now beat it before I call the cops!"

She heard Bobby curse, then kick the door. The kick was so hard she thought the door would cave in. She almost expected him to knock it down, he was just that mad, but she didn't care. How dare he come over to her house in another woman's vehicle? She peeked out the window. He had gotten back in the truck and was speeding off.

"Bastard," Rachel muttered. "You'll be sorry."

12

JONATHAN FOUGHT BACK TEARS. He was a grown man and he was determined not to cry about this.

"So, is it somebody else?" he asked. Jonathan had just returned from a brief visit with Tracy at Houston Intercontinental Airport. Tracy was on the way to Los Angeles to visit family, and they agreed to meet at the airport during a two-hour layover. Although things started off fine, in the end, their visit hadn't gone too well and Jonathan had stormed out, leaving Tracy standing alone in the terminal. As soon as Jonathan had set foot in the house, he'd called Tracy's cell phone so they could finish the conversation.

"Answer me!" Jonathan demanded when Tracy didn't respond.

"Yes," Tracy softly responded. "I didn't mean for it to happen. It's just I didn't know what was going to happen with us. When you left Atlanta, I thought it was over."

Jonathan cupped the cordless phone between his head and shoulder and began pacing back and forth in his room. He knew Tracy was upset about him leaving Atlanta and moving back home. They had agreed that once Jonathan graduated, he would try to find a job there and they'd live happily ever after. But this was no fairy tale. When the time came, Jonathan said he was just too confused and bolted back to Houston to "get his head together." Granted, that was a few months ago, but he never thought Tracy would turn to someone else. "So this is how you solve an argument? By running into someone else's arms? You throw away everything we had, just like that?"

Tracy sighed heavily. "Look, they're calling for my plane. But Jon, you have to realize you threw us away when you left. I'm sorry. It's just I'm so tired of being with you the way we've been. Sometimes you act like I mean the world to you. Other times you treat me like I don't even exist. I can't keep going through that. You have been promising to tell your family about us and that has yet to happen."

"Is that what this is about? I told you that would come in time!"

"So you said, Jonathan. You've been telling me that for the last year. I told you from jump, I'm not ashamed of being gay and I just can't be with someone who is."

Jonathan had met Tracy at an off-campus party three years ago. They had immediately clicked and began hanging out. Jonathan knew from the start that Tracy was gay, but he found himself drawn to him. Eventually, Tracy implied that they should take their friendship to the next level, something Jonathan seemed open to trying. And things had worked out great, for a while. But then, Tracy wanted everyone to know that they were a couple, and that was something Jonathan wasn't ready for.

"Now, Tracy, you know that's not it."

"No, I don't know anything," Tracy calmly responded. "Except I'm tired and for the first time in almost a year, I feel happy. I owe it to myself to be happy, Jonathan. And yes, I'm sorry, but Martin makes me happy."

Why don't you just stick the knife in further and turn it a little bit more? Jonathan didn't know what to do. The love of his life was slipping through his fingers. Part of him wanted to cry and beg Tracy not to give up on them. But the other part was telling him to have some dignity and let it go. "Fine. I won't bother you again. Be happy!" Jonathan didn't give Tracy time to respond. He slammed the phone down and once again tried to fight back the tears.

Jonathan fell down across the bed in his room. He had converted the attic into his bedroom when he was a freshman in high school and his parents seldom ventured up there, giving him the privacy he desired. His parents had left everything just as he had it when he was in high school. From the TLC poster on the wall to the honor society achievement certificate resting in a frame on his dresser, everything was just as it had been.

Jonathan glanced at the yellow church program lying on his nightstand. Sister Hicks's granddaughter, Veronica, had written her number on it after church last Sunday. Jonathan hadn't planned to use it, but now, that didn't seem like a bad idea. He knew that wasn't the way to solve his problems, but at this point he didn't care. He was starting to feel like Tracy had been a big mistake and maybe this was his way to make things right.

Jonathan gazed at the sexy young female sitting across from him. She had to be one of the most beautiful women he had ever seen. Her shoulder-length tresses framed her delicate honey complexion perfectly. Her smile was seductive and sensuous. Still, Jonathan couldn't get his mind off Tracy.

"Hel-lo. Is anyone home?" Veronica waved her hands in front of Jonathan's face.

He smiled. "I'm sorry. I was lost in thought."

Veronica leaned back and seductively crossed her long, sultry legs. "Wow, I must be pretty boring, because from the look on your face, you weren't thinking about me."

Jonathan began toying with his napkin. "Veronica, I'm sorry. I have to be honest with you. It's been a long time since I've dated. I've been in a relationship for three years."

"So, is that relationship over?"

Jonathan tried to shake the look of melancholy from his face.

"Yeah. It's over."

"Tell me about her."

Jonathan twiddled with his drink next, swishing the ice around. Veronica had been receptive to his call, agreeing to meet him immediately. But now that he was actually here, he wasn't exactly comfortable, although he was trying hard to relax. "You know what? Why don't we change the subject? I'm not out with a beautiful lady to talk about my past. That's something that never should've happened."

"Whatever you say."

They continued eating dinner and making small talk. As they were finishing their raspberry soufflé, Jonathan said, "Why don't we go back to your place?"

"What? Is the preacher's son propositioning me on the first date?"

Jonathan didn't know what he was doing. All he knew was he had to get Tracy off his mind.

"Veronica, I don't normally do this. It's just, I was in this relationship for so long. I was faithful. But the last few months were pretty bad. We barely even spoke. And, let me just say, it's been a long time since I've . . ." Jonathan's voice trailed off. He couldn't believe what he was doing, but he needed to find a release and this beautiful woman sitting in front of him had to be just what the doctor ordered.

Veronica didn't take her eyes off him. "I think that's what I need," Jonathan finally continued. "In no way do I want to use you. I think you're attractive, lovely, and very, very sexy. And I think spending time with a woman like you is just what I need to make me forget my troubles."

Veronica looked like she was taking it all in. She smiled. "Jonathan. I appreciate your honesty. I'm sure you've heard the stories about my reputation. I've heard them, too. Some of them are rumors and some are the truth. I like sex. I especially like sex with fine men. And you are a fine man. So, I'm down." She leaned in, making sure her breasts were resting on the table. "Let Veronica make you forget all about your ex. I promise you, when I'm done, you won't even remember her name."

Jonathan smiled. That's just what he wanted to hear. Maybe he needed to return to his so-called ho days. He glanced at the check, pulled out three twenty-dollar bills from his wallet, laid them across the table, and reached out for Veronica's hand. Veronica took it and eased out of the chair.

She wet her lips before turning to walk in front of Jonathan. His eyes made their way down her back and to her behind, where the skirt hugged her full hips. He noticed other men in the restaurant checking her out, too. The way her body swayed as she walked out the door was enough to get a rise out of any man.

Jonathan looked down to the crotch of his pants. Nothing. "Come on, fella," he whispered to himself. "I need you like I never needed you before. Forget Tracy. That's not what's meant for you. This is."

Veronica paused in the doorway, turned, and waited for Jonathan to catch up. "Would you come on? We got some business to handle." She giggled and sashayed out to the white Ford Mustang Jonathan got his senior year in high school.

Jonathan moved his jacket in front of his body and began discreetly massaging himself as he walked out of the restaurant. Part of Veronica's reputation included her bragging on her sexual prowess, so he was determined to give her something to brag about with him.

It took nearly thirty minutes to get back to Veronica's apartment. She spent the entire drive nibbling his ear, singing seductive songs, and massaging Jonathan between his legs. All that, and he was still limp as a wet rag.

"You'll have to excuse the mess," Veronica said once they were inside her apartment. "I've been busy and haven't had a chance to clean up. Make yourself at home. I'm going to grab us some wine."

Veronica disappeared into the kitchen and left Jonathan standing in the cluttered living room. He picked up a pair of thong underwear off the sofa and dropped them to the floor. He wondered, had she left them there after having sex with someone else.

"What am I doing?" He sat down and muttered to himself. As soon as the thought entered his mind, he heard Tracy's voice telling him it was over. He imagined what this Martin person looked like and what they were probably doing right now.

"Forget this," he mumbled. "I'm here with one of the sexiest women in the church and I'm thinking about that sorry, good-for-nothing . . ."

"Here's your wine." Veronica reached over Jonathan's

shoulder and handed him a glass. He didn't normally drink, but maybe the wine would help ease his mind. He took the glass, stood up, and turned around. Veronica was standing there in her bra and panties, a brown lace set that looked like it was sculpted for her. Jonathan's eyes scanned her body. He would have to be a fool not to be turned on by this gorgeous woman. She sipped her wine, then set the glass down.

"Bad news, baby. I got a visit from my monthly friend. I know it doesn't bother some people, but I don't get off like that."

Jonathan stared at her with the glass in his hand. He didn't know whether to be happy or sad. He really wanted to try to have sex with her. He *needed* to have sex with her. But if he couldn't perform, he would never have been able to forgive himself. Maybe this was a blessing.

"But, I'm not one to tease and leave," she continued. She took Jonathan's glass, sipped some wine, set the glass down, then pushed Jonathan down on the sofa. Veronica began unfastening Jonathan's pants. She eased her hands inside his underwear.

Jonathan watched Veronica at work, unsure of what to do. He took a deep breath, grabbed his glass, and gulped down the remaining wine. He closed his eyes just as Veronica's head lowered into his lap.

A small smile crossed his lips as he felt himself becoming erect. Veronica's head rhythmically bobbed up and down. Jonathan's smile grew as he felt his hormones flare. This confirmed it. He wasn't gay. He could still be turned on by a woman. Maybe what he felt for Tracy hadn't been real, a youthful experiment. "Yes, baby. Like that," Jonathan whispered.

Jonathan moaned, groaned, and grunted. He felt like a volcano on the verge of eruption. Just when he thought he couldn't take it anymore, he exploded and Veronica laughed as she savored his juices.

"I knew it," he whispered as he gently rubbed her hair.

"Knew what?" Veronica softly said as she slid up on the sofa next to him.

"I knew you would make me forget all my troubles." Jonathan leaned in and kissed Veronica on the forehead. "Thank you."

Veronica giggled. "My pleasure, baby. My pleasure."

Jonathan wrapped his arm around Veronica and leaned back, a huge smile across his face. Maybe getting over Tracy would be easier than he thought.

13

RACHEL PATTED THE WAD of cash in her jacket pocket. This was her fifth time checking it since she and her mother left for the mall an hour ago. She didn't want to put the money in her wallet, fearing a thief might try to snatch her purse once they were there. If anybody wanted this money, they'd have to wrestle her to the ground for it.

Eight hundred dollars. Rachel was still in shock over the unexpected gift. Lester had shown up at her parents' house last night. When she first saw him, she immediately jumped on the defensive, but then he'd handed her a bouquet of flowers and an envelope of cash. It turned out Lester had received a large check from his father's insurance policy. Lester's father had died a couple of months earlier in a tragic car accident. His mother had died two years prior, and Lester was an only child. The only other relative he had was an aging grandmother.

When Rachel saw all those crisp one-hundred-dollar bills, she thought she was going to faint. She did make a half-hearted attempt to return the money, praying the entire time that Lester would say no. Her wish came true. Lester claimed he had no one to spend all that money on. All Rachel heard was his reference to "all that money." She wanted to ask him just how much money he received, but decided against it. Lester made her day even more when he insisted that she take the money and go shopping, something he knew she loved to do. He said he wanted her to pamper herself. The only thing he'd made her promise was that she buy something for the kids. He also told her not to spend any of the money to pay bills. He promised to help her with that later if she needed it.

Rachel wanted to jump for joy. She'd never been on a shopping spree, other than back-to-school shopping, and with her father's tight rein on the money, that had never been much fun. Rachel was so excited that she threw her arms around Lester's neck and planted a juicy kiss right on his lips. She closed her eyes, so it hadn't been totally repulsive. The kiss had caught them both by surprise and left them both speechless. Rachel had felt so guilty about accepting the money that she agreed to go out to dinner with him the next night.

Her father, who along with her mother had witnessed the whole exchange, called her a high-priced hooker for taking the money, then agreeing to a date. At first Rachel was mad, but the more she thought about what she'd buy, the less her father's words stung.

"Rachel, I still don't think it's right, you taking that boy's money," Loretta said as they pulled into the parking garage at Baybrook Mall.

Rachel exhaled loudly. Maybe bringing her mother along wasn't such a good idea, but Loretta hadn't been looking good lately. Rachel attributed it to years of putting up with her father.

She knew her mother was stressed, so she wanted to take her to get a manicure and pedicure, maybe even buy her some nice clothes, too.

"Mama, you were standing right there. You heard Lester say he wanted to give this money to me, no strings attached."

"Yeah, but you wouldn't be going out with him if he hadn't given you that money."

"That's not true. I've been out with Lester before," Rachel protested.

"Usually right after he pays your rent or does something else nice for you." Loretta shook her head. "Doesn't that boy know he can't buy love?"

"He only helped me with my rent one time. Besides, Lester and I are just friends. He doesn't really have anyone, so he clings to me. That's it. Plus, he knows my heart belongs to Bobby."

Loretta pursed her lips and gazed out the window. "Don't get me started on that."

"Please, don't say anything," Rachel mumbled. "I really . . ." Rachel's voice trailed off when she noticed the black Ford Expedition parked in an aisle near the front of the mall entrance. The license plate read "Miss S."

Rachel turned up her nose with contempt. So Shante was at the mall. "I'm sure she's spending up a storm in Lane Bryant, trying to find something cute to impress my man."

"What are you talking about?" Loretta said. "And why are you stopping?"

Rachel shook herself out of her trance. "Oh, nothing. There's a space over there." Rachel pointed to the next aisle, then maneuvered her mother's van down it, swinging into a parking space.

They had just stepped into the mall when Rachel turned to

her mother. "Mama, I'll be right back. I think I dropped my sunglasses when we were getting out of the car."

"I didn't see you with any glasses."

"Just go on. I'll meet you in the children's section of Dillard's in just a minute."

"Okay, fine," Loretta said. Rachel waited until her mother had gone up the escalator before she turned around and dashed back out the store entrance. She scanned the rows of cars to see where it was she'd seen Shante's truck. "There it is," she mumbled when she spotted the Expedition sitting between a Ford Taurus and a Chevy Suburban. "Too bad it's so close to the front."

Rachel ducked to the side of the Suburban that was parked farthest from the mall. She pulled up her purse and began sifting through it. Where was a good pocketknife when you needed one? She spotted her metal nail file and pulled it out. Rachel looked around to make sure no one was watching, then she took the file, leaned down, and jabbed it into the sidewall of the Expedition's back tire as hard as she could. Nothing. Rachel drew her arm back and jabbed again, and again, and again, until finally she heard the air hissing out of the tire. Rachel moved to the front tire, repeating the process. She did it two more times on the other side until all the tires were flat. By then, her arm was throbbing with pain. Rachel stepped back and admired her work. She then looked around one more time to make sure no one had spotted her. When she was sure it was safe, she ran her fingers through her hair, and dropped the nail file back into her purse. She spotted her keys and her eyes lit up in thought. Rachel removed the keys, pulled out the longest one, then positioned it between her fingers before running it along the side of Shante's truck. Rachel whistled with a nonchalant look across her face as she ran the key back and forth several times. Satisfied with what she'd done, Rachel dropped the keys in her purse and walked back inside the mall.

She had just stepped off the escalator when she spotted her mother pressed up against a wall. She had a pale look across her face. "Mama, are you all right?" Rachel asked.

"Sshhh!" Loretta put her finger to her lips.

Rachel looked confused. Her mother looked like she was straining to hear the conversation that was going on right around the corner. Rachel listened intently. It must be something important because it wasn't like her mother to eavesdrop.

"Do you know what I could do with a hunk of man like Simon Jackson?" one of the voices said.

Rachel's eyes got wide. "Who is that?" she whispered to her mother.

"Delilah," her mother whispered back. "And Carrie Thompson from church."

Rachel frowned up. She recognized Delilah's sultry voice.

"Are they talking about Daddy?"

Loretta motioned for her to be quiet.

"Girl, who wouldn't love to get them some Simon Jackson? Honey, that is one good-looking man," Carrie responded.

"Tell me something I don't know," Delilah said. "Five minutes. That's all I need and I could turn that man out. He'd think God himself had sent me down for his personal pleasure."

Carrie laughed. "You know his old, plain-Jane, chunky wife ain't turning nothing out but a plate of biscuits every time you turn around. I just can't for the life of me understand why he stays with her."

"I've stopped trying to figure that out. I've just come to the conclusion that it's a charity case. You know, like maybe he just feels sorry for her. I just know if I was first lady of the church, I would come in every Sunday morning in a brand-new suit with a matching hat, gloves, and shoes. You know I'd be working it."

"I know you would, girl. Hell, you look and dress better than Loretta anyway. You look like a first lady should look."

"The problem is convincing Simon of that. I can't tell you how many times I've all but thrown myself at that man. I put these 36DDs up in his face and he just ignored them. No man can resist these!" Delilah exclaimed.

"Well, I'm sure you won't give up until you get him. You're a determined woman." They both burst out laughing.

Loretta became paler and paler. Rachel stood with her mouth wide open. She was furious and had had enough. She didn't care what they said about her father, but they weren't about to sit there and disrespect her mother like that. "Unh-unh." Rachel started heading around the corner. Loretta grabbed her by the arm. "No!"

"What?" Rachel heard Delilah and Carrie's laughter grow distant and she peeked around the corner. They were heading toward the lingerie section. "Mama, I know you're not going to let them talk about you like a dog and you not say anything."

Loretta looked like she was fighting back tears. She swallowed. "We came here to do some shopping, so we're going to do some shopping."

Rachel stared at her mother in disbelief. She knew her mother didn't have much of a backbone with her father, but this was too much.

Loretta ignored Rachel and walked over to a rack. She picked up a blue jean jacket and matching pants. "I saw this for Jordan when I first walked in. Don't you think it's cute?"

Rachel followed her mother, stunned. "Mama, I don't believe you. What is wrong with you? Don't you have any pride? This is ridiculous. I mean, I've heard of weak women in my life, but you take the cake. They called you fat, ugly, and Delilah all but said she was going to take your husband. And you just stand there. How can you be so spineless? Don't you even care how—"

Rachel was unprepared for the slap she received from her mother's right hand. The blow stunned Rachel and stopped her from finishing her sentence. She looked at her mother, dumbfounded. Not only because they were standing in the middle of the department store but also because her mother hadn't struck her in years.

"Shut up! Shut up right now!" Loretta said. "I can't do anything about those hussies disrespecting me, but I won't have my own child disrespecting me!"

Rachel felt tears welling up. Where had that come from? The blow hurt like hell. She also had never seen her mother that angry. Loretta's cinnamon complexion had turned red in fury.

"Don't you think I know what those women say about me? It's not the first time I've heard that nonsense," Loretta hissed. "I know people wonder why Simon is with me. They've been wondering for years. Do those comments still hurt? Yes. But if I don't know nothing else, I know my husband loves me. For me."

Rachel rubbed her cheek, taking in her mother's words. "But Mama, he treats you so bad."

"How? He doesn't beat me, cheat on me. So what makes him a bad husband? Because he asks me to clean and cook? Because I'm submissive to him? Let me tell you something, Rachel." Loretta leaned in close to her daughter. "I submit to him because I *choose* to. I choose to follow God's words and let the man lead. I know you new-age women can't understand that, but that's what I do. And I do it with my head held high. I love cooking, cleaning, and being a good wife. I love taking care of my husband and if that makes me a disgrace to womankind, then I'm sorry. But I won't apologize for who I am, or how I am."

Rachel stared at her mother in amazement. It had never crossed her mind that her mother actually liked being submissive, let alone doing it for biblical reasons.

Rachel removed her hand from her cheek. "Well, I guess I'll never be married. Because I refuse to let a man treat me the way Daddy treats you."

"Your father treats me just fine. Do I wish he spent more time with us? Absolutely. Do I agree with the way he treats you and David? No. But Simon is struggling with his own demons because he feels like a failure as a father. But if I don't know anything else, I know he loves me and each one of you kids. Now, I'm grateful that the Lord blessed me with a man like Simon, whose biggest fault is he spends too much time in his church."

Rachel sniffed and wiped away the single tear falling down her face. Her father felt like a failure? That was news to her. Still, she couldn't agree with her mother's rationale.

"I'm sorry, but I still think you're mad at Carrie and Delilah and taking it out on me."

Loretta's voice turned gentle. "Rachel, I'm not mad at them. I'm happy with who I am, all 228 pounds of me. That's what you don't understand; beauty is from within. You're always talking about Shante, how fat she is. But I'd be willing to bet, Bobby fell in love with her mind. When you have that, everything else falls into place."

Rachel's heart sank at the mention of Bobby loving someone else. She sucked it up and tried to force a smile. While she didn't agree with her mother, she felt a newfound respect for her.

Loretta straightened her back and held her head up. "Now, come on, let's go do some shopping."

14

WHY WAS LIFE so complicated? Jonathan thought being with Veronica would return his life to normal. No such luck. He lay across the bed in his room, staring at a picture of his family. He, David, and Rachel were all little on that picture. It was taken in Virginia Beach, at one of the few family vacations they had ever taken. His dad looked like a proud father in that picture. Over the years, slowly but surely, that proud look had faded as far as David was concerned. Then Rachel. Jonathan knew it was only a matter of time before it would be gone for him as well.

The phone rang, breaking the silence that had settled in the room. Jonathan looked at the Caller ID. It was Veronica, again. He really didn't mean to avoid her, but the other night proved he just wasn't ready for another relationship. Not yet anyway. Granted, she finally gave him an erection, but with her off her cycle, she'd want to have full sex. What if he couldn't come through? It was all he'd thought about since that night. The last three women he'd been with before Tracy had all been a bust, including his last time with Angela. He had lied and told them he was on medication, but it was still embarrassing.

The phone continued to ring. It was like she hung up, waited two minutes, and called right back. Did she know he was avoiding her calls? Jonathan had to get his head together. He thought being with Veronica would make him forget Tracy, but it only made things worse. He had to decide if he was going to love Tracy all the way or not at all. Why couldn't he just make up his mind?

Jonathan leaned in and cut off the ringer on his phone. This was her eighth call today. She had left a nasty message on his cell phone talking about how she didn't appreciate him not returning her calls. A soft knock on the door startled Jonathan out of his thoughts.

"Hey, Dad," Jonathan said, answering it.

"Hey, Son." Simon eased into the room, looked around and smiled. "You've been here weeks and your room is still immaculate. Rachel and David would have had this place in shambles by now."

Jonathan managed a slight grin and sat on the edge of his bed. He knew his father always favored him, that's why it was so difficult to be honest with him. He wasn't sure that being a preacher was his calling. He wasn't sure if he was even worthy of being a preacher. He could never tell his father that. It would tear him up.

"You know I've always been a neat freak, Dad."

"I know. I remember you talking about how it drove your roommate crazy." Simon laughed. "But that's my boy. You got it together all the way around."

If only you knew, Jonathan thought. "So, Reverend Jackson, what brings you into this neck of the woods?"

Simon sat down in the black leather chair across from

Jonathan's bed. "I just wanted to talk to you, Son. You don't look the same. Oh, you put on a good front, but I see it in your eyes. Is something wrong?"

Jonathan gazed at his father. How he wished he could tell him the truth, but that would never, ever happen. Jonathan looked down. He didn't want to tear up.

"Is it Tracy?"

Jonathan's mouth dropped open. How did his father know about Tracy?

"It is, isn't it?" Simon continued. "I heard you on the phone with her the other day. I wasn't eavesdropping, but you sounded very upset." Simon patted Jonathan on the knee. "You can talk to me, Son. Is Tracy your girlfriend?"

Jonathan didn't know what to say. "No."

"Not any more?"

"Something like that," Jonathan responded. He desperately wanted to end this conversation.

"So you two broke up? Is that why you decided to move back home? Is that what has you walking around here so gloomy?"

Jonathan looked away so his father couldn't see the tears in his eyes.

"Son, it's okay. We all get our hearts broken at one time or another. I remember the only other woman I loved besides your mother. Her name was Lillian Butler. She was like a cool glass of lemonade on a hot summer day." Simon smiled at the memory. "That woman was spectacular, and she broke my heart in a thousand pieces. Up and married some doctor. Said she couldn't spend her life as a preacher's wife. I never thought I'd heal from that. Probably like you're feeling right now. But two months after that, I met your mother, and she made me forget all about Lillian. So see, I promise you, you'll find you another young woman to steal your heart. Although, honestly, I think you've found her already. That Angela is something else. You really should try to work things out with her. Everything happens for a reason. We may not understand God's motives, but He knows what's best for us. Turn to your faith now, son. It'll help you be strong, and it'll help you heal."

Jonathan let his father ramble. Faith. He would need a lot of that. He didn't understand why he was hurting so much. When he left Georgia he thought he was doing the right thing, but now, with the emptiness he felt inside, he wasn't so sure.

"Do you understand what I'm saying to you, Son?"

Jonathan hadn't heard any of his father's last comments. He nodded nonetheless. "I know I'll meet someone else. I'll be fine."

"Good. Before I get into what I came up here about, I was just wondering about you and Angela. You know she's good for you?"

"Dad, please."

"I'm just saying, personally, I think you and Angela should really try and work things out. That's a good woman if I've ever seen one. And you two already have a solid foundation. I'll never for the life of me understand why you broke up in the first place."

Jonathan knew how crazy Simon was about Angela. Not just because she was a dedicated member of their church but because she was simply the type of woman everyone fell in love with. She was good-hearted, sweet, respectable, mannerable, and didn't have an evil bone in her body. It had always been Simon's dream that they would end up married.

"Dad, Angela has no interest in me. She's moved on."

"No, I don't think so," Simon said, shaking his head. "That girl still pines for you. I see it in her eyes every time she asks about you, or someone mentions your name. That's why you never ran into her on any of your trips home. Whenever she found out you were coming home, she'd skip service, and that girl never misses church. I just think she couldn't bear to see you because she still loves you."

"Anyway."

"Okay, you don't have to get back together with her, but at least do your old man one favor and work with her on the planning for the youth celebration next month."

Jonathan eyed his father suspiciously. "Come on now. As if she needs my help."

"She does. She has only a few other members working with her, and from what I've heard, she's doing all the work. So could you do that for me? You know how good you are with the kids." Simon smiled mischievously.

Jonathan didn't feel like arguing. Maybe the distraction would do him good. Unlike Veronica, he wouldn't have to worry about Angela being all over him. She was way too classy for that. "Fine, I'll help her."

"Good, I'll let her know, unless of course you want to call her."

"No, I think I'll let you handle that. She may tell you she doesn't want to work with me."

"I'll talk to her. Now that that's all settled, I really came up here to talk to you about your future. I know it has always been your plan to go to seminary school, but did you know some of the best preachers never set foot in a theological classroom?

"I think you have what it takes to lead already. The church needs you." Simon hesitated as a huge grin crossed his face. "Andrew has been offered his own church in Dallas. He told me in confidence, he's going to take it."

Jonathan nodded. Andrew Cooper was the associate pastor

at Zion Hill. Jonathan had heard rumors he might be leaving, but he never thought there was any truth to it.

"Really?" Jonathan said.

"Yes, he is. And I know the perfect person to take his spot."

"Who?" Jonathan had barely gotten the word out when he realized where his father was heading. "Dad, no . . ."

"Nothing would honor me more than to have my son take his rightful place by my side as associate pastor."

Jonathan didn't want this job. Besides, he didn't even know if he was going to stay in Houston. He had just come home to get his head together. He had planned for his future to be in Atlanta, but Tracy's decision to break up had changed that. At this moment, he didn't know where his future lay.

"And I think you can get a job down at the Y mentoring troubled youth," Simon had been rambling on, mapping out Jonathan's future. As usual, Jonathan had little input. "Deacon Riley works down at the Y. I know you won't have any problem getting on with him. Of course, you can stay here as long as you like. Hopefully, in a year or so, you'll meet you a good, clean Christian woman, preferably Angela, settle down, and give me some grandkids."

Jonathan decided not to tell his father that he wasn't going to be a minister. At least not yet. But he knew, at some point, he was going to have to get over his fear and tell his father the truth.

15

DAVID BALLED UP HIS FISTS and began silently counting. He was determined not to get mad. But he couldn't help the rage that was building inside of him. Tawny was leaning back against the wall in the abandoned apartment. Her eyes were closed and judging from the look of euphoria on her face, the crack from the pipe gripped tightly in her hand was having its desired effect.

But that wasn't what had David so furious. It was the pot-bellied, scraggly-haired man standing over Tawny with a cheesy grin plastered across his face. He was fastening up his pants.

"Damn, baby, I have to say it again. That was good. Next time I'll double up and give you six rocks," he said.

"Umm-hmmm," Tawny moaned.

David could no longer contain his anger. He rushed in, pushing the man to the floor.

"What the—!" the man screamed.

"David!" Tawny yelled as she tried to get up off the floor. "What are you doing?"

"No, the question is, What are you doing?" David said through clenched teeth.

"Why you come up in here trippin'? This Tommy, you hooked me up with him in the first place. You remember?"

David stared at the man, who remained cowering on the floor. "That was six months ago. What you doing with him now?"

Tawny pulled herself completely up and started nervously glancing around. "I was just . . . ummm . . . I was walking down the street and I bumped into him and he asked me if I wanted to ummm, you know, get high." Tawny shrugged and gave a weak laugh. "And you know I ain't never been one to pass up a free high." She stepped toward David and put her arm around him. He slapped her arm away.

"Come on, baby, don't be mad."

"It wasn't free, Tawny. You fucked him. For three rocks," David spat.

"Damn. What you getting all worked up about? You wasn't saying nothing when you had me sleeping with him so *you* could get high."

David noticed Tommy scurrying away out of the corner of his eye. He decided to let him go. Right now, he had to deal with Tawny.

"You know we were at a low point when that happened. We said it wouldn't happen again," David said. He rubbed his temple, trying to figure out how his life had been reduced to this. Why did he even stay with Tawny? She didn't do anything but bring him down. "Tawny, I told you I wanted us to leave the drugs alone. Don't you want something better for us?"

"Whatever." Tawny was shaking her head. "You need to go on with that shit. You fucking up my high."

David stared at Tawny in disgust. He had told her he

wanted to try to get clean. After leaving his family at church, he sat Tawny down in one of her rare sober moments and had a long talk. He'd told her this wasn't how he wanted to live his life. He wanted kids of his own. He wanted more to life than his next high. Part of him wondered why he even stayed with Tawny because that was all she was concerned about. But the other part felt like he wasn't any better than Tawny, so they deserved each other.

David had begged her to work with him so they could both get off the drugs. Of course, he'd slipped up a few times, but for the most part, he was trying to stay clean. Last week, they were mugged after coming back from buying drugs and David had said that was the last straw. He made Tawny go with him the next day to the community center to see a drug rehab counselor. Although Tawny had fidgeted through the whole session, David thought they were making progress.

Then when David came home today and the little boy next door told him he saw Tawny leave with a fat white man, David knew exactly where to find her. This abandoned apartment was her favorite place to turn tricks.

David groaned as he thought about how he had condoned that at one point, even going so far as finding men like Tommy. David had gotten tired of that real quick. High or not, he couldn't stand knowing another man was having sex with his woman. But Tawny was persistent, saying it was an easy way to get money and drugs.

"Tawny, I thought we said we were going to try and let this stuff go."

"You said that shit. Not me. I don't want to let it go." Tawny plopped back down, picked up a baggie off the floor, and took out a rock. David watched as she put it in the pipe, flicked her lighter under it, and let the flames dance around it. With her eyes half closed, she leaned in and inhaled the smoke from the pipe. David knew he should just leave her there. Just leave, period. There was no hope for Tawny. But there was hope for him. He could just walk away. *Then why don't you,* a little voice kept saying in his head.

"Baby, this is some high-quality shit," Tawny taunted. "It'll make you feel real good."

David stared at the pipe, it was mesmerizing. "I told you. My family. I'm trying to do right."

"Man, fuck your family. You can never touch a drug again and you'll never be anything in their eyes. Isn't that what you're always telling me?" Tawny wrapped her lips around the pipe and slowly inhaled again. David watched as her chest heaved, then she slowly sank back against the wall. "Awww, yeah," Tawny moaned. "Baby, you don't know what you missing. Come on. Just one hit." Tawny held the pipe out. David stood firm, although it was becoming more and more difficult.

Tawny puffed again after David didn't move. She slowly exhaled and looked David directly in the eyes. "You said yourself, your father ain't got no love for you. You think just because you give up something you enjoy, something that makes you feel good, you think all that will change? You ain't got no job, no future. All we got is each other and this," Tawny said, caressing the crack pipe. She lowered her voice to just above a whisper. "Don't punk out on me now, baby." She extended the pipe again. "And when we finish this, I know where we can get some more."

David's vision was getting blurry. Was Tawny right? Was he desperately fighting to let the drugs go for nothing? Even if he was clean, it's not like he was all of sudden going to become Simon's pride and joy. Tawny was right about one thing, neither one of them had a future. No skills, no job, no money. He got depressed as he thought about his life. What was the use? He had given it his best shot. He simply couldn't do it. Besides, that pipe did look so inviting and Tawny looked like she was feeling really good.

"Fuck it. Give it here," David said, snatching the pipe out of Tawny's hand. She smiled as he put the pipe to his mouth, deeply inhaled, and let the smoke wash away all thoughts of his family.

16

SIMON SAT IN THE LIVING ROOM laughing at his favorite TV show, *Sanford and Son*. No matter how many times he saw each episode, it still made him crack up. Maybe because Fred Sanford reminded him of his own Uncle Cleo, the black sheep of their minister-laden family.

This was about the only thing he ever watched on television, with the exception of his church programs and the news. It was the only luxury he had time for. However, tonight he needed to be going over the church budget, but he felt utterly exhausted. He had spent all day at the hospital with a church member whose son was in a coma from a drug overdose. The boy wasn't but eighteen years old. It was a shame. Simon saw David there or dead in just a few months. He felt a twinge of pain as he imagined his eldest son dying from drugs. Although David had always been a little mischievous, he had had a promising future. Simon reflected on what he could've done differently to alter David's path. He seldom went to any of David's games because they usually fell on Friday nights and he had Bible study on those nights, but he'd always made sure David knew he was proud of his achievements. Maybe he'd been too hard when David was injured. He'd tried to push David to go to rehabilitation daily so that he could heal. But it was only because he knew how bad David wanted to play football. David had taken Simon's efforts the wrong way, even going so far as asking, "Will you not love me if I'm not this great football hero?" It was absurd to Simon, but apparently David felt that way. Simon wondered if maybe he'd not done enough to convince David he would love him regardless.

He shook off his doubts. There was no sense in wondering about maybes now. David had chosen to seek solace in drugs. And if it was God's will to take David, so be it. Simon had washed his hands of his oldest son. He had disgraced his family for the last time.

"Sweetheart, are you coming to bed?" Loretta poked her head into the living room. She had on a long, white cotton night-gown with yellow flowers all over it. Her hair was in pink curlers, which poked from underneath her satin cap. Still, Simon smiled at the sight of his wife. She was the most beautiful woman he had ever seen.

"I'm going to finish watching this episode. It's where Fred meets Lena Horne and nobody believes him."

"You've only seen that a thousand times," Loretta said, laughing.

"I know, but you know I love me some *Sanford and Son.*"

"I know you do. Well, I'm going to bed. Good night."

Simon stopped her before she turned to walk away. "You know what else I love?"

"God, of course," Loretta answered without hesitation.

"Of course. And you." He flashed that seductive smile he knew had won her heart so many years ago. They had met at a gospel concert on campus. Simon was actually trying to make eye contact with her friend, but his eyes met Loretta's and they just sort of clicked.

Loretta walked over and kissed Simon on the head. "I love you, too."

Simon pulled her onto his lap. They seldom did anything together anymore and their sex life was all but nonexistent. It wasn't that he didn't desire her. He was just too busy. But once upon a time, he and Loretta were like rabbits in a cage. Maybe now was the moment to revisit the cage. "You sho' are looking mighty sexy in them there pink curlers," Simon joked. "You goin' make me turn off *Sanford and Son*."

Loretta giggled and kicked her legs like a giddy schoolgirl. "Simon, what are you doing? Behave yourself. Jonathan may walk in."

"Nah, he left with Kevin to go somewhere. Said he wouldn't be back until later." Simon started nibbling at his wife's neck. "Ummm, you taste so good!"

"Simon!"

"What? You're my wife, aren't you?"

"Well, yes . . . but, it's been so long."

"That's why Mr. Wiggle Man wants to come out and play," Simon joked. He couldn't believe himself. It had been years since he acted like this, but somehow his weariness was gone and he actually felt himself burning with desire for his wife. He didn't have to worry about them going too long. They were both past the point of all-nighters. "So, whatcha wearing underneath that sexy, cotton muumuu you have on there?"

Loretta jumped up, still giggling. "Stop, Simon."

Simon stood up after her. "Your lips say no, but your body

says yes. Come here, woman!" Simon laughed and playfully lunged toward his wife, who let out a small yelp when she toppled over on the sofa. In a second, Simon was on top of her. "Don't fight it, baby," he quipped. Loretta was cracking up. Simon could tell she was enjoying every minute of it. He began nibbling on her neck again when he heard a loud pounding on the front door. The noise was so intense, both of them stopped and turned their attention to the door.

"What in the world?" Simon said. He eased up off his wife and made his way to the door. The pounding was louder, almost frantic. "Who is it?" Simon yelled.

"Dad, open the door! Open the door!" It was David and he was screaming at the top of his lungs.

Simon stood glaring at the door. Loretta sat up on the sofa, a look of fear across her face. "Oh, my God," she whispered.

"What do you want?" Simon yelled through the door.

"Daddy, not now, please!" David screamed. "Just open the door before they kill me!"

Simon felt his anger building. David was caught up in some madness, no doubt because of drugs. And here Simon was thinking after that day at the church, maybe David would actually clean himself up. "Get away from my door! I told you you're not welcome here!"

"Daddy, please. They're going to kill me!" David sounded like he was crying, and out of breath.

"Simon, let him in." Loretta was clutching the top of her gown, her eyes transfixed on the door.

"I'm not letting him bring his drug-infested behavior in our home!" Simon spat toward his wife. They both jumped as they heard a loud thud against the front door. It was followed by several men yelling and David screaming and crying even louder.

"Simon, do something NOW!"

Simon briefly stared at his wife. "Oh, for Christ's sake!" He raced to the hall closet where he pulled out a locked rifle case he kept on the top shelf, pushed all the way to the back. He quickly punched in the combination and removed a loaded 12-gauge shotgun before throwing the front door open.

"Get away from my house!" Simon yelled with the shotgun aimed directly at the head of one of the three people attacking his son. All three stopped beating David, who was lying on the front porch, bleeding.

"Yo, Pops, we ain't got no beef with you. Go on back inside," said a tall man in a black leather jacket.

"As long as you're on my property, you got a beef with me. Now go!"

"Like I said, this between us and David," the man repeated.

Simon didn't move the gun from the man's head. "Loretta, call the cops, right now!"

The man nearest David's head motioned like he was going toward his jacket. Simon quickly aimed the gun his way. "Ah, ah, ah. I wouldn't do that if I were you. Just because I'm a man of God doesn't mean I won't blow you to kingdom come."

"Come on, man, let's get out of here before the cops come," a short, muscular boy, who looked like he couldn't be any more than seventeen, said.

"Yeah, we'll catch this fool slipping," the second guy replied.

The tall man who had been doing all the talking held his hands up. "Aw'ight, Pops, you win. This time. But tell that crackhead son of yours that you don't get something for nothing. And the next time he or his anorexic girlfriend even so much as thinks about smoking some of my stuff and not paying up, I'm goin' put a bullet in his head, her head, yo head, and that pretty little wife of yours' head. And I'm going do it all right in the middle of Sunday morning service." He never took his eyes off Simon the entire time he spoke. Somehow, Simon knew this man meant every word he said.

"Thank you for the warning, Mr. Drug Dealer. Now get off my property," Simon said sternly.

The man smiled, kicked David one last time for good measure, then motioned for his boys to leave with him.

David coughed, sputtering up blood. Loretta raced out onto the porch, dropped down, and lifted David's head until it was resting on her lap. Both of his eyes were swollen, and a cut above one was bleeding. He moaned and clutched his ribs.

Loretta cried and rocked David back and forth.

"It's goin' to be okay, baby. Hang on, we're gonna get you some help." Loretta looked up at Simon. "Go call an ambulance."

Simon just stood there, staring at David.

"Go!" Loretta repeated.

Simon shook his head in disgust. "You reap what you sow," he said, as he turned inside to call for help.

17

JONATHAN STOOD NERVOUSLY at the door to the small meeting room. He couldn't believe he let his father talk him into this. Angela was more than capable of planning the youth day celebration without him. This was just his father's way of pushing them together.

Jonathan actually cared very deeply for Angela. But after Tracy, he didn't know what he wanted anymore.

Angela looked up and saw Jonathan standing in the doorway. "Hey, come on in. Your dad told me you were coming, although honestly, I didn't think you'd show."

Jonathan shifted.

"Have a seat. I already have the first activity planned. I was thinking a church lock-in for the kids."

Jonathan relaxed. Angela was getting straight to business so he didn't have to worry about any uncomfortable moments between them.

Angela spent the next hour detailing her plans for the week and soliciting Jonathan's input. After they wrapped up,

Jonathan felt like he hadn't been much help, but she seemed to value his advice.

Angela had been perky throughout most of the meeting, but her mood was suddenly changing. Jonathan figured she must have been thinking about them.

He tried to make small talk, but she didn't seem receptive. Finally, she looked him directly in the eyes and said, "Are you sure it wasn't another woman?"

Jonathan could see how much she was still hurting. "No. I promise you that." He wished he could talk to her. That was one thing he'd loved about their relationship, they could talk about anything. Anything but the real reason he left.

"Angela, it was never you. It was just me." He gazed at her beautiful hazel eyes and smiled at the memories of the fun they used to have.

"You know you really hurt me." The words came out slow and deliberate.

Jonathan's mind went back to his last conversation with Tracy. They hadn't talked since that day at the airport. Tracy had moved on. It was time he did, too. With Veronica it was all about lust, but he could honestly say what he still felt for Angela went far beyond that.

Jonathan gently rubbed his hand across Angela's cheek. "That was never my intention."

Angela inhaled, then nodded, fighting off tears. Jonathan stood, walked over, and pulled her up into his arms. "I'm sorry."

She didn't cry, but her body sank in his embrace. Her perfume tingled his nose. He, too, felt relieved as he hugged her tightly. "I'll always love you," he whispered.

Angela looked up at him. "Jonathan, don't say stuff you don't mean."

"I mean it, Angela." He didn't know where all this was coming from. Just holding her brought back so many memories. Or was he just trying to escape Tracy? Either way, Jonathan knew it felt good to have her in his arms again.

The next thing he knew, his lips were moving toward Angela's. When they met, he felt the electricity he thought was long gone and he kissed her with passion and intensity.

"Now as happy as I am to see this display of affection, I don't think the church is the place for it."

Angela and Jonathan jumped apart at the sound of Simon's voice. He was standing at the entrance to the room with Loretta by his side.

"Dad—" Jonathan stammered. Angela looked down at the floor.

"That's okay, son. Nothing to be ashamed about. It warms my heart to see you two together. I pray this is a sign of good things to come."

Angela never removed her eyes from the floor. "Reverend Jackson, that kiss . . . it was nothing."

"Nonsense," Simon said. "I saw the sparks before I stepped into the room. You two are destined to be together. God knows it and soon enough, you'll know it, too." Simon beamed with pride. "Now, let me see what great things you two have planned for our young people!"

Destined to be together. Jonathan pondered the thought. Maybe that's why his relationship with Tracy had failed. Because his destiny lay here at home.

18

SIMON STARED AT HIS OLDEST SON sprawled out across the sofa watching television. The sight of him made Simon sick. He kept trying and trying to give David the benefit of the doubt, and David kept messing up.

David's ribs were taped up with white gauze. Both his right eye and his lips were swollen. He had spent two days in the hospital, a bill that Simon had to foot. Then Loretta had been adamant about David staying with them until he got better. At first, Simon said no, but Loretta wouldn't let up. Since she very seldom spoke up about anything, he eventually just let it go. He didn't like it, but for the sake of his wife, he'd deal with it for a couple of weeks.

Now, watching David lounging on his sofa, flipping the channels, he felt his anger rising again. All this because of drugs.

Simon decided not to get into it with David because Jonathan was in a chair in the corner fast asleep.

Simon walked over to the sofa, snatched the remote out of David's hand, then returned to his seat in the recliner. David looked like he wanted to protest, then thought better of it. Simon flipped to the religious channel and began watching a church service.

David groaned loudly. "Do we have to watch this?"

Simon didn't take his eyes off the TV. "No, you don't have to watch anything. You can go back to your place and watch whatever you'd like."

David exhaled and gently flipped over, turning his back to his father.

"Maybe if you did watch programs like this from time to time, your life wouldn't be so messed up."

"Oh, here we go. I knew this was coming. I'm just surprised it didn't come up sooner," David said, from the wall.

Simon flipped the TV off and leaned forward. If he woke up Jon, then so be it. "What's wrong with you, boy? Why do you defile your body like that?"

David didn't respond.

"Answer me!"

David turned back over to face his father. "Defile my body like what?"

"You dang near got killed trying to cheat somebody out of some drugs. Do they make you feel that good? I'm just trying to understand." Simon threw up his arms in frustration.

"As a matter of fact, they do. They help me forget my troubles."

"What troubles? You live with your girlfriend; you don't work. What troubles you got?"

David glowered at his father. "How about a father that can't stand me."

Simon leaned back and exhaled loudly. "Of course, this has to be my fault. It all comes back down to what a horrible father I am."

David shook his head. "I didn't say that."

"So, what are you saying then? That I'm the reason you got hurt in school? I'm the reason you weren't man enough to pick yourself up? I'm the reason you turned to drugs?"

David wouldn't respond. He covered his eyes with his hand.

"Look at your brother here." Simon pointed to Jonathan, who had awakened but was trying to stay out of their argument. "You're the one who's supposed to be setting an example. But it's Jon who has himself together. A college graduate."

"Oh, that Jonathan," David sarcastically responded. "He should get a Nobel Peace Prize. He's right up there with Jesus."

"Say what you want about Jon. It's a good thing I got him, because you and Rachel, y'all could shame the devil!"

Simon threw the remote on the table, got up, and stormed out.

Jonathan and David sat in silence for a few minutes.

"Man, I'm sorry about that," Jonathan finally said.

David laughed, removing his hand from his face. "Hey, it ain't nothing new."

Jonathan cast his eyes downward. Unfortunately, he was right. Even growing up, he was always the favored one. He was always the one that Simon praised, doted over, and compared everyone else to. It had caused his siblings to be bitter toward him and made his childhood miserable.

"I'll never live up to King Jonathan. I've stopped trying," David continued.

"Just be yourself, David."

"Myself?" David laughed. "Naw, man. I am now, and forever will be, a worthless piece of shit in the eyes of the honorable Reverend Simon Jackson."

"It's just the drugs. He can't stand seeing you on drugs."

"Jon, quit fooling yourself. I've always been worthless to him. The bad little son who was always shaming the good reverend. It got so the only time he ever showed me any attention was when he was getting on my case about something I did. Then I discovered I could play football. That's the only thing that made me halfway decent in his eyes. So when that was gone, what was left?"

"You can't blame Dad for your doing drugs."

"I'm not blaming him. I get high 'cause I like getting high. I don't have to think about shit when I'm floating in the air."

"Man, watch your language. Mama's right in the kitchen."

"See? Good ol' Jon, always minding his manners."

Jonathan surveyed his brother. He looked horrible, and not just from the beating he had sustained. "Why are you so bitter?"

"You'd be bitter too if you spent your whole life trying to live up to your little brother. It's bad enough we gotta compete with that damned church, but then I gotta compete with you, holier-than-thou Jonathan."

Jonathan hated that people had that attitude about him. "I'm not holier than thou."

David snickered. "Oh, yeah, you are. Or at least you want everybody to think you are. You have sex; that's your downfall. I've heard the stories. Not from you, 'cause you want everybody to think you're so perfect. But I heard about all the women you be bonin'. You can't even admit to your own brother that you're having sex. Why? You're a grown man."

"I never said I don't have sex. I just don't talk about it."

"My point exactly. What twenty-three-year-old man you know don't talk about it? That's because you don't want people to know. More specifically, you don't want Dad to know. It would just break his heart to know you bone and move on."

"I'm not like that anymore."

"Whatever you say, man. Can you pass me the remote, please?"

Jonathan got up and walked over to the table. He reached down, grabbed the remote, then threw it at his brother. "I'm just saying things would be so much easier if you would just give up the drugs. I mean, you're not that hooked. You've been here three days without them."

David caught the remote, switched the TV back on, and began flipping channels. "Yeah, that's why I'm about to go crazy. But that's all right, Tawny will be here in a little while to bring me a hit."

Jonathan looked at his brother in shock. "I know you're not going to sit in their house and get high."

"Of course not. We goin' go out back," David laughed. "You need to try it yourself. It'll help you relieve some of that pressure from trying to be Mr. Perfect."

Jonathan debated what to do. He contemplated telling his father, but he knew he would kick David out so fast it wouldn't be funny.

Loretta appeared in the doorway. "Hey, boys. Are you all hungry?"

Jonathan shook his head. "No, thank you." His mind wasn't on food. He was thinking of David's words and how tired he was of trying to live up to that perfect image. He even found himself questioning his relationship with Angela. They had been hanging out more and more in the last few weeks. It's like she was the icing on his picture-perfect life. That's why everyone was pushing for them to be together.

"Mama, are you all right?" David asked.

Jonathan was so caught up in his thoughts he hadn't noticed his mother lean against the wall and grab her chest. She looked pale. Jonathan walked toward his mother. "Are you okay?"

"I'm fine. Just a little chest pain," Loretta responded.

Simon walked into the room. "It's probably all the added stress around here," Simon said, glaring at David. He patted his recliner. "Here, sweetheart, have a seat."

Loretta didn't move. She was still rubbing her chest. "No, I need to finish cooking. Dinner's just about ready."

Jonathan spoke up. "Mother, I'll go in and finish."

Loretta weakly smiled like she was actually grateful to be off the hook for dinner. "Okay, baby. If you all don't mind, I'm going to go lie down. I'm not feeling too well. It's probably just a little indigestion. You know how I love to nibble as I'm cooking."

"Do you need some help?" David asked.

"As if you'd be able to help her," Simon snapped.

"Now you all stop all this fussing. No, I don't need any help. I'm just going to go upstairs and lie down. You all just enjoy your dinner. Rachel and the kids should be by shortly."

Loretta hadn't gotten out of the room good before Simon spun toward David. "Do you see this? You're making your mother sick!"

David relaxed back on the sofa and turned his attention back to the TV.

"Do you hear me talking to you?" Simon shouted.

David quickly sat up, moaning at the pain of moving so fast. "Of course, this would all be my fault. The rising price of gas is my fault. All the madness and mayhem in the world, yep, I'm responsible for that as well, as usual."

Simon stomped over and stood in front of his son. "This is your fault! Bringing this nonsense into our house. Having thugs scare your mother half to death." Simon stopped talking when he noticed a shadow out on the patio. He peered outside. The figure ducked down behind the rose bushes. Simon raced to the patio doors, threw them open, and yelled, "Who's over there? You better come out right now, or I'm calling the cops." He waited for a response. "Jonathan, call the police! The last thing I need is those thugs coming back to the house to finish what they started."

"Wait! Wait! Wait!" Tawny stepped out from behind the rose bushes. She looked a mess. Her stringy hair was still matted to her face. Her clothes were dirty and she looked like she hadn't slept in days. "Ain't no need to call five-oh."

Simon surveyed the woman with disgust. "Are you David's girlfriend?"

"Yeah." Tawny held up her head. "I came to see my man."

Simon pointed to the small brown paper bag in her hand. "What's that?"

Tawny moved the bag behind her back. "Um. Nothing. Just a little somethin', somethin' to help David get better. Where is he?"

David had managed to struggle off the sofa and was leaning over Simon's shoulder looking out the patio door. "Yo, Tawny, I'm busy right now. I'll get with you later."

Tawny strained to see David. "What? I know you ain't had me catch the bus, coming all the way over here, just to send me home!"

"Tawny, now ain't the time."

"I tell you what." Tawny held up the bag and shook it. "If I leave I'm smoking this shit by myself."

David put his hands on his head in frustration. Simon scrunched up his brow in disbelief and turned to face David. "I know you didn't have this scandalous woman bring drugs to my house."

"He damn sho' did!" Tawny yelled. "So, David get your old man to let me in, or bring your ass outside!"

Simon twirled back around to face Tawny. "Young lady, I think you need to leave," he said, in as civil a voice as he could muster.

"Yeah. Beat it, Tawny. You can't come over to my mama's house acting a fool!" David shouted.

Tawny went ballistic. "I'm out here tricking so your ass can get a hit. That ugly, fat-ass man you sent me to damn near suffocated me. Then turned around and gypped me and only gave me half the stuff he promised."

"You slept with him?" David yelled. "I told you not to sleep with him!"

"Whatever! How was I supposed to pay him, stupid? I did all that," she held up the bag again, "and I get over here and you want to play me for crazy! You done lost your damned mind! Hell, naw, we fixin' ta smoke this right now!"

Jonathan was standing in the window, his mouth hanging wide open. Simon whispered, "Lord Jesus, have mercy on my soul. Not only is my son a drug addict, he's a pimp to boot."

"Daddy, I ain't no pimp. Don't be listening to Tawny. She high." He hobbled around his father. "Girl, you better take that crap somewhere else! Coming over here disrespecting my people!"

"Mother—" Tawny stopped talking, looked around, spotted a brick stacked up against the side of the house, then picked it up and hauled it toward David. Simon and David both dove out of the way, just as the brick smashed into the window next to the patio. Glass went everywhere. "You sorry, good for nothing, trifling-ass dog!" Tawny continued to search for more things to throw.

Loretta appeared in the den's entrance. "What in the world is going on down here?" She looked at the busted window, then peered outside. "What happened and who is that out there acting crazy?"

Jonathan just shook his head. "That's Tawny, David's girl-friend."

"She ain't my girlfriend no more!" David shouted, pulling himself up off the ground. "I'm through with stupid hos!"

Loretta rubbed her chest and sank in the recliner. "Oh, Jesus."

Simon was still in shock and remained stooped on the ground. Jonathan decided it was time for him to get this situation under control. He eased outside in front of his brother. "Tawny," he called out. "David didn't mean any of that. He's on painkillers. That's why he's talking crazy."

Tawny looked skeptically at Jonathan, a brick nestled in her hand ready for launch. "Who the hell are you?"

"I'm David's brother, Jonathan. Why don't I just give you a ride back home?"

Tawny started rapidly tapping her foot. "I want David to come here and talk to me."

"I ain't coming nowhere!" David yelled.

Suddenly, Simon stood and spun on his son. "Yes, you are! Get out! Get out of my house!"

David looked at his mother, his eyes pleading for her to come to his aid. Loretta looked like she was too tired to argue. Simon never took his eyes off David. "I am sorry, Loretta, but I will not allow this sorry excuse for a son to defile my home, bringing in his drug-infested friends, and blatantly disrespecting me. I don't care how sick he is, I want him out! And it's not open for discussion!" Simon turned and stormed out of the den. Loretta sighed heavily, muttered, "I'm sorry, David," then got up and followed Simon out of the room.

David started after Loretta to protest. Jonathan stopped him. "Don't, man. Maybe you need to go home with Tawny, at least until we get this all straightened out."

Tawny had made her way onto the patio and was standing just outside the door, with a victorious look across her face.

"Fine," David said, "I don't want to stay in this stuffy-ass place anyway." He wobbled over to the sofa, stepped into his shoes, and looked around for his car keys. He noticed them sitting on top of the TV. He turned to Tawny. "Grab my keys and let's go."

"Yes, baby." Tawny's whole attitude had changed. You'd have never known she was just in their backyard throwing bricks and acting a fool.

Tawny grabbed the keys, clutched the brown paper bag, and strung her arm around David. "Let me help you to your truck, baby." David glared at her. Tawny got an innocent expression across her face. "What, I'm sorry, okay? You know how I get sometime. I just need a little hit and some of you."

David looked at her, then Jonathan, before finally starting toward the door. "Me, too, baby. Me, too. Let's roll."

Jonathan watched as they stepped over the shattered glass and walked outside and around to David's truck. He was convinced that they were both crazy. He shook his head as his mind replayed the scene that had just unfolded. Maybe he should've stayed in Atlanta. This family drama was almost as bad as what he was dealing with back there.

19

It had been just over two months since he'd talked to Tracy. While it'd been hard, Jonathan had been able to make it through because of the beautiful young lady who stood in front of the choir directing the young voices through a glorious rendition of "His Eye Is on the Sparrow."

Angela beamed as the young soloist belted out the words that sent the congregation into a frenzy. The little girl, Alicia Patterson, sang like she was thirty years old, even though she clearly couldn't be any more than seven or eight.

Jonathan stood with other members, applauding as the youth choir wrapped up their selection.

Angela motioned for the children to sit, then turned to the congregation and smiled. Her eyes met Jonathan's and he broke out into a huge smile as well.

They had seemed to pick up where they left off, spending almost all of their time together these past few weeks. At first, it was simply a distraction from Tracy, but soon Jonathan got to the point where he was actually looking forward to their time together.

Jonathan watched Angela walk back to the choir stand as his father called for one more round of applause for the choir and soloist.

Their youth day event had been a success, even though he felt he hadn't done much but offer his opinion, one that generally mirrored that of Angela's. Still, she seemed appreciative of his assistance.

Simon's sermon was short today, something about asking God for forgiveness. Jonathan had been in another world throughout the sermon. Right after his father began, Jonathan started to wonder if God would ever forgive him for his relationship with Tracy. He spent the next twenty minutes thinking about all the reasons he shouldn't be with Tracy, and all the reasons he should pursue a relationship with Angela.

In the end, he decided there was no question about it, he needed to be with Angela.

"So, what did you think?"

Jonathan and Angela were sitting across from each other in a booth at Carrino's, Angela's favorite Italian restaurant. It was her twenty-fourth birthday and much to his mother's dismay, Jonathan had agreed to take her to dinner after church. Loretta wanted them to come eat at her house, but Jonathan knew Angela wanted to be alone with him on her birthday; she'd been hinting at it all week. The atmosphere was perfect. The restaurant was dimly lit, a small tea lamp shining from the back center of the table. Most of the people in the restaurant looked like they were in love or trying to get there.

"You did an awesome job today," Jonathan said, taking Angela's hand.

"*We* did an awesome job," she said, squeezing his hand tightly. "We make an awesome team."

Jonathan loved seeing the happiness etched in her face. "That we do." He hesitated, never taking his eyes off her.

"I wonder where our food is," Angela said, trying to get his gaze off her.

Jonathan continued to stare. How could he have ever let this woman go, let their relationship go? How could he have given up something that seemed so right, so natural, for something so . . . unnatural?

"Why are you staring at me?" Angela finally asked.

"Angela, I was a fool," Jonathan replied.

"I know that." She smiled, trying to lighten the moment.

"Seriously, I never should have let you get away. We were meant to be together."

"Well, I'm just glad you finally realized there were no better fish in the sea," she said, half-kidding.

"I told you—"

"I know. I know. You didn't leave me for another woman." Angela turned her head. "Look, let's not talk about why you left."

Jonathan paused as the waiter sat their food in front of them. Angela had ordered the shrimp scampi pasta. He had stuck with the tried-and-true spaghetti.

"Can I get anything else for you?" the waiter asked.

Angela shook her head.

"We're fine," Jonathan responded. He eyed Angela's food. "That looks good."

"You haven't changed. We come to the best Italian restaurant in the state, and you order spaghetti and meatballs."

Jonathan dipped his fork into his noodles and twirled them around before bringing them to his mouth. He made a funny face, causing Angela to break out into laughter.

Jonathan talked incessantly throughout the rest of the dinner. He was trying not to let thoughts of Tracy seep into his head.

"Boy, you were just a little chatterbox tonight," Angela said, after they had paid the check and were on their way back to her apartment.

"Oh, I'm sorry." Jonathan searched for words to explain his behavior. "It just feels good talking with you again."

Angela smiled and took his hand. She leaned her head back against the seat in his car and closed her eyes. Jonathan kept her hand gripped tightly as he navigated his car down Interstate Ten toward her apartment.

It wasn't long before Jonathan found himself standing in front of Angela's door, waiting for her to get it unlocked. The sun was setting and cast a shadow on Angela's back.

"Thank you for dinner. And a memorable birthday," she said, turning to face him.

"It was my pleasure." Jonathan looked into Angela's eyes. She seemed happy, yet cautious. He realized then just how much he'd hurt her.

"I will always love you."

Angela's shoulders sank with relief. "I will always love you, too." She leaned in and kissed Jonathan. A slow, deliberate, and passionate kiss. It sent fire through every inch of his body. He hadn't felt like that since Tracy. He closed his eyes. There was Tracy invading his thoughts again. Jonathan kissed Angela harder, hoping his passion would will thoughts of Tracy away.

He opened his eyes and pulled back from her. "Can I come inside?"

"I don't know if that's a good idea." If ever there was a time when the phrase "her mouth said no, but her eyes said yes" applied, this was it. Angela looked like she wanted him, desperately.

"Please. I need you." Jonathan desperately wanted her, too. This was different from Veronica. He needed to be with Angela to prove how much he loved her, that he was making the right decision by letting Tracy go.

"Jonathan, I haven't been with anyone since we broke up. I . . . I promised God if he just let me get over you, I'd honor Him and stay celibate until I got married." Angela's breathing was heavy. It looked like it was taking every ounce of her power to get those words out.

"I need you," Jonathan repeated, leaning in and kissing her even more forcefully.

He felt the hesitation in Angela's body. But he also felt her start to relax the longer he kissed her. She wanted him just as much as he needed her.

Angela pulled herself from his touch. She stared at him through misty eyes. "Jonathan, I can't be hurt again."

Jonathan stared back. His thoughts were cloudy. All he knew right now was that more than anything he wanted to be with Angela. "I'll never hurt you again." He kissed her again, this time easing her through the front door and inside the apartment. Angela pulled back, dropped her purse on the floor, and pushed the door shut. "Do you promise?"

"I promise," he said, taking her into his arms.

Jonathan didn't know if he'd be able to keep that promise, but right now, he knew that from the bottom of his heart, he meant it.

20

RACHEL BRUSHED OUT THE WRINKLES in her dress as she stepped to the doorway. Her heart was racing. Bobby had actually called and asked her to come over without Jordan. She knew he'd come around. She had raced to the mall and bought the multicolored wrap dress now hugging her body. The strappy, high-heeled sandals were the perfect topping, showing off her smooth legs. She felt as good as she knew she looked.

Rachel had her auburn-tinted hair in spiral curls, just the way Bobby liked it. She ran her fingers through the curls and tossed the few loose strands out of her face before ringing the doorbell. This was the opportunity she'd been waiting for. She was determined not to mess it up again. All she needed was another chance. She could make Bobby love her again.

"Rachel?" Bobby called from the other side of the door.

"Yeah, it's me."

Bobby eased the door open. "Come on in." He had a serious look on his face. Rachel didn't let it bother her. She knew she'd have a smile on his face before she left.

"How are you?" Rachel asked as she strutted in. She was making sure her hips swayed as she passed Bobby. He used to always tell her how fine she was: she had kept her figure despite having two kids.

"I'm doing okay." Bobby closed the door.

"I'm glad you called." Rachel turned, paused, then looked Bobby dead in the eyes. "I've missed you so much." Rachel stepped forward and began to raise her arms for a hug. Bobby backed up.

Rachel stepped back. *Slow down, girl. This may be a little more work than I thought.* "Sorry, I didn't mean to scare you off. It's just that I've been waiting so long for this moment."

Bobby stepped around her. "Rachel, I think you have the wrong idea—"

Rachel rushed out her words. "I knew you never stopped loving me. I could tell in your voice. I sure as hell never stopped loving you. I just want us to be a family again."

"Rachel, listen. That's not why I called you over here."

"Bobby, let's stop playing games. We were meant to be together. I know it, and you know it too. I think we've just—" Rachel stopped midsentence and stared at the entrance to the living room. "What in the hell is she doing here?"

Bobby slid over to where Shante was standing.

"Is everything okay, Boo?" Shante asked.

"Boo???" Rachel felt her temper flaring. What kind of game was Bobby playing? *Calm down,* she told herself. This is the new Rachel, the one that doesn't act a fool. "Bobby, what is going on?" she asked, her hands positioned defensively on her hips.

Bobby took Shante's hand. "Baby, I'll handle this. You go on in the back."

Shante patted his hand. "No, I think I'll stay." She walked

over to the love seat, sat down, picked up an *Essence* magazine, and started flipping through the pages. Bobby looked like he wanted to protest but just let out a deep sigh.

"I'm going to ask you again," Rachel said, crossing her arms. "Tell me what that bitch is doing here."

So much for being civilized. Maybe it just wasn't in her blood.

"This bitch belongs here," Shante snidely responded. She scooted to the edge of the seat like she was preparing for a fight.

Bobby jumped in before anyone could say anything else. "Look, Rachel, I called you because I needed to talk to you. Will you sit down, please?"

"Why does she have to be here, though?" Rachel didn't know whether to cry or wring that smug-looking heifer's neck.

"I told you," Shante interjected forcefully, "I'm here because, as Bobby's woman, I have every right to be here."

"Shante," Bobby snapped, "can I handle this, please?"

"Well, handle it then," Shante said, while glaring at Rachel.

Bobby motioned for Rachel to have a seat on the sofa. Rachel refused to move.

"Please," Bobby said.

Rachel stood with her arms crossed a few more seconds, before finally sitting down.

"So talk, Bobby," she said.

Bobby took a deep breath. "Rachel, you know I care for you. I always will care for you because you are the mother of my son."

"So is that the only reason you care for me?"

"Will you let me finish, please?"

Rachel threw her hands up. She didn't know where this was going, but it looked like her whole plan to get back with Bobby was falling apart.

"We have been through a lot, things that will never make us the same."

"Bobby, don't say that."

Rachel started tearing up. She suddenly didn't care that Shante was sitting across the room staring at them. "You loved me so much and I loved you. Don't say we can never get that back."

"Rachel, you're right, I did love you, once upon a time. That was a long time ago. What we had is over. It has been for a long time."

The tears were falling freely now. Rachel's heart felt like it was being torn out. She slid to the floor on her knees.

"Bobby, don't do this; please, don't do this. Jordan needs you; I need you." She grabbed Bobby around the legs. "We can make this work. We can! We can!" Rachel was near hysteria.

Bobby tried to pull Rachel's arms from around his legs.

"Rachel, calm down. You know it's over between us. Don't act like this."

Rachel continued crying. "Bob-by, don't do this. I need you!"

Bobby freed the lock on his legs and grasped her wrists tightly as he pulled her up and gently shook her. "Rachel, stop it! Stop it! Listen to me!"

Rachel continued sobbing, her body growing limp. Bobby eased her down onto the sofa.

"Is this what you called me here for? To tear my heart out in front of your new woman?" Rachel buried her face in her hands.

"No," Bobby replied.

"Then why?" Rachel sobbed. She lifted her head and stared at Bobby. "Why are you doing this to me?"

Bobby carefully placed Rachel's hands in her lap then got

up and walked toward the living room window. He took a deep breath. "Rachel, Shante and I are getting married."

Rachel's sobbing quickly stopped. Bobby was standing with his back to her. "What did you just say?" She must have heard him wrong.

Bobby turned around. "We're getting married, and we want joint custody of Jordan."

Rachel's eyes grew wide. Not only was she *not* going to get Bobby back but he was marrying another woman and he wanted to take her son. Rachel felt her fury rebuilding. "You just didn't say—"

"Yes, Rachel," Bobby continued, "we're getting married. We don't want any drama. We were hoping we could handle this like adults."

"You have lost your damn mind!"

Rachel stood up. No need to act civilized. Bobby was gone. She might as well let the real Rachel out. She wiped the tears from her face. "If you think for one New York minute that I'm going to let you and that fat bitch anywhere near my son, you are as crazy as she looks!"

Shante jumped up. "That's your last time calling me a bitch," she said, lunging at Rachel. Rachel jumped out of the way just in time.

"Stop it!" Bobby screamed as he grabbed Shante.

Shante gained her balance and glared at Rachel. "Get this psycho out of here!"

Rachel started backing up toward the kitchen. "You wanna see psycho! I'll show you psycho!"

Bobby and Shante looked stunned as they tried to figure out what she was doing. Rachel snatched open a cabinet drawer and pulled out a butcher knife.

"Come on, bitch!" she screamed, waving it at Shante. "I'll

show you psycho!" She dove at Shante who screamed and jumped across the sofa.

"Rachel!" Bobby yelled, blocking her path. "Stop it!"

Rachel was a madwoman. Her curls were becoming disheveled, her cheap mascara was running down her face, and her eyes were crazed. "Move out of the way, Bobby! You love me. I know you do. This tramp is just making you think you don't. If I slice her up real good, maybe she'll get the message and leave us alone."

"I'm calling the police!" Shante screamed, racing toward the phone.

Bobby remained calm although he looked scared to death. "Rachel, put the knife down. You don't want to stab anybody. Think of Jordan."

Rachel swung the knife at Bobby, barely missing his chest. "Don't you dare say his name," she cried. "Don't you ever say his name again! Were you thinking about Jordan when you left me?"

Bobby stepped back and said, "Rachel, I didn't leave you. You slept with Tony, remember? You left me."

Rachel started crying again, but she kept the knife firmly pointed at Bobby. "You slept with Tony, remember," she said, mocking. "Of course, I remember; you won't ever let me forget!"

"So, I didn't leave you. I loved you." Bobby started taking baby steps toward Rachel.

Rachel's shoulders sank. "Then why couldn't you forgive me that one little mistake?"

"It wasn't exactly little, Rachel. Remember Nia?"

"Nia is a beautiful child. You could've learned to love her."

"She is a wonderful child, but I couldn't get over you sleeping with my best friend."

"You make mistakes, Bobby! I forgave you when you took that girl's phone number that time! Right in my face."

"Rachel, that's not the same."

Rachel jabbed the knife toward Bobby. He jumped back, skirting the wall. Rachel closed in, pointing the knife at his throat. "Like my daddy always says, no one sin is greater than the next!"

Bobby didn't take his eyes off the knife. "Rachel, let's not rehash the past. Give me the knife, please!"

"No!" she screamed. "If I can't have you, nobody can!"

Rachel felt like she had stepped out of her body. Never in a million years would she have dreamed she'd be standing in Bobby's living room, ready to slice his throat.

"Ma'am, put the knife down!"

Rachel was so hysterical, she didn't hear the two uniformed officers come in. But there they were, standing with their guns drawn at her like she was a common criminal. She looked at them, then at Shante hovering behind them. She slowly turned back toward Bobby. He looked terrified. Her eyes made their way to the six-inch butcher knife that was just inches from Bobby's throat. *What the hell am I doing?* Rachel dropped the knife and collapsed to the floor in tears. The snap of the handcuffs around her wrists was the last thing she remembered.

21

RACHEL LOOKED AROUND the dingy, musty room. It had to be one of the dirtiest places she had ever been in. She still couldn't believe she was there. She had never been in any real trouble. The worst thing she'd ever done was skip school a couple of times. Sitting in a jail cell was something totally new. Actually, they called this a holding cell, but it might as well have been a jail cell. The four walls were bare, a pale, dusty gray color. There was a small window, but that was it.

Thankfully, they had let her keep on her own clothes and she didn't have to change into one of those awful orange jumpsuits.

When are they going to let me make my phone call? Rachel had been downtown for over an hour and she still hadn't gotten the one phone call she was entitled to. If she didn't learn anything else from her years of watching *New York Undercover,* she knew she was supposed to get one phone call.

"Hey!" Rachel started banging on the window. "Can I make my call now please?" The white-haired lady sitting at the desk outside the cell didn't look up from her magazine. Rachel knocked harder. "Excuse me! Can I make my phone call now?"

The woman looked up, irritated. She muttered something to herself, then picked up the phone and dialed a number. After a few minutes on the phone, she pulled out a set of keys, then walked over to the holding cell.

Without saying a word, she opened the door and stood back for Rachel to come out. Rachel looked at the lady, contemplating saying something smart, but decided against it. The officer looked at her like she dared her to say something.

"Thank you very much," Rachel said instead, with as little sarcasm as she could muster.

"You got three minutes," the officer snapped. She pointed to a phone sitting on an empty desk.

Rachel hadn't given much thought to whom she'd call. The last people she wanted to call were her parents, but she knew they were really the only ones that could help. Twyla would be useless. She was about as broke as Rachel.

Rachel took a deep breath, then picked up the phone to dial her parents' number. Part of her hoped no one would be at home. The other part, the part that desperately wanted to get out of this dump, was praying that someone would answer, preferably her mother. But, of course, luck wasn't on her side.

"Reverend Jackson speaking." Her father picked up the phone on the first ring. Rachel hated the way he answered the phone. He had done that for as long as she could remember. Why couldn't he answer the phone like normal people. His brass demeanor scared off many of the boys who were interested in her.

"Hello, is anyone there?" Simon said.

"Daddy?"

"Yes, Rachel?"

"Daddy . . . I'm in some trouble . . . I need you." Rachel could just picture the look on her father's face.

Simon sighed heavily. Rachel knew he was thinking about how much of a disappointment she was. "What kind of trouble is it this time, Rachel? I know you better not tell me you're pregnant again, because if you are—"

Rachel cut off her father before he got on a tirade. "No, Daddy, it's nothing like that. I'm . . . I'm downtown."

"Downtown where?"

Rachel hesitated before responding. "In jail," she whispered.

"In *where?*" Simon screamed.

Rachel started crying, partly to manipulate her father and partly because she was truly upset. "Daddy, please, can you just come get me? I got into some trouble over at Bobby's and—"

"Bobby? Rachel, when are you going to leave that boy alone! He's done made it clear that he don't want you. You got Lester trying to give you a chance and you won't give him the time of day!"

"Daddy, please. Now is not the time. Can you come get me? They say they'll release me into your custody. Please, Daddy, I can't take it down here."

Simon grunted. He paused for several seconds before saying, "You should've thought about that before you did whatever you did to land you down there." He hesitated again. "What did you do?"

"Daddy, please," Rachel begged.

"What did you do?" Simon repeated.

Rachel lightly banged her head against the wall. No sense in trying to dance around it, she had to tell him straight. "I pulled a knife on Bobby and his girlfriend."

Simon was quiet a moment before saying, "Father Jesus."

"Will you come get me?"

Simon didn't respond quickly. "Rachel, I'm sorry you got yourself in that predicament, but I'm due over at Ebenezer Baptist Church for their vacation bible school finale. I'm on the program," he finally said.

Rachel couldn't believe her ears. "Daddy, did you not hear me? I'm in jail. I need you."

"So do the folks at Ebenezer. They're counting on me to be there to represent Zion Hill, and unlike you, I honor my commitments."

Rachel was in a full-fledged crying mode now. "Daddy, please don't do this to me."

"Rachel, you did this to yourself. Now, I will leave a note for your mother. She had to go visit Brother Thompson in the hospital. She can come see about you when she gets back."

"So what am I supposed to do until then?" Rachel cried.

"I suppose you should just sit down there and think about what you did to land yourself in jail and how this should be a sign for you to get your life together." Simon paused again, then inhaled deeply. "Now, I'm sorry, I know you think I'm being harsh. But we keep bailing you out of these predicaments and you've got to learn. Sometimes that means you have to learn the hard way. You had one child and we stepped in and made everything all right. Then you had another, and, reluctantly, we did again. It's time for you to grow up and think about the consequences to your actions."

Rachel couldn't be sure, but she could've sworn she heard her father's voice cracking.

"I have to go now," Simon continued. "The vacation bible school program starts in an hour and I don't want to be late."

Rachel heard the phone click in her ear. She held it for a minute, in stunned disbelief, then she fell to the floor in tears.

She was crying for the hurt she heard in her father's voice, but more so for the fact that he was actually going to leave her here.

The lady officer raced over to her. The coldness in her face had softened. "Hey, come on now."

"He's just going to leave me here!" Rachel cried. "He's leaving me here for another church's vacation bible school!"

The officer didn't say anything. She just gently patted Rachel on the back and handed her a box of tissues. Rachel snatched two out of the box and wiped her face. Her father had missed many of her youth activities because he was so busy with the church. He had missed her first date because he was at a revival out of town. She always believed she came second to that damned church. Now she knew that to be the case without a shadow of a doubt.

22

Simon stood outside the church conference room doors and leaned in. He was trying desperately to hear what the deacons were saying.

"I tell you I saw the boy and he was all hugged up," he heard a voice whisper. It sounded like Brother Davis but Simon couldn't too sure.

"Maybe you were mistaken," another voice said. "You know your eyesight ain't been too good these days."

"I know what I seen!" Simon could tell that it was definitely Deacon Elijah Davis talking. But who was he talking about? And why were they whispering? Simon didn't take part in the church gossip, and he had never paid it much attention, even with all the horrible rumors swirling about Rachel. But his curiosity had peaked these last few days due to the nonstop whispering that always seemed to end abruptly when he entered the room.

"Tell him exactly what you saw, Brother Davis. They won't believe me." That was the voice of Deacon Jacobs.

"It was him sure as I'm standing here," Deacon Davis repeated. "And they was looking all lovey-dovey."

"Well, maybe you just read too much into it." That was Simon's friend, Mitchell Baker, talking. Simon felt guilty standing there. Maybe he should just walk in and ask them what they were saying.

"I didn't read too much of nothing," Deacon Davis responded. "What I want to know is, is anybody goin' say something?"

Deacon Baker spoke up again. "No, I think you ought to just let this drop. You ain't got no proof and y'all know Brother Davis ain't got but one good eye anyway."

Deacon Davis huffed. "Fine. This one good eye know what it saw. Just don't say I didn't try and tell y'all when he shame this church."

Simon couldn't take it any longer. If one of his members was doing something that could shame the church, he wanted to know about it. He pushed open the door. All of the deacons immediately sat up, a tense look across their faces. "Deacons," Simon said, nodding in their direction. "No need to stop your conversation." He scanned the room. Every man in the room had a nervous look about his face. "Somebody wanna tell me what's going on?"

Several deacons cast their eyes down.

"Who are you talking about?" Simon asked.

Elijah stood up. "It's your son."

Everyone looked at Elijah surprised. Simon took a deep breath. "Okay, what has David done now?"

Mitchell took the opportunity to jump in. "I'll handle this," he said.

Simon looked at his friend. "Don't beat around the bush, Mitchell. Just tell me what you know. Ain't nothing you can tell me about David that is goin' shame me more than he already has."

Mitchell cleared his throat. "Well, a couple of our members saw David and some woman at the mall shoplifting. They didn't get caught, but we're still worried."

Elijah let out a long sigh and shook his head. "You wrong, Mitchell," he said.

"No, I feel we need to tell Simon. He needs to know what's going on in case someone brings it up to him."

"They were shoplifting?" Simon hung his head. Would David ever stop embarrassing him? "What about him being hugged up? I heard someone say something about that."

Mitchell looked around nervously. "That's how they were getting the things they were stealing. They would act like they were hugged up together as they stuffed the items in their jackets." Mitchell paused and looked around the room. "Well, we just wanted you to know."

"I appreciate that, Mitchell. I'll do my best to handle it." Simon couldn't quite make out the look on the other deacons' faces. Maybe they were just as sick of David's shenanigans as he was, but, somehow, Simon wondered if there was more to the story.

Simon couldn't believe he was parked again in the front of David's beat-up apartment. He didn't even know how he'd ended up there. The last thing he remembered was leaving the church, his vision clouded in anger. He was sick and tired of David. What if he had gotten caught? They probably would've found drugs on him. It would've been all in the papers. Simon felt he had to do or say something, anything. He had given up on trying to get David to turn his life around. That was a cause only for the Lord to work out. He had come here today to try and talk David into moving out of Houston.

Simon had a brother in Philadelphia who worked with drug offenders. He'd invited David to come stay with him for a while and Simon was now determined to get David to go.

A loud bang against the car window startled Simon out of his thoughts. A dark-skinned man with long, dirty dreadlocks and food stuck in his matted beard was knocking on his window.

"Hey, you wanna buy a VCR?" the man asked.

Simon waved for the man to go away.

"Forty dollars," the man said, holding up the dual-deck Sony.

Simon looked at the man's hands to make sure he didn't have any weapons. When he saw nothing but the VCR, he stepped out of the car. "No, I don't want to buy a hot VCR." Simon closed and locked his car door and started toward David's apartment.

"Okay. Thirty dollars then," the man yelled, following Simon. "You can't beat this for thirty dollars, man. You can watch two tapes at the same time."

Simon shook his head. "I said no, thank you."

"Aww, come on," the man called out as Simon quickened his pace. "Twenty dollars then; that's as low as I can go. Come on!"

Simon looked back over his shoulders with disgust. If he could ever get his hands on the person who brought drugs into their community, he probably would lose every ounce of his Christianity.

Simon knocked once and the door to David's apartment opened. Tawny was sitting on the sofa, her head, tied in a black scarf, hung low. She looked worse than she did at his house.

Tawny looked up. "What's up, Pops?" Her words were slurred.

Simon stiffened. "Hello. Is David here?"

"Somewhere around here." She yelled for David, then said, "He's probably in the back."

Tawny struggled to get up, then slowly made her way to the back of the apartment. Simon waited in the living room.

Tawny's scream sent him running down the hall.

"Oh, my God! David! David! Wake up!"

Tawny was on the floor, next to David, whose eyes were rolled up in the back of his head. Drool was coming out of his mouth and a thick rubber band wrapped was around his forearm. A needle stuck from the bend of his arm. Tawny snatched the needle out and began violently slapping David. "Wake up, baby!"

Simon stood there in shock.

"Mmmmmm," David moaned.

"Wake up! Wake up!" Tawny kept repeating.

Simon looked at his son lying on the bedroom floor. His emotions changed from sickness to anger to disgust. Most of all he felt sorry for what his son had become.

"Is he dead?" Simon stoically asked.

Tawny slapped David's face some more. He flinched, then moaned again.

"No, no. He's still alive," she cried. "Baby, wake up. Damn. I knew that shit was too strong." She was shaking her head, blubbering and crying.

Simon pursed his lips together, then turned around and walked out of the room.

"Where are you going?" Tawny called after him. "Pops? I can't believe you just gonna leave him! Asshole!"

Simon ignored her screams as he walked through the living

room, out the front door, and back to his car. As he unlocked it and stepped inside, his mind replayed the horrible scene of his son lying on the floor, near death, with a needle stuck in his vein.

Simon buried his head in his hands and for the first time in his life, cried uncontrollably.

23

"WHAT'S UP, TERRI?"

Jonathan felt the tap on his shoulder and turned toward the sultry voice coming from behind his booth. He was at Bennigan's Restaurant waiting to meet Kevin for lunch.

"Uh, hey, Veronica. How are you? And why'd you call me Terri?"

"As in McMillan. You know, *Disappearing Acts.*"

Jonathan didn't know whether to laugh at Veronica's attempt at humor, but the stoic look on her face told him that it probably wasn't such a good idea.

"I'm listening," she said as she slid in next to Jonathan.

"What are you talking about?" Jonathan said.

"Oh, so now we're playing stupid? I'm talking about the fact that you just outright ignored my phone calls."

Jonathan had been dreading the inevitable confrontation with Veronica. He sighed deeply. He hoped he wouldn't offend her with what he had to say.

"Veronica, part of the reason I wanted to go out with you was because I knew you were a no-strings type of woman. I knew you weren't looking for a committed relationship."

Veronica held up her palm. "Wait, hold up. Nobody said anything about commitment. All I'm talking about is returning a phone call. Seems like we've got some unfinished business." Veronica threw Jonathan a pouty expression. "I thought that I pleased you that night at my place."

Jonathan displayed a small smile. "You did."

"Then what's the problem?" Veronica said, returning the smile.

Jonathan glanced at his watch. Kevin was already thirty minutes late. He wished he would appear and save Jonathan from this conversation.

"Did you hear me? I said, 'What's the problem?'"

"I told you I was going through some things, that's all."

Veronica ran her finger along Jonathan's arm. "And you also told me that I helped you forget about those things."

Jonathan thought quickly and said, "Look, Veronica. The real reason I didn't call you back was because I'm involved with someone."

"Is it Angela?" Veronica didn't give him time to answer. "I heard you two were kicking it."

Jonathan didn't respond. He and Angela hadn't officially committed but they were spending more and more time together.

"Well, I'm not a man-stealer," Veronica said, seductively leaning in, "although I could be one if I wanted to."

She grabbed Jonathan's hand, maneuvered it under her skirt, and placed it between her legs. She wasn't wearing any panties. Jonathan tried to jerk his hand away, but Veronica had it firmly gripped. Jonathan looked around nervously. They were in a booth, but Jonathan still felt uneasy. Veronica acted like she couldn't care less.

"It's such a shame that you won't get to experience the full range of this." She pushed his hand deeper in her crotch. "I'm almost willing to bet you've never had anything this good." Still holding onto his hand, Veronica eased it away. She lifted it to her mouth, seductively running his index finger across her tongue. "Oh, well, give me a buzz if things don't work out." Veronica dropped his hand, slipped out of the booth, ran her hands down her hips, and sauntered off without looking back.

Jonathan leaned his head against the back of the booth and closed his eyes. He refused to entertain any more thoughts of Veronica or having meaningless sex. That's one of the reasons he enjoyed being with Angela. Despite their initial time together, there was no pressure to have sex. And until he cleared his head up, he needed to stay sex-free.

Jonathan felt a pair of eyes on him. He looked up and saw Kevin staring at him in amazement. "Man, who was that that just left?"

"That was Veronica," Jonathan said, nonchalantly.

"Veronica, the freak? The one that you were telling me about?"

Suddenly Jonathan regretted telling Kevin about his night with Veronica.

Kevin was the only friend Jonathan had kept in touch with after he went away to college. A consummate ladies' man, it was in his footsteps that Jonathan had followed prior to meeting Tracy.

"Yeah, that's her."

"Man, that's the best-looking freak I've ever seen." Kevin sat down across from Jonathan. "Tell me I did not see her stick your hand up her skirt?"

"How long were you standing there gaping?"

Kevin grinned. "Long enough. Is that what she did?"

"Yeah. Can we order now? I'm starved." Jonathan motioned for the waitress. He ordered a Sprite and a dish of potato skins as an appetizer. Kevin ordered a Bud Light and asked for a few more minutes to figure out what he wanted to eat.

"Wow. I didn't know you had it like that," Kevin said, once the waitress had walked off.

"I don't; believe me, man, I don't."

"So, what did she want?"

"To finish what we started."

"And you ain't all over that? Man, you've lost your mind." Kevin noticed the melancholy look on Jonathan's face. "Don't tell me you're still hung up on ol' girl in Atlanta?"

Jonathan had told Kevin a little about Tracy. He had been careful not to tell everything, as he was sure Kevin wouldn't understand.

Moments later, the waitress returned with their drinks. Kevin smiled at her. "Thank you, beautiful. You can bring my drink anytime."

The waitress rolled her eyes like she was used to tired pickup lines. "Have you all decided what you want?" she said, looking at Jonathan.

"Give us the double order of fajitas, please."

The waitress scribbled the information on her pad, stuck the pencil in her apron, then asked, "Anything else?" She never looked at Kevin.

"That'll be it," Kevin snidely remarked. "Just bring my man's potato skins. If we need anything else, we'll summon you." His hand flicked to shoo her off. The waitress threw him a hateful look before walking off.

"So much for her tip." Kevin didn't handle rejection very

well. He usually didn't have to. His half-Venezuelan background saw to that. His flawless caramel color, accented by
light brown eyes and wavy black hair, and coupled with his out-
going and humorous personality, usually made the women find
him irresistible.

"You need to let Tracy go," Kevin said. "Don't make no
sense for a man to be wrapped up in a woman like that. There's
too many of them out there. You're walking around in a deep
depression, turning down a woman like Veronica. You have to
be crazy. The best advice I can give you, let that girl go."

Jonathan looked at his friend. He wanted so bad to talk
about what was going on with him and Tracy, but the longest
relationship Kevin had ever been in lasted only three months.
He wouldn't understand. Besides, Kevin definitely was not the
most liberal-minded person on the face of the Earth.

Kevin noticed Jonathan still looked sad. "Man, what did
that girl do to you?"

Jonathan didn't respond—he didn't have to. Kevin's attention had already shifted to the two women in the booth across
the aisle.

"Hold that thought. I'll be right back."

Kevin slid out of the booth and walked over to the two
young ladies. Both of them were beautiful. One had a short,
cropped red Afro. Jonathan usually didn't find women with
masculine hairstyles attractive, but it fit her perfectly. The other
woman had long, curly hair and big, puppy-dog eyes. They
were sitting down, but Jonathan could tell they had the figures
to match the faces. Kevin slid in next to the woman with the
Afro. She looked like his type, exotic and intriguing.

The two women began giggling and whispering to Kevin.
Five minutes later, he returned to their booth and pushed a
napkin Jonathan's way. "Janine, the one on the right, said to

give her a call. I told her you had just broken up with your girl-friend and needed some comfort."

Jonathan wanted to ball the napkin up and throw it at Kevin. "That's how I got in the mess I'm in with Veronica," he said. "Plus, me and Angela are hanging pretty tight."

Jonathan didn't want to embarrass Janine, who was looking at him, smiling, so he took the napkin, folded it up and put it in his jacket pocket. Both women waved, then eased out of their booth to leave. Janine mouthed, "Call me" as they walked out of the restaurant.

Jonathan nodded. He'd never had a problem getting women, especially hanging out with Kevin. Which is why he had been so promiscuous in high school.

"I can't believe you and Angela are back together," Kevin said.

"Me either. And truth be told, I don't even know how it happened."

The waitress returned, and without saying a word, sat their fajitas on the table and walked off.

"What is her problem?" Kevin said loud enough for her to hear. "Somebody needs some good loving in their life."

The waitress stopped, turned around, then stomped back to their table.

"For your information," she said, wagging her finger in Kevin's face. "I get good loving *every* night. Better than you could ever dream of giving. And the *woman* that gives it to me does things that you wouldn't even begin to know how to do!"

She threw her nose in the air, then turned and walked off.

"A dyke!" Kevin said, his mouth gaping wide open. "I should've known since she wouldn't give me the time of day. Man, I'll never understand what a woman thinks another woman can give her that a man can't." Kevin shook his head, then reached in and began loading fajitas on his plate. "That's what's wrong with the world today, all these messed-up people. You can't tell the gay people from the straight ones. That girl looks perfectly normal." He glanced back over at the waitress who was glaring at him from the corner. "Damn, what a waste. 'Cause that sister is fine."

Jonathan shifted uncomfortably over his friend's comment. Nope, he thought, Kevin could never know he was one of those "messed-up people." He simply wouldn't understand.

24

"RACHEL, DON'T BE STUPID."

Twyla had been on the phone for the past hour trying to talk some sense into her best friend. Rachel wasn't listening to a word she said.

"Twyla, I'm tired of discussing this. I'm going and that's that." Rachel surveyed herself in the mirror, the phone nestled between her head and shoulder. She had to make sure she was looking the best she possibly could. She had to make sure Bobby knew what he was giving up. Last time, she had lost her cool, but this time would be different.

"I'm begging you, don't do this. Haven't you made yourself a big enough fool behind this man?"

Rachel was getting irritated now. She was tired of people always doubting her love for Bobby, and Bobby's love for her. She knew it was still there. She could just tell in the way he talked about getting married. He said it like it was something he *had* to do and wasn't his choice. He had even called her to make sure she had gotten home safely from jail. Granted, he just talked to her mother, but the fact that he even bothered to call at all spoke volumes. Then he refused to press charges against her. That clinched it for Rachel. She knew he still loved her.

"Twyla, you just don't understand. Nobody does. I'll never forgive myself if I don't give it one last try."

"But, Rachel, it's his wedding day!"

"All the more reason for me to get off this phone and get going. Besides, as rushed as this wedding is, I know that ain't nobody but Shante pushing it. Bobby wouldn't want to throw together a wedding in two months."

Twyla let out a long sigh. "Fine."

Rachel smiled. She could just picture Twyla shaking her head in amazement. "Twyla, I know what I'm doing, okay?"

"Whatever you say. Call me when you get back. And don't get yourself arrested again."

"I will be the epitome of finer womanhood. I'm just going to make one last appeal to his heart."

Rachel wiggled her hips in the mirror and smiled at her reflection. She was wearing a mustard-colored sundress that matched her skin tone perfectly. The front dipped just enough to show cleavage without being trashy. The dress hugged her size eight figure in all the right places.

"Like I said, whatever you say. Just call me. Bye."

Rachel hung up the phone, determined not to let Twyla spoil her mood. She planned to ease into the church unnoticed and try to talk some sense into Bobby to call this wedding off.

Rachel took one last look in the mirror, smiled confidently, and snapped off the lights before stepping out of her meager little apartment. As usual on Saturday nights, her mother was watching the kids. If her prayers were answered, she could bring Bobby back to her place after all this wedding nonsense was over.

Rachel was still having a hard time comprehending that the love of her life was going to get married in her father's church. She knew Shante had been a member since she was six years old, but she was never there. Sure, her parents were active members of Zion Hill, but they knew Bobby was Rachel's man, so they should've paid for their old stank daughter to have her wedding somewhere else. Bobby didn't go to church, so it wasn't like they could get married at his parents' church, but they still could've found a nice garden or something. The fact that Shante was adamant about getting married at Zion Hill showed she had no respect for Rachel. And Rachel was not the least bit fazed about crashing her wedding.

Rachel swung her little Ford Escort into a parking space in the back of the church. The parking lot was already filling up and the wedding wouldn't start for another hour. Rachel noticed her father's car parked in the pastor's spot and her stomach turned even more flips. She was too through with him. He was actually going to officiate this ceremony, even though he knew how much it hurt her. As always, he tried to feed her that mess about his obligations as pastor. What about his obligations as a father? Even her mother had pleaded with him to let one of the associate pastors handle the wedding. But no, he didn't want any church members talking about him for not performing the ceremony.

"Fine," Rachel muttered as she got out of the car. "Reverend Jackson, you're going to feel like a fool when Bobby calls this thing off."

Rachel made her way into the back of the church. She heard giggling coming from the main choir room and figured that's where Shante and her bridesmaids were getting dressed. She definitely didn't want them, or anyone from Shante's family, to see her. They probably would tackle her to keep her from getting to Bobby.

Rachel eased past her father's office and down the hall on the opposite wing. The groom usually got dressed in the old choir room just down the hall. It was a lot smaller, but perfect for guys who didn't need nearly as much room as women.

Rachel hadn't yet figured out how she would get Bobby to talk to her. She hadn't figured much of anything out. She was just following her heart and praying that it would all work out.

For a minute, it seemed like God was on her side. Travis, Bobby's best man, had just come out of the choir room. He was humming a tune, a huge smile across his face. Rachel broke into a smile herself. Travis had always liked her and Bobby as a couple. He told her on more than one occasion how he wished they could work things out.

"Travis." Rachel's voice was just a whisper. She had ducked into the men's restroom and was now peering from behind the door.

Travis turned toward Rachel. The smile immediately left his face. "Rachel. What are you doing?"

Rachel looked up and down the hall, making sure it was safe to come out. "Travis, where's Bobby?"

"Getting ready to get married." Travis had a genuine look of concern across his face. "What are you doing here?"

"I just need to talk to him. Can you go get him?"

Travis walked toward Rachel and took her hand. "Rachel, you know you're my girl, but don't do this. Don't mess up this day for Bobby."

Rachel's heart sank. Even Travis was turning against her

now. "Please, Travis. Just go get him. Tell him to come talk to me and I'll leave. Otherwise I'm not going anywhere."

"Rachel," Travis pleaded with exasperation.

"I promise I won't act a fool; just go get Bobby."

Travis sighed, but seemed resigned that the sooner he went and got Bobby, the quicker this would be over with. "Wait right here." He turned and went back into the choir room.

It seemed like he was gone a long time, but Rachel's watch said it had only been a few minutes. Bobby slowly opened the door to the choir room and stepped out. He was wearing a black, double-breasted tuxedo with a gold bow tie and matching cummerbund. Although he looked amazingly handsome, he still seemed to have the weight of the world on his shoulders.

I knew he didn't want to get married, Rachel thought, breaking out in a big, seductive smile.

"Hey," she said, stepping out of the restroom.

"Rachel, what's up?" Bobby bore a cautious expression.

Rachel began fidgeting with her purse strap. "I just wanted to see you, just in case you changed your mind or something." She laughed nervously.

Bobby took a deep breath and closed his eyes. After a few seconds, he opened them and said, "Rachel, I'm not going to change my mind."

There was an awkward silence between the two of them for a moment. Rachel said a silent prayer. This was her last chance. "I'm sorry, Bobby."

"For what?"

Her voice cracked. "For everything. For Tony. For giving you a hard time. For not being the woman you wanted."

"Rachel, that's in the past."

"Just tell me one thing," Rachel said, sniffing.

"What?"

"Do you still love me?"

He didn't answer.

Rachel continued, although she knew she was grasping at straws. "You've got to still care for me. You called to make sure I was okay after I got arrested. You didn't press charges."

Bobby sighed. "Rachel, you will always be special to me because you're the mother of my child."

Rachel searched his face, hoping desperately to see the love. "Is that all?"

"And because of what we once shared. But now, I'm marrying Shante. You've got to accept that." Bobby looked at Rachel sympathetically.

Rachel stared down at the floor, despair written across her face. "So this is it?"

"Yeah, this is it. We're still going to have contact. We have to for Jordan. But for you and me, it's over."

Rachel slowly lifted her head. She looked defeated, but that quickly changed when she noticed Shante storming down the hall, wedding dress and all. Rachel decided to act fast. "I understand. Good-bye, Bobby." She leaned in, wrapped her arms around him, and planted the deepest, most ferocious kiss she could on his lips.

Bobby didn't push her off and throw her to the ground like she feared. He kissed her back, albeit briefly, but he kissed her! Rachel knew he still felt something for her!

Bobby clutched her arms and pushed her away.

"Rachel—" he began.

Too late. "I know you didn't!" Shante shouted at her. She clawed out at Rachel but Rachel moved just in time. She mockingly laughed as Shante spouted out obscenities.

"Remember, you're in a church," Rachel said as she jumped

behind Travis, who had run out from the choir room. She wasn't scared of Shante, but even she knew hell hath no fury like a woman scorned on her wedding day.

"Shante!" Bobby shouted.

"I saw it!" Shante said, crying. "You kissed that tramp on MY WEDDING DAY!" One of her bridesmaids was now behind her and trying to restrain her. A huge crowd had started to gather.

"He sure did kiss me, sweetheart," Rachel taunted. "That's because his heart still belongs to me. It will always belong to me!"

"You two-bit slut!" Shante screamed. She lunged at Rachel and caught some of her hair. She jerked so hard she sent Rachel flailing to the ground. Before anyone could move, Shante was on top of her pounding her face. "You try and mess up my day!"

Rachel could only cover her face and try to ward off the blows. It took Bobby, Travis, and several bridesmaids to get Shante off Rachel.

They were still trying to restrain her when Simon came running down the hall. "What in Sam Hill is going on down here?" Simon asked.

"Ask your whorish daughter!" Shante screamed. "Ask her why she would come and try to ruin my wedding day!"

Rachel struggled to get up off the floor. She felt her lip and left eye swelling. Even though she hadn't touched Shante, the bride looked like she had been dragged through the mud. Her veil was knocked off, the beaded bodice was torn, and there was a rip in her train.

"Rachel, what are you doing here?"

Rachel didn't answer her father. She just rolled her eyes at all the people looking at her with a mixture of pity and disgust.

"Get into my office, young lady!" Simon ordered. When Rachel didn't move, he bellowed, "Now!"

Rachel huffed, threw one last smug look at Shante, then sauntered off, limping because one of the heels on her sandals had been broken. She heard her father trying to comfort Shante and tell her and Bobby to go talk. Rachel smiled as she walked right past her father's office. She had no intention of waiting on him. Rachel headed out to her car, a look of satisfaction crossing her face. She didn't care that everyone was probably talking about her like a dog. All that mattered was she had broken up Bobby and Shante's wedding. Her mission had been accomplished.

25

RACHEL PRAYED that her father would be late in returning from church and that she would have to deal only with her mother. She had been sitting in her car outside their house for almost an hour now, waiting to pick up her kids. She knew her father would yell at her about the scene at Bobby's wedding yesterday. That's why she didn't go to church this morning; she didn't want to deal with him, and she didn't want people looking at her like she was crazy. Both her mother and father had tried calling her all last evening, but she did not answer the phone. She was only at the house now because Jonathan had refused to drop off her children, saying he wasn't getting in the middle of that mess.

Rachel looked as her mother's minivan turned the corner. She strained to see if her father was in the car. He wasn't. Thank God for small miracles. Rachel jumped out of the car and met her mother just as she was pulling into the driveway.

"Mama, please don't start," Rachel said as soon as she saw her mother's chastising look.

"I ain't goin' say a word. You're the one that's got to walk around with folks knowing how much of a fool you acted."

Loretta got out the car, pushed the front seat forward, and unstrapped Nia from the first car seat. She lifted the toddler onto her shoulder and motioned toward Jordan. "Get him and bring him on inside. Try not to wake him."

"Actually, I thought I'd just take them on home," Rachel said.

"Nonsense," Loretta snapped as she struggled to pull her purse up on one shoulder and keep Nia positioned on the other. "These babies ain't had nothing to eat and I know you ain't got nothing over there for them to eat."

Rachel really didn't feel like arguing; she just wanted to get out of there. "I'll swing through McDonald's."

Loretta threw her a crazy look before walking up the sidewalk to the house. "McDonald's. On Sunday?" She called out behind her. "Don't be silly. Now come on."

Loretta stopped, turned around, and noticed Rachel hadn't moved. "Get that boy out the car and come on inside. You can't hide from your daddy forever." Loretta shifted Nia, unlocked the door with the keys from her purse, and went inside.

Rachel stood there debating her next move. She couldn't just leave, but she didn't want to see her father either. Simon's car turning onto the street ended her dilemma. Rachel silently cursed, then quickly leaned over to get Jordan out of his car seat. She had just made it to the front door when her father pulled into the driveway.

"I thought I told you to wait on me yesterday," Simon said as he got out of the car.

Rachel struggled to open the door with Jordan lying across her shoulder. "I need to get Jordan inside," she said without looking back. Once inside, she quickly raced upstairs and laid her son across the bed in David's old room, now a room for the kids.

There was no more putting off the inevitable; Rachel slowly made her way back downstairs. Simon was waiting for her in the living room.

"Sit down," he commanded.

Rachel let out a long sigh and did as she was told.

Simon paced back and forth. "What do you have to say for yourself?"

"I ain't got nothing to say." Rachel sat there defiantly.

Simon shook his head. "How dare you come into the church, on that boy's wedding day, and create a scene! Do you know how bad you made me look?"

"Oh, yeah. We gotta make sure Reverend Jackson doesn't look bad," Rachel snidely remarked.

"Girl, don't think you're too old for me to bust your head to the white meat," Simon threatened. Rachel tried not to snicker. Growing up, her father had always threatened them with some crazy country saying. But he seldom carried through on his threats. The last time he whipped her was when she was six years old. As the baby, she usually got away with a lot. She assumed her parents were just tired after raising two boys.

"Are you listening to me?" Simon bellowed.

Rachel knew the sooner she agreed with her father, the sooner all this would be over with, so she just nodded, trying to soften her look of defiance.

"I'm sorry, okay? I just love Bobby so much."

"Love?" Simon looked at his daughter like she had lost her mind. "You're nineteen years old. What do you know about love?"

"You fell in love with mama around my age."

"That was a different day and age. Besides, we were mature, which is more than I can say about you."

Rachel let out a grunt. "Well, I know I love Bobby. And he loves me." She was getting agitated again. No matter how civilized and respectful she tried to be with her father, he always managed to make her mad.

Simon laughed, a deep, maniacal laugh. "If he loves you so much, then why did he marry Shante?"

Rachel stared at her father in disbelief. "They . . . still got married?"

Now it was Simon who looked defiant. "They sure did. He convinced her that you were crazy, not that it took a lot of doing. Your shenanigans delayed the wedding, but they didn't stop it."

Rachel was speechless. Bobby was married. They had actually gotten married. Rachel felt tears forming. Her heart had never ached the way it did right now.

Simon's anger softened at the sight of his daughter's tears. He sat down beside her on the sofa and awkwardly put his arms around her. "Rachel, it's for the best."

Rachel couldn't hold it in any longer. She buried her face in her hands and started sobbing.

Simon sat for a few minutes, like he didn't know whether to pull her into an embrace or not. He finally decided to hug her tightly. "Maybe this will finally get you to move on," Simon said.

Rachel pulled back and looked up at her father, though she could barely see, the tears were so heavy. "And you married them?"

Simon pulled his arm away and stood up. "We've already had this discussion. I told you as pastor of Zion Hill, I can't let my duties interfere with some obsession my daughter has."

Rachel's anger rose again. "Heaven forbid you would do something to jeopardize your pastoral duties!" Rachel shouted. "Who cares how much it hurt your daughter. All that matters is Zion Hill! Zion Hill! I hate that church!"

All their commotion had Loretta running into the living room. "What is the problem?" she asked.

Simon stood facing Rachel as he spoke. "Your daughter has lost her everloving mind. You best talk some sense into her before she's crossed off the welcome mat at this house."

Rachel stood up. "So you goin' ban me like you did David? Just kick me out of your life, too?" She gestured mockingly. "Oh, but you'll still have your precious Jonathan! I bet you would've never married one of his ex-girlfriends!"

The veins in Simon's neck started bulging. "Loretta, you deal with this child because she goin' make me lose my religion!" Simon grabbed his newspaper off the mantle and stormed down the hallway and out to the deck. Rachel watched as he settled down into a lawn chair, flipped the paper open, and started reading.

"Rachel—" Loretta eased up behind her daughter.

"Mama, how could he?" Rachel sobbed. "How could he do this to me?"

Loretta took Rachel into her arms and squeezed her tightly. "Get it all out, baby," she said soothingly as Rachel buried her head into Loretta's shoulder. "I know it hurts but God heals all wounds."

"How could God do this to me? He knows how much I love Bobby."

Rachel had grown up in the church. Sure she cursed and had a little sex every now and then, but she still considered herself a Christian. So why did God treat her so unfairly? She couldn't understand.

Loretta continued rubbing Rachel's back. "He also knows what's best for us, even when we don't. And the fact that Bobby married that girl means God has a greater plan for you."

Rachel lifted her head, wiped her eyes and sniffed. "Like someone better than Bobby?"

Loretta brushed the loose strands of hair out of Rachel's face. "Like someone better than Bobby."

Rachel wanted desperately to believe her mother's words, but, right now, she didn't think she'd ever find anyone she loved as much as Bobby.

26

JONATHAN FELT BETTER than he had in months. He was really enjoying his time with Angela, and if he could just get his mind off Tracy, everything would be fine. He thought about seeking professional help because he couldn't for the life of him understand how he was in love with both a man and a woman. It was a thought that quickly passed because if he couldn't come clean with his family, he sure wouldn't be able to tell a complete stranger.

The fact that he loved Angela proved he couldn't be gay. And just labeling himself bisexual seemed too farfetched. But he didn't know what else to call it. He kept telling himself that Tracy was an experiment. That's not the way life was supposed to be.

"You seem to be in another world." Angela's voice jolted Jonathan out of his thoughts.

"Oh, I'm sorry. What was it you wanted to talk to me about?"

"Isn't this place beautiful?" she said. They were sitting on a blanket in the grass at Transco Towers, a waterfall-laden garden area near the Galleria shopping center. Several couples were strolling through the area. One young woman was having her bridal portraits taken near the waterfall. Right next to them, a boy was throwing a Frisbee to his dog.

Angela leaned back and inhaled. "I love coming out here. It's so peaceful. And I just love the smell of the water."

Jonathan looked at Angela strangely. She had been doing and saying weird things all week. Sure, the waterfall was pretty, but as for smelling good? "What's going on, Angela?"

Angela closed her eyes and began talking. "You know, when you left me I was devastated. I just knew you had gotten down there and fallen for some college coed."

Jonathan interrupted. "Angela, I told you—"

"Just let me finish." Angela kept her eyes closed, lying down with her hands behind her head. The mist from the waterfall lightly sprinkled her face. "I wanted some answers. I needed some answers. But they never came. So, I just prayed for peace of mind and finally that came. Then when I saw you that day at church, everything I thought I had buried came rushing back. Still, I never dreamed we'd get back together."

"Angela, where are you going with this?"

"Jonathan, I'm pregnant." The expression across her face was strained, but she never opened her eyes.

Jonathan stared at her in disbelief. They had only had sex that one time. Angela was consumed with guilt afterward, saying she had really built her relationship with God during their time apart and she was adamant about remaining celibate. That was just fine with him because after their rendezvous, he was more confused than ever. He had hoped since he once truly loved Angela that being with her sexually would help him get over Tracy. Of course, it wasn't working.

Jonathan wasn't stupid, he knew it took only one time, but

he never would've dreamed that's what she wanted to talk to him about.

They sat in silence for several minutes. "So?" Angela finally said.

"So what?"

"Do you hate me?"

"Angela, I could never hate you. Besides, you didn't get pregnant alone." He looked off, taking in the scenery. A baby. How could he have been so careless? She'd told him she wasn't on birth control. Of course, that was after they'd already slept together. She said she'd stopped taking it after they had broken up and because she had vowed to remain celibate, had never bothered to get back on the pill. Still, he never thought he would've gotten her pregnant.

"You don't have to be there. I can do this by myself," Angela offered.

Why is it women always said that? As if he'd be able to just forget his flesh and blood. "Angela, that's absurd. I'm not just going to leave my child."

Jonathan turned toward Angela. She was now lying with her eyes wide open, staring at the sky. They were misting and her chest was heaving up and down. Jonathan took her hand and began stroking it. "Angela, we'll get through this." He had to make her believe that, because he sure didn't.

"So an abortion is out of the question?" Kevin was munching on Pringles in between gulps of his Rolling Rock.

Jonathan had rushed right over to Kevin's apartment after dropping Angela off at home. He had to talk to someone about the news. They were now stretched out on Kevin's Italian leather sofa.

"Yeah, I wouldn't even suggest that. She'd go berserk and probably damn me to hell."

"You're the religious one. Maybe this baby is a sign for you to get over ol' girl," Kevin said, with a mouthful of chips.

"Who?"

"The chick from Atlanta." Kevin swallowed the last of his beer and continued talking. "So, you don't think she did this on purpose, do you? I mean you were her first love, and maybe this is just her way of trying to get you back."

That thought had crossed Jonathan's mind, albeit briefly. Angela simply wasn't that type of woman. "Naw, she didn't even want to have sex. I practically had to beg her."

Kevin didn't look swayed. Finally he shrugged. "You know, having a baby isn't the worst thing that could happen. At least you know Angela ain't crazy and you won't have to deal with any baby mama drama like Rachel be dishing out."

Jonathan narrowed his eyes at Kevin. "Leave my sister alone."

"All I can say is I'm thankful you never let me get with her. Because if I had been unlucky enough to shoot some of this up in her fertile ass, I'd never be able to deal with her crazy behind. Man, I just think of some of the stuff she's done, and it's enough to get me to make sure I wrap it up with whoever I'm with."

Jonathan let Kevin ramble on. Even though he hated people bad-mouthing his sister, he didn't let the ranting get to him because he knew Kevin loved Rachel like she was his own flesh and blood.

"Anyway," Kevin continued, "Angela is good people. If there was anyone I'd want as a baby's mama, it would be her."

"That's just it. I don't want a baby's mama."

"So what does that mean?" Kevin paused, his mouth dropping open when he realized what Jonathan was saying. "Don't tell me you're thinking of marrying Angela?"

Jonathan sat up and started thumbing through the various sports magazines strewn out on Kevin's coffee table. "I know that's what she wants. She kept hinting at it all the way home, talking about how she never saw herself having a baby out of wedlock."

Kevin looked shocked. "Man, that's deep. Are you ready for that?"

"I don't know. Angela is the type of woman men dream of marrying. *If* I wanted to get married, she'd be perfect." Jonathan didn't know if he should even be considering marriage. Especially, not with lingering feelings for Tracy.

"But still, marriage? Everybody and their mama got babies these days. Nobody gets married anymore just because they knocked someone up."

Jonathan sighed. "Angela isn't just *someone*. I really care for her and it's going to be so embarrassing for her to walk around pregnant and not married."

"Embarrassed? Who the hell cares about her being embarrassed? And if she's that damn embarrassed, tell her don't have it."

Jonathan knew Kevin wouldn't understand what he was going through. Angela was held in high regard at the church. It would really affect her to have people talking about her having an illegitimate child, but not nearly as much as having to endure an abortion.

"I told you, man, she doesn't believe in abortions," Jonathan said.

"Well, dog, I don't know what to tell you on that one." Kevin patted his chest. "I know, ain't no woman tying the big man down until I'm good and ready. And even then, I don't know if I'll be able to be faithful until death do me part."

"It seems real easy for my dad. And he has women throwing themselves at him."

"You know some of them church women are the freakiest ones of all." Kevin leaned in. "You really think your dad ain't hit on none of them?"

"Naw, man, I really don't think so. The way those women treat my mother, they'd probably love to throw something like that in her face. My father ain't having that."

"See, that's why I couldn't be no minister. I'd be trying to get my freak on in the choir stand."

Jonathan laughed. Kevin wasn't lying.

"I'd probably get shot by one of the deacons for sticking this snake in his daughter," Kevin said, grabbing his crotch.

Jonathan shook his head at his friend. "That's why you haven't been called to preach."

Kevin's smile turned serious. "What about you? Does your dad think you still want to be a preacher?"

Besides Tracy, Kevin was the only person who knew Jonathan didn't want to be a preacher. But he didn't know the real reason. "You know I can't tell him that."

"So why are you so adamant about not being a minister and all now? Besides the fact that you're a closet stud?"

"I just don't think that's my calling is all."

Kevin shrugged. "Whatever you say. I just know if you do become a minister, I can't be hanging with you no more. You'd cramp my style."

"Well, you don't have to worry about that." Jonathan had all but ruled that out, even though he'd yet to tell his father. He figured if he stayed with Angela, his father would never have to know about his relationship with Tracy. Sure, he'd be disappointed about Jonathan fathering a baby out of wedlock, but nowhere as much as he'd be if he knew his youngest son was gay.

Kevin eyed the clock. "Hey, I don't mean to rush you. But I got some honeys coming over tonight and I'm not in the mood to share."

"Honeys, as in plural?"

"Yep. Kashanna and Dayanna. Twins, baby!"

Jonathan shook his head at his friend. The sad part was society would more easily accept Kevin's behavior than his monogamous relationship with Tracy. Jonathan stood up and began making his way toward the door. "I'll leave you with your twins. I got some things I need to work out in my head anyway."

"Well, give me a call if you need to talk. In the morning, that is." Kevin grinned.

Simon was sitting at the kitchen table poring over some scripture notes. Jonathan stood silently behind him for a few minutes, trying to gather up his nerve.

"Hey, Dad."

Simon looked up and smiled. "Hey, son. What's shaking?"

"Dad, no one says 'what's shaking' anymore," Jonathan said, pulling out a chair and taking a seat next to his father.

"Excuse me. I'm not up on today's lingo." Simon closed his Bible, set his pen down, and removed his reading glasses. "I'm glad you came in. I needed a break." He leaned back, folding his arms in front of him. "I just wanted to tell you how happy I am to see you and Angela back together. That's a sweet girl if I ever saw one. Have I ever told you how much I like her?"

"Only a thousand times."

"Well, I hope you're serious about her. Because she's just the type of woman a good preacher needs by his side."

Jonathan knew that now was a perfect time for him to tell his father about his decision not to be a preacher, but that was not what he had come here for. Besides, since he was pursuing a future with Angela, maybe he could still have a career in the ministry. The only reason he was deciding against it was because he knew if he chose a gay lifestyle, being a minister was out of the question.

"Dad, I wanted to talk to you about Angela."

"Talk away."

"She's pregnant."

Simon sat in stunned silence, his arms across his chest, his glasses dangling from his hand.

"Say something," Jonathan said.

"What do you want me to say? That I'm happy for you?" Simon asked, a stern expression across his face. Jonathan lowered his eyes, like he had just been chastised.

"Look, Son," Simon continued, finally unfolding his arms and leaning forward. "I can't lie and say I'm not disappointed, but we all make mistakes. I know you'll do right by that girl and give that child a name. So, I won't judge you."

That was not quite the reaction Jonathan expected. His father didn't seem upset at all.

"Of course, I didn't want it to be like this," Simon continued. "But I guess I got my wish about having Angela in the family after all. She'll make a good wife." Simon put his glasses back on, opened his Bible back up, and resumed writing like the discussion was closed.

Jonathan didn't reply. As usual, his father had decided how his life would turn out.

27

DON'T DO IT. Rachel heard the little voice in her head. The one that always tried to keep her out of trouble. The voice of reason. The one that she usually ignored.

Rachel looked at Bobby and Shante's wedding program that she had swiped from inside her father's Bible a week ago. She had the whole thing memorized, including the names of all the bridesmaids, the groomsmen, even the musician.

Rachel looked at the black line drawn through Shante's name. Above it she had written her own. She knew if anyone saw the program, they would think she was crazy, but she wasn't. She was just in pain and imagining what could have been.

I've got something that can make you feel better, too. There went that little voice again. Rachel had been fighting it all afternoon. As usual, she was sprawled out on the sofa at her parents' house. Her electricity had been cut off for nonpayment, which was really trifling because for once she had the money to pay it.

She just had been so depressed that she never made it down to the light company. Since it was Friday, she would have to wait until Monday to get it turned back on.

Just do it. The little voice was driving her crazy. For two days the idea to do more damage to Bobby and Shante had been haunting her. She was trying to heed her mother's words to move on, but she wasn't having any luck.

Rachel finally decided the only way to get the voice out of her head was to go forward with what it wanted. She threw back the afghan she'd been lying in and eased quietly off the sofa, making sure not to wake Nia at the other end. Jonathan had taken Jordan to the circus. They had tried to get Rachel to go, but Nia had an ear infection. Besides, Rachel was in no mood to sit up in a circus and act like everything was peachy-keen in her life.

Rachel made her way over to the telephone. She hesitated before punching in the 800-number.

"Good afternoon, Reliant Energy. This is Carla, may I help you?"

Rachel took a deep breath. No turning back now. "Um . . . yes, this is Shante Wilson, I mean Clark. I live at 25 Northwest 51st. And um, I need to have my electricity cut off. I just got married and we're moving out."

"Okay, Mrs. Clark. For security purposes, we'll need your mother's maiden name."

Rachel smiled. Good thing Lethora Stewart-Wilson was a modern woman who used a hyphenated name. "It's Stewart."

"Thank you, Mrs. Clark. Is there an address you'd like this service moved to?"

"No, not right now. We're staying with family. We'll call back when we're ready to get service hooked up again."

"Mrs. Clark, we'll get you all taken care of. Thank you for being a valued customer of Reliant. Have a great day."

Rachel hung up the phone with a look of satisfaction across her face. She knew Bobby's lease was up at the end of the month, so they were most likely staying at Shante's condo. Now let them stay in the dark, Rachel thought.

Rachel decided not to stop there. She picked up the phone again and called information, asking for the number to the gas and phone companies.

She repeated the process for both places. She ran into a snag with the phone company because they wanted the last four digits of Shante's Social Security number, which she didn't know, but Rachel managed to convince them that she just couldn't remember it. She gave them Lethora's maiden name again and they seemed content with that.

Rachel relaxed in her father's recliner. She was pleased with her handiwork and glad she had listened to that little voice. Granted, this would only be an inconvenience to them (a big one), but not a matter of life or death. It would, however, fulfill Rachel's goal to piss off Shante.

"What are you sitting in here grinning about?" Loretta asked as she walked into the den. "What have you done now?"

Rachel looked at her mother standing in the doorway with her arms crossed. She realized she was still holding on to the phone. She slammed it down in the cradle. "What are you talking about, Mama?"

"You've been walking around here depressed with your lips to the ground for the last week. Now, you're sitting in here with an amused look across your face. So I repeat, what have you done now?"

Rachel let out a deep breath. "Mother, you underestimate me. Maybe I just realized it's time to move on."

"And maybe I've got some swampland in Florida to sell." Loretta eyed Rachel suspiciously. "Come on in here and help me with these dishes."

Rachel rubbed her stomach. "I don't feel too good."

Loretta threw her daughter a stern look. "Don't debate me on this. I don't ask you for much. You come over here to eat, drop your kids off, and wash your clothes. I never say a word, so the least you can do is help me with the dishes. Now come on."

"But I have to watch Nia!"

"Girl, if you don't get on in here. Nia is sound asleep."

Rachel stomped behind her mother into the kitchen. "Why don't you all get a dishwasher?" Rachel complained.

"We have one, you."

"Where's the almighty Reverend Jackson?" Rachel asked as she started running dishwater and stacking up the mounds of dishes from their dinner.

"He's taking a nap. He has the revival at Greater St. John in about an hour."

Rachel peered under the cabinet for some rubber gloves. She had just had her nails painted with little intricate designs, and didn't want to risk them wearing off.

"Why do people have revivals on Friday nights anyway?" she asked as she put on the gloves, shut off the water, and started scrubbing a dish.

"Souls need saving seven days a week," Loretta said. She was wiping down the stove.

The doorbell rang and Rachel seized the opportunity. "I'll get it," she said, racing out of the kitchen.

When she pulled back the little curtain on the door and saw the figures on the other side, her mood became sour again. Rachel snatched the door open.

"Hello, Miss Rachel." Delilah spoke first, displaying a big fake grin. Carrie was standing next to her, looking innocent. Rachel couldn't believe they had the audacity to show their faces at her mother's home.

Delilah's eyes made their way down to Rachel's gloved hands. "Did we interrupt your domestic duties?"

Rachel's attitude was written all over her face, and she didn't care what they thought about it. Both of them looked taken aback by her cold demeanor. "May I help you?" she asked.

Delilah and Carrie glanced at each other with confused looks. Delilah shrugged her shoulders and turned back toward Rachel. "We're here to see Simon, I mean, Reverend Jackson."

"He's asleep." Rachel didn't move from her spot.

Delilah held up a stack of papers. "Well, he wanted me to drop these scripture copies off for the revival tonight."

"I'll take them." Rachel stuck her hand out.

Delilah grasped the papers close to her chest. "There's some things on here I need to personally explain."

Rachel rolled her eyes. "Just tell me and I'll tell him when he wakes up." Her attitude was getting more intense.

"Rachel, let our guests in." Loretta had walked up behind her daughter. Rachel turned around and her mouth dropped open. Her mother's long, thick hair was down, hanging past her shoulders. Rachel hadn't seen her mother wear her hair down in years. She always wore it pinned up tightly in a bun or a French roll. She had also taken off the apron that had become her domestic staple.

Rachel stepped aside and let the women pass.

"Good afternoon, ladies," Loretta said.

"Good afternoon to you," Delilah responded. "I do love your hair like that."

Carrie nodded. "Yeah, I didn't realize it was that long. It looks good."

Rachel felt like she was going to be sick.

"I was just telling Rachel I needed to get these papers to

Reverend Jackson," Delilah said. "And there are some things I needed to go over with him, because they didn't quite come out the way he wanted them to."

Rachel stared at Delilah's outfit. As usual, her cleavage was showing. She also wore a skintight, leopard miniskirt. The woman had to be forty-five years old and still dressed like she was seventeen.

"Well, I'll go wake Simon. I'm sure if he has any questions, he'd like them answered before the revival tonight." Loretta turned toward her daughter. "Rachel, you can go finish what you were doing."

"Thank you," Delilah remarked.

"Make yourself comfortable. I'll be right back."

Loretta went upstairs to wake Simon.

Rachel cut her eyes at the women before heading back down the hall. When she was out of sight, she stopped within earshot of their conversation. She knew she was eavesdropping as always, but she wanted to find out why they were really there.

"Did you check out Miss Thang's hair?" Carrie whispered.

"Girl, yes. It don't matter though. She still looks like somebody's grandmother in that frumpy old housecoat."

"She is," Carrie said, laughing. "You know her scandalous daughter has all those babies."

It took everything in Rachel's power not to go back in there and give them a piece of her mind.

"And get a load of this house," Delilah continued, rubbing her hand along the sofa. "She has it decorated like a funeral parlor. It's horrible. This hard sofa, those old antiquated tables. I would be living large if I was the first lady."

"But you're not."

Both women jumped up at the sight of Loretta. She had entered the living room through the kitchen entrance. Rachel broke out into a big smile. Her mother must have come down the back stairs that led to the kitchen. Loretta knew exactly what she was doing. Rachel had to see this up close. She stepped out from behind the door where she had been listening, walked into the living room, and leaned against the wall with a triumphant look across her face.

Loretta gently walked within inches of Delilah's face. "You know, for years I have been listening to you degrade me, talk about me. I have watched your worthless attempts to steal my husband. And I have remained a true Christian, just turning the other cheek, because I have faith in my husband. You can consider yourself the most glamorous, sexiest diva there is. But the bottom line remains. I still have what you want." Loretta had a smooth, confident look across her face. Rachel had never been so impressed. Delilah, however, looked stunned.

"*I* am Mrs. Simon Jackson. *I* am the first lady of Zion Hill. *You* are nothing but a lonely, bitter, washed-up wannabe who cannot keep a man, and must therefore try to steal everyone else's."

Rachel wanted to give her mother a high five. She wished she were taping this. David and Jonathan would never believe it. Her mother was telling Delilah off with such dignity and class. Rachel knew that if it was her, she and Delilah would be rolling on the floor.

Loretta stood firm, not taking her eyes off of Delilah. "I'm about fed up with you. Therefore, I would advise you to begin looking for another job, because I will be speaking with my husband regarding your dismissal and finding someone with morals, values, and respect. And much to your dismay, I guarantee you, my feelings will come before yours. Now, if you would kindly hand over those papers and get the hell out of my house!"

With that, Rachel couldn't help but laugh. She had never heard her mother curse. This was too much.

Delilah looked dumbfounded, but didn't move.

"If you can't find the door, my foot would be happy to help you," Loretta said calmly.

Carrie took the papers from Delilah, threw them on the table, then grabbed Delilah's arm. "We'll be leaving now."

She pulled Delilah toward the door. Rachel had raced over and pulled it wide open. The women scurried out without looking back.

Rachel closed the door and turned toward her mother. "Oh, my God, Mama. That was off the hook! I can't believe you finally said something to them."

Loretta looked at her daughter and smiled. "Even Christian women have their limits. Now let's go finish the dishes."

Rachel proudly beamed at her mother. "Gladly, Mama. Gladly."

She draped her arm through her mother's arm and led her back into the kitchen.

28

ANGELA SAT ON the floor of the Jacksons' home. She was playing with Nia, looking so happy. Jonathan, on the other hand, had never been more confused. He believed without a shadow of a doubt that he loved Angela, so why did his insides feel like they were all jumbled up?

These last three months with her had been wonderful. He had forgotten just how much he enjoyed her company. For a while, she actually made him forget his troubles with Tracy. Jonathan didn't think anyone would ever be able to do that. He started telling himself that this was all part of God's master plan.

Simon appeared in the doorway. "How is my most favorite granddaughter?" he asked, bending down to kiss Nia.

Nia giggled. "She's wonderful, Reverend Jackson," Angela replied.

Simon smiled, before turning to Jonathan. "Can I talk to

you a minute, Son?" He motioned toward the patio door. "Let's just go out on the deck."

"Are you going to be all right?" Jonathan asked Angela as he got up.

"We'll be just fine," she replied, tickling Nia's stomach.

Jonathan followed his father outside. Simon had a huge grin across his face as he turned to face his son. "Jon, since the day you entered this world, you've made me proud of you. The only way you can make me happier is to take this." Simon opened up his hand to reveal a stunning one and a half carat ring encased in white gold.

Jonathan's eyes narrowed. "That's Mom's ring."

Simon grasped the ring between his index finger and thumb and lifted it. "This belonged to your Grandma Naomi. And it belonged to her mother before that. She gave it to me; I gave it to Loretta, and now we want to give it to you. It would make us both proud if you would take this ring and make Angela your wife."

Jonathan gazed at the ring in amazement. He knew everyone expected him to marry Angela; he was even seriously considering it. But by no means had he intended on doing anything anytime soon. He and Angela had never discussed marriage, although he knew she desperately wanted it. She would sink into these silent bouts and Jonathan knew it was because she was wrestling with her feelings about having a baby out of wedlock.

"Dad, I don't know if we're ready for this," Jonathan said. "We've only officially been back together a few months."

"It's not like you don't know her, have a history with her. You two had solid years together. I know you were in high school but you both have always been so mature. You need to do right by that girl and make her your wife before that baby is born. That child deserves to come into this world with two parents . . . parents who are married."

Jonathan thought about what his father was saying. The last thing he wanted was for Angela to be a single mom. Granted, he would always be there for his child, but it wasn't the baby's fault he had pressured her into having sex. It's not like he didn't love Angela. Maybe this was the sign he was asking for to help him get his head together.

Jonathan took the ring and stared at it briefly, before easing it into his pocket. Simon smiled broadly and patted his son on the back. "I knew you'd do the right thing."

"Let's go back inside. I'll get your mother and you can propose to Angela in front of everybody," Simon said.

His father wasn't wasting any time. He wasn't even giving Jonathan time to digest everything. Before Jonathan could respond, Simon was gone.

A few minutes later, his parents walked back into the den.

"Let me take Nia," Loretta said to Angela, trying to conceal her excitement.

Angela looked like she wanted to protest, she was having so much fun.

Jonathan touched her arm. "Let Mama have her just for a moment." He looked over at his father, who gave him a reassuring nod.

Angela handed Nia over to Loretta, a look of confusion across her face.

Jonathan turned back toward Angela. "I know this isn't how we planned on anything happening, but obviously this was God's plan. I don't want to bring a child into this world without the Jackson name. So," he hesitated, pulling out the ring, and dropping to his knee. Angela stood before him, her eyes wide. "Will you marry me?"

Jonathan took the tears forming in Angela's eyes as a yes. She eased her hand out, her face beaming with excitement, tears welling up in her eyes. As he slid the ring on her finger, Jonathan said a silent prayer that he was doing the right thing.

29

THIS WAS SIMON'S favorite part of each service, standing outside and greeting the congregation as they left church. It gave him a chance to interact with his members.

"Pastor, you sho' spread the word of God today," said a lady in a big yellow hat with fruit on it.

Simon leaned in and kissed her on the cheek. "Thank you, Sister Perkins. I'm just a vessel for the Lord. You tell that husband of yours we'll be looking for him next Sunday."

Constance Perkins nodded. "He's been a little under the weather. But I'm going to drag him here next Sunday. If he ain't here, it's 'cause he died." She laughed.

She moved on and shook the hand of Rachel, who was standing next to Loretta. Simon looked down at his daughter. Jonathan was standing on the other side of her. Simon could tell Rachel didn't want to be here, but having the family greet the congregation was a tradition that had been going on at Zion Hill since he took over.

Rachel shot her father a look saying, "Can I go now?" When

he made sure everyone was just about out, he turned to his daughter and whispered, "Just say hello to Lester, then you can go."

Rachel rolled her eyes as Lester made his way out of the church.

"Good sermon, Reverend Jackson."

"Thank you, Lester."

"And Mrs. Jackson, you sure look lovely today. Is that a new dress?"

"It sure is, Lester. Thank you for noticing," Loretta responded, fluffing up the shoulders of the bright purple silk dress she was wearing.

"I think I'm going to be sick," Rachel mumbled.

"Did you say you're sick?" Lester asked.

"Huh? Uh, no. I'm fine," Rachel responded, irritated. "How are you, Lester?"

"Better now that I got a chance to see you." He grinned widely, showing off the spacious gap in his two front teeth.

Rachel didn't respond.

"Rachel, I was wondering . . . well . . . Grandmother cooked her special fried chicken today and she always cooks too much . . . and well . . . I was just wondering . . . if maybe you and the kids . . . would like to . . ." Lester stopped mumbling when he saw the man in a sheriff's uniform walk toward them. Everyone turned and stared at the officer.

"May I help you?" Simon asked.

"I'm looking for Rachel Jackson."

Rachel froze. This couldn't be about those grapes she ate in the grocery store the other day. They wouldn't arrest her for that, would they? Simon pointed toward his daughter. "This is Rachel. I'm her father. What is this about?"

The officer ignored Simon and pulled an envelope out of

his pocket. "Rachel Jackson, you've been served." He handed Rachel the envelope, then turned and walked away.

Rachel stared at the envelope in her hand.

"Well, open it!"

Simon's voice snapped her out of her daze. Rachel tore open the envelope.

"I don't believe this," she said as her eyes scanned the legal document.

"What is it, baby?" Loretta asked.

"It's Bobby. He's suing me for joint custody of Jordan." Rachel didn't remember much after that. Her whole world turned black.

Rachel inhaled deeply as she stood outside the door of Simon's office. She and her father hadn't had a civil conversation in years, but now she needed him. For a change, she needed his influence as pastor of Zion Hill. Having him testify on her behalf would surely speak volumes with the judge. She refused to share custody of Jordan with Bobby and Shante, and if that meant sucking up to her father, then so be it.

After a few minutes of waiting, she realized her father wasn't there.

She made her way back into the hall to search for him. At the conference room she stopped and decided to check inside. The door was closed and she was just about to knock when she heard someone shout.

Rachel leaned in closer to make out what they were saying.

"I don't care how, I just want him out!"

"Keep your voice down. Simon is still in the church."

Rachel's interest was piqued. She always was one for a piece of good gossip. The first voice sounded like Deacon Jacobs, the chairman of the church board. Rachel couldn't make out the other voice. She put her ear to the door.

"Y'all know I don't particularly care for Simon anyway," Deacon Jacobs said. "If I had my druthers, we would've gotten rid of him long ago. Now, my nephew needs his own church, and Zion Hill is just the place for him. So, I don't care how we do it, we just need to get Simon out!"

"How?" the other person asked.

"I don't care! Catch him embezzling some money, set him up having an affair—it doesn't matter."

Rachel raised her eyebrows. Were they trying to kick her father out of Zion Hill? Granted, nothing would make her happier than seeing him give up this church, but Rachel wasn't quite sure about him being set up.

"I'm going to push to get Simon Jackson out of here so that my nephew can take his rightful place as pastor of this church! Besides, he should've had the job when they hired Simon in the first place."

Rachel turned to go find her father and bumped right into him.

"Were you eavesdropping at that door, Rachel?" Simon asked.

"No, I was looking for you."

"I saw you. You were eavesdropping. Then you goin' stand right in the church and lie about it."

"But, Daddy, I need to tell you—"

Simon cut her off. "I don't believe you, Rachel. Have you no shame? No, of course not. What was I thinking? You fornicate, you lie, and you're disrespectful, so what's a little eavesdropping to the list? You know, I am so disappointed in you. You really need to get yourself together."

Rachel glared at her father. She couldn't win for losing

with him. Simon ignored her icy stare. "Come away from that door," he snapped. "What are you doing up here anyway?"

Rachel debated whether she should go ahead and tell her father what she'd overheard, but his look of contempt made her decide against it. Let them kick her father out. It would serve him right.

Rachel let out a long sigh. "I came by to make sure you were going to be at the court hearing. It's at two o'clock."

Simon looked at his watch, then blew his breath. "I need to finish up some paperwork here, but I guess I'll be there."

"No guessing. You have to be there."

"Fine, although I think you ought to do right by that boy and let him see his son. Maybe Jordan would be better off in a more stable environment anyway."

Nobody asked you what you thought, Rachel wanted to say, but she also wanted him to show up in court. Instead she said, "We'll just let the courts decide that."

The conference room doors opened and Deacon Jacobs walked out. He was followed by Deacon Joseph Riley, who had to be the other person talking. Both of the deacons smiled at Simon.

"Afternoon, Pastor," Deacon Jacobs said.

Simon nodded. "Gentlemen."

"That was a wonderful sermon you preached last Sunday," Deacon Riley said.

"Yeah," Deacon Jacobs added. "It sure hit home for a lot of people."

Simon smiled appreciatively as they walked away. Rachel smiled, too. They were playing her father for a fool. Grinning in his face, then plotting behind his back.

Good. Losing his church would knock her father off his

self-righteous pedestal. Rachel couldn't wait to see how this all would turn out.

"What are you standing there grinning at?" Simon asked. "I hope you're not plotting some other way to try and mess up things for Bobby and Shante."

"No, Daddy. I have to go. Just please don't be late to court."

"I'm always on time! It's you who has the tardiness problem."

Simon spun on his heels and returned to his office.

"I'll say a prayer that Deacon Jacobs gets his wish," Rachel muttered as she watched her father walk away.

30

RACHEL SAT AT the large table next to the stocky attorney her parents had hired. She still couldn't believe they were in court. It had been only two weeks since she was served. She'd quickly learned that Shante used to work for a judge—that had to be the only reason they were in court this fast.

As the attorney scanned the documents in front of him, Rachel fidgeted with everything within her reach. First, twirling the pen, then swishing the water around in the small glass that sat on their table. After getting bored with that, she turned to look at her parents in the front row. Her father refused to make eye contact with her, shaking his head like he was mad at her for wasting his time. Her mother gave her a reassuring smile. Jon and Angela sat next to her. Jon gave Rachel a "thumbs up," then poked at a dozing David and whispered something in his ear. David looked up, smiled, then gave Rachel a "thumbs up," too. Sitting at the end of the row was Lester. He looked as scared as Rachel felt. Lester mouthed "I love you" to her. That threw Rachel for a loop and she quickly turned back around. She always knew Lester was crazy about her, but love? He'd invited himself to the hearing, but Rachel couldn't complain; right now, she was thankful to have as many people in her corner as possible.

"Rachel, I think you should try to give just a little," the attorney said, leaning in and snapping Rachel back to the present.

Rachel huffed. They had been down this road a thousand times in the last week. She was not budging. She refused to give Bobby and Shante joint custody. She refused to let Shante be around Jordan, period. Her parents had told her she was being ridiculous, adding that Bobby had rights. The attorney had preached that same sermon, but Rachel wasn't trying to hear it.

Rachel looked over her shoulder as Bobby and Shante walked into the courtroom. Their hands were gripped tightly together. She noticed the rock glistening brightly on Shante's hand. Rachel struggled to fight back the tears. That should have been her ring. That should have been her all hugged up with Bobby. Shante glared at Rachel with a smirk on her face. She was eating this all up.

It seemed like Bobby's whole family had accompanied him to the hearing. His parents, all five of his sisters and his two brothers, none of whom ever liked Rachel, were gathered in a circle, taking up the entire aisle. Bobby's oldest sister leaned in and whispered something in Shante's ear. They both looked at Rachel and burst out laughing. Rachel was just about to get up and give them a piece of her mind when the bailiff entered the courtroom. Bobby squeezed Shante's hand, released it, then shuttled to the table on the other side of the room. His attorney, a distinguished-looking black man, smiled as he approached the table. Shante and the rest of

Bobby's family took up two rows behind Bobby and his attorney.

"All rise," the bailiff said. "The honorable Patrice Russell presiding."

Everyone stood up as the blond-haired judge made her way onto the bench. Rachel grinned. She was happy to have a female judge. Hopefully, a woman would be more sympathetic to her case.

"You may be seated," the judge said. "This is a matter of Bobby Jordan Clark versus Rachel Nichelle Jackson, over the custody of the minor child, Jordan Kobe Clark. Are both parties present?"

Both attorneys stood up and simultaneously spoke. "They are."

The judge briefly studied Bobby and Rachel before looking over the documents.

"Am I correct that the child is in the custody of his mother?"

"That's correct, Your Honor," said Rachel's attorney.

"Have you advised your client how I take into account both parties' willingness, or unwillingness, to reach a resolution prior to court?"

The attorney straightened his back and shot Rachel an "I told you so" look. "Yes, I have, Your Honor."

"Very well, then. You may proceed."

Rachel's attorney glanced over his papers briefly before stepping out from behind the table. "Your honor, my client feels the hostile environment created by the presence of Miss Shante Wilson is—"

"The name is Clark. Shante Clark," Shante stood up and yelled out.

Bobby turned around and threw a hostile look at Shante. Several people started laughing. Bobby's sister grabbed

Shante's arm and pulled her back down into the seat. The judge slammed her gavel down. "Order! There will be no outbursts in my court or you will be asked to leave."

Shante leaned back and crossed her arms defiantly. "It's Clark," she muttered.

"As I was saying, Your Honor, my client feels it is in the best interest of the child if he be allowed only supervised visits with his father, Bobby Clark." He turned and pointed toward Shante. "That is indicative of the reason my client doesn't want joint custody. She feels her son would be subjected to outbursts like that by Mr. Clark's wife."

Rachel smiled as she looked over and saw the frustration on Bobby's face. She told him not to mess with her. Now he'd be lucky to see Jordan at all.

Rachel's attorney continued presenting his case, calling on Loretta and Simon to talk about the role they played in Jordan's life. Rachel was proud. She knew her mother would deliver, but her father had actually described her as a loving, doting mother. Those words had to be some of the nicest things he'd ever said about her. For once, her father had come through.

Rachel's attorney took just over an hour presenting her side. By the time he was through, Rachel was certain that she would emerge victorious. She knew if it boiled down to Bobby choosing between Shante and Jordan, he'd choose Jordan. And since she and Jordan were a package deal, they'd end up together after all.

Rachel sat back confidently as Bobby's attorney made his way to the front of the judge. Her smile slowly faded as she listened to him describe how she became "impregnated" by another man while in a committed relationship with Bobby. He talked about her inconsistency in jobs, even pulling out her employment records to show how she always left within eight months.

How could he have gotten his hands on that? Rachel wondered.

The attorney ran down every despicable thing she had ever done. He talked about the arrest after she had come to their home and physically assaulted both Bobby and Shante. He even had Shante take the stand and recap the incident where Rachel had Jordan knock on her door.

"Your Honor," the attorney said, after Shante had returned to her seat, "we're not asking for anything out of the ordinary. Just the God-given rights due to Bobby Clark, Jordan's biological father. We're not asking to take the child from his mother, even though my client believes the child would be better off in the stable environment he and his wife could provide." Shante smirked at that comment. "We just want little Jordan to know his father loves him and wants to take part in raising him."

Rachel was near tears by the time the attorney finished. He had made her sound like a horrible, vengeful mother. Loretta leaned forward in her seat and gently rubbed Rachel's back.

Judge Russell took a few moments to look through her papers. Both sides sat in silence. Bobby nervously fiddled with his cufflinks. Rachel tried desperately to ward off the tears.

Finally, the judge raised her head. "This case is pretty cut and dried." She turned toward Rachel. "Miss Jackson, your behavior is childish, petty, and downright vindictive. I believe if Mr. Clark had chosen you instead of his current wife, you wouldn't have had any problems with him spending time with his son. Your motives are purely personal and not in the best interest of the child. With that in mind, I am awarding the petitioner's request for joint custody."

Bobby and his entire family clapped and began loudly congratulating each other. Rachel lowered her head and began sobbing.

The judge pounded her gavel for order, then turned her attention back to Rachel. "Miss Jackson?" Rachel lifted her head and tried to stifle her tears. "Consider yourself lucky that Mr. Clark did not seek sole custody because, based on the information presented here today, I would have had to award it to him. I genuinely believe he does not want to separate you from your son. For that you should be grateful; now get yourself together. Court is adjourned." She pounded her gavel one last time, then exited the bench.

31

JONATHAN STARED at his image in the mirror. He looked elegant in his coal black Italian-made tuxedo. He adjusted his hunter green bow tie and wiped away the beads of sweat forming on his brow.

You're doing the right thing, he told himself.

It was a message he had been repeating nonstop for the last two weeks. Angela was a good catch. She would make a wonderful wife. But Jonathan couldn't help but wonder if he would make a good husband, especially if he couldn't completely give his heart to her.

He glanced at his watch. The ceremony was set to start in fifteen minutes. His father would be in any second to walk him to the front of the church. Simon was so proud. This was a moment he had dreamed of. Backing out now would not only crush Angela, it would devastate Simon as well.

"That's not an option," Jonathan muttered. He felt so confused. Part of him loved Angela without a doubt, but was it enough to make a marriage work?

Out of the corner of his eye, Jonathan noticed the huge cross hanging on the wall of the small choir room. He thought about the last time he'd prayed. It had been so long ago. He'd strayed from praying while he was with Tracy. He was too consumed with guilt. But now, he felt maybe prayer could provide some answers.

Jonathan took a deep breath and decided it was worth a try. He closed his eyes and bowed his head.

"Hey, God, long time no talk to. I'm sorry I haven't been turning to you much, it's just . . . well, you know why. Lord, tell me I'm doing the right thing. Help me get Tracy out of my heart, so I can give Angela all the love she deserves. Amen."

Jonathan looked up at his reflection again. He couldn't believe how unhappy he looked.

"God meant for you two to be together, Son." Jonathan quickly turned to see Simon leaning against the wall.

"How long have you been there?"

"Long enough. You are doing the right thing. If God had meant for you to be with Tracy, it would've worked out. But you were led back home. That's because He had something better in store. Angela." Simon smiled. "You look great, Son. And I just saw the bride. Once you lay eyes on her, there won't be any doubt. I've never met Tracy, but I'd be willing to bet she can't hold a candle to Angela."

Jonathan cast his eyes downward. Simon walked over and patted him on the back. "You can do this. Most grooms get wedding-day jitters."

Jonathan inhaled deeply. "I know. I also know I'm doing the right thing. I want my son to come into this world with both his parents."

"So, you already know it's a boy?"

"That just slipped out." Actually, Jonathan was hoping for a girl. How could he teach a son to be a man when he had doubts about his own manhood?

"Well, I believe you're doing the right thing, too," Simon remarked. "Now, let's go do it."

Jonathan managed a slight smile and eased his chair back. "I'm ready." At least, as ready as I'll ever be, he wanted to say.

His father was right. Angela was absolutely beautiful. She was wearing a white fitted bridal gown, with intricate pearls sewn across the bodice. It dipped slightly at her shoulders. Her face was uncovered, the veil hanging from a crown atop her head. She showed no signs of the life growing inside her.

They had chosen a small ceremony, with only close family, friends, and members of Zion Hill. The bridal party was small as well, just Kevin as Jonathan's best man and Angela's sister as the maid of honor.

Jonathan felt himself relax as Angela walked down the aisle to Kenny G's "Wedding Song." Angela's cousin was playing the song on his saxophone. He sounded almost as good as Kenny himself. Her father, a tall, husky attorney with graying hair—who looked like he could break anyone's neck who hurt his daughter—escorted Angela.

Jonathan shifted uncomfortably at the gaze Angela's father was throwing him. He knew how protective Mr. Brooks was, another reason he didn't want to hurt Angela.

Angela's eyes shone as they met at the altar. She seemed so happy. Her enthusiasm was contagious and Jonathan began to smile himself. His smile quickly faded when he glanced out into the crowd. Sitting in the second row of the groom's side, nestled between a distant cousin and a Zion Hill church member, was Tracy.

Jonathan began to shake nervously. He had written Tracy a letter telling him that he was getting married. Part of him did it to hurt Tracy. The other part wanted the letter to serve as confirmation that he was actually moving on with his life. But Jonathan never dreamed Tracy would show up. Had he come to ruin this day? *Please, God, no,* Jonathan thought. After the debacle with Rachel at Bobby's wedding, Simon would probably go ballistic if there was any drama during these nuptials.

"Son, are you going to take her hand?"

Simon was smiling at his son. Jonathan looked down and noticed Angela waiting for him to take her hand and help her up the two stairs to stand at the altar.

"Oh, sorry." Jonathan nervously laughed.

"You know these young grooms," Simon said. The audience chuckled, with the exception of Mr. Brooks.

Jonathan stepped down, took Angela's hand, then led her back up to stand in front of his father.

Simon began talking about marriage being a commitment and some other things Jonathan couldn't quite make out. He wanted desperately to turn around and see what Tracy was doing. Was he going to make trouble? But Jonathan looked straight ahead the entire time Simon talked. He couldn't even bring himself to look at Angela, fearful that if he did, his eyes would make their way back to Tracy.

"If there is anyone here today that thinks this couple should not be joined in holy matrimony, let them speak now or forever hold their peace," Simon said.

By this point, Jonathan felt like he would pass out. He couldn't breathe as he waited for Tracy to come running down the aisle, imploring the wedding to stop, begging Jonathan to come out of the closet. Jonathan had the entire scene played out in his mind. It was his worst nightmare about to come true.

Simon waited a minute, then continued. "Since everyone is in agreement that these two young people belong together, Jonathan James Jackson, do you take this woman to be your lawfully wedded wife, to have and to hold, in sickness and in health, for richer or for poorer, forsaking all others so long as you both shall live?"

Jonathan took a deep breath. "I do."

Simon turned to Angela. "And do you, Angela Renee Brooks, take this man to be your lawfully wedded husband, to have and to hold, in sickness and in health, for richer or for poorer, forsaking all others so long as you both shall live?"

"I do," she confidently proclaimed.

"Well, then, by the power vested in me by the state of Texas, I now pronounce you man and wife. Son, you may kiss your bride."

Jonathan's shoulders slumped in relief. He managed a smile, then leaned in and gently kissed Angela on the lips.

"Ladies and gentlemen, I present to you Mr. and Mrs. Jonathan Jackson."

Angela turned toward the crowd first. Jonathan followed as Natalie Cole's "Our Love" began playing in the background. Everyone stood up and clapped as Jonathan took Angela's hand and they made their way down the center aisle. He nervously glanced over to where Tracy had been sitting. The spot was empty.

It's for the best, Jonathan thought. *My future is with Angela.*

Jonathan turned his attention back to the crowd of well-wishers throwing rice at them. For the first time that day, he truly felt like he'd made the right choice.

32

THE STEAM FROM the shower permeated Jonathan's nostrils. The water was hot, scorching his back. But Jonathan refused to move. He needed cleansing. He needed to wash away all the ill thoughts he had, continued to have, of Tracy.

He was a married man now. To everyone who saw him, a happily married man. But inside, his soul was in torment.

A month had gone by since he and Angela had exchanged vows. They were settled in a nice townhouse, compliments of her parents. Angela had already decorated the place. From the Persian rug that lined the hallway to the soft leather sofa and loveseat, she had made the house feel like a home. But instead of enjoying his blissful newlywed status, Jonathan had never been more miserable.

What have I done? he thought as he let the drops of water slide down his back. Jonathan had prayed every night for God to banish Tracy from his heart, but so far, God wasn't listening.

"I'm trying to do right," he muttered to himself. "I'm trying to live a normal life." That had become his daily mantra. The words he needed to get himself through each day.

Angela was seemingly oblivious to his feelings. That was probably because he put on a good act, being the loving husband, showering her with affection. But he was just going through the motions. He thought marriage would change the way he felt, wipe away any lingering feelings of Tracy. Instead, those feelings had only intensified.

Maybe the saying "absence makes the heart grow fonder" was true. Jonathan tried to call Tracy two days after the wedding, but Tracy never returned the call. Or the numerous messages Jonathan left after that. The one and only call he'd received from Tracy had been a voice mail left on his cell phone this past Sunday, when Tracy had known Jonathan would be at church.

"You've got your 'Leave It to Beaver' family. So now, leave me alone," was all it had said. But just hearing Tracy's voice made Jonathan's heart pine even more.

Then he'd watch Angela doting over her protruding stomach, getting more and more excited about motherhood. She was out now buying stuff for the nursery, making plans for their future. Jonathan couldn't help but wonder what in the world he'd gotten himself into.

He flipped the water off when he heard the phone ring. His body seemed to breathe a sigh of relief once the scorching water stopped. Jonathan grabbed a towel and raced out of the shower and into the bedroom. Call Notes was set to pick up on the sixth ring, but Jonathan made it to the phone before it rolled over.

"Hello," he said, gasping for breath. His skin felt raw as he tried to wrap the towel around his waist. "Hello," Jonathan repeated when there was no reply.

"Hi."

Jonathan felt his heart drop. "Tracy?"

"I'm sorry for calling your house. The number was on my Caller ID from when you called. And your cell phone isn't working." Tracy seemed to be choosing his words slowly.

"Yeah, I just changed providers." Jonathan sat down on the edge of the bed. "I miss you." He couldn't help it. He had to say that, he'd been wanting to say it for so long. It felt so good to finally get it out.

Tracy paused. "I miss you, too. I've tried to stay away. I just can't stop thinking about you."

Jonathan moaned. "I know the feeling."

"Can I ask you a question?"

"Go ahead."

"Why'd you marry her?"

Jonathan stared at the picture in a silver-plated frame on the nightstand next to the queen-size bed. A wedding guest had snapped that picture at the reception. Angela looked so beautiful as she rested her head on his shoulder. They looked like a happy, normal couple. "I love her," Jonathan finally responded.

"More than you love me?"

Jonathan fell back on the bed, the towel dropping from around his waist. Despite the warmth of the room, he felt himself shiver. He closed his eyes and took a deep breath. "I don't think I can ever love anyone more than I love you."

"Then why?" It sounded like Tracy was softly crying now. "I sat there in the wedding, watching, waiting for you to come to your senses. When your father called for anyone who objected to speak, it took every ounce of my being to stay quiet. I left when you kissed her. I just couldn't believe you went through with it."

"Tracy, I'm sorry."

"Are you happy?"

"It's only been a few weeks."

"Are you happy?" Tracy repeated with firmness.

Now it was Jonathan's turn to let the tears loose, let out everything that had been consuming him since he boarded that plane leaving Atlanta. "I want to be with you so bad it hurts. I think about you nonstop. I touch my wife and I pretend she's you. Only it's not working. I can't get you out of my system. But I'm trying to do the right thing. For my baby, for Angela."

"What about for yourself?"

"Tracy, don't do this."

Tracy exhaled slowly. "I know you love me. I know you want to be with me. I hear it when you call here and say nothing on my voice mail. I feel it in my heart."

"I know, Tracy. I'm just so confused."

Tracy's voice resonated with conviction. "You tell me to leave you alone; that you really and truly love this woman and want to spend the rest of your life with her; that you didn't marry her because it's what everyone expected of you. Tell me that and I will go and never call you again."

Jonathan was silent. He closed his eyes to ward off the tears. "I can't." Suddenly, Jonathan heard a woman's sob, then what sounded like a phone dropping to the floor. He jumped up, snatched back the curtain and looked outside the window. Angela's red Mazda Miata was parked in the driveway.

"Oh no," Jonathan mumbled. "Tracy, I'll call you back!" Jonathan pushed the off button on the cordless phone, waited a few seconds, then turned the phone back on. No dial tone. "Angela . . ."

He raced down the stairs. Angela was sitting on the floor at the bottom of the staircase, a shocked look across her face. The phone was lying on the floor next to her. She still clutched a Babies "Я" Us plastic bag in one hand.

Jonathan eased toward her. "Angela, I can explain . . ."

Angela started shaking her head like she was in a daze. "The phone was ringing when I walked in. I . . . I just answered it." Her chest started heaving. She dropped the bag, clutched her stomach, and began rocking back and forth. "I never meant to keep listening, but . . . oh, my God. I don't believe this is happening."

Jonathan slowly kneeled down next to her. "Please, let me explain."

Angela kept shaking her head. "Explain what? That my husband is gay? That he married me in some quest to find his manhood? This can't be happening to me."

Jonathan reached out to try and take her hand. "I love you."

Angela jerked her hand away. *"DON'T! Don't you dare say that to me, you liar!"* Angela scooted back against the wall, a crazed look across her face. She grasped her head with both hands. "You're gay? And your lover was at our wedding?"

She began sobbing uncontrollably. Jonathan didn't know what to say. He couldn't explain away what she'd heard; he wouldn't even know where to begin.

He had to at least try to say something, though.

"Angela, it's not like that. Tracy and I are over."

"So you admit it?" she asked, trying to catch her breath.

Jonathan took a moment to gather his words. "No, that's not what I'm saying. I mean, yes, I did have a relationship with Tracy, but it's over."

"It doesn't sound like you want it to be. For God's sake, you were crying!"

Jonathan leaned back on the wall next to Angela. He had no idea what to say to her.

"I thought if I got married, then—"

"Then what? You wouldn't be gay?" Angela screamed as she stood up. Her eyes made their way up and down his naked body. "Were you planning on having phone sex with him or something?"

Jonathan looked down, just realizing he didn't have any clothes on. "Angela, no. I just got out of the shower when the phone rang."

Angela looked like she was about to faint. Jonathan stood up. "You shouldn't get upset. The baby."

Angela's eyes widened as she grabbed her stomach. "My baby. Our baby. Oh, my God, what am I gonna do?" she sobbed.

"I'm so sorry, Angela." Jonathan tried to reach out and hug her. Angela jumped away from his outstretched arms.

"Don't touch me! You disgust me! Don't ever touch me again! Just leave me alone," she cried. "Get out. Go be with your lover."

"Can we talk about this, please?"

"GET OUT!"

Jonathan backed up, looked at his wife standing there sobbing, and knew he had hurt her to the point of no return. "I'm sorry," he repeated before heading upstairs to put on some clothes.

Ten minutes later, Jonathan was back at the bottom of the staircase. He had stuffed some of his clothes and toiletries into a duffle bag. Angela was sitting on the living room sofa, her eyes beet red.

"I'll give you some time to cool off, then hopefully we can talk through this."

"Your stuff will be packed and waiting on you tomorrow," she said calmly.

Jonathan couldn't look her in the face, he was so ashamed. "Angela, please?"

"Get out, Jonathan. And don't ever come back." Angela gently rubbed her stomach as she spoke. "My father will get in touch with you regarding the annulment papers."

Jonathan looked down at the floor, before raising his head back up. "You'll never know how sorry I am. I never meant to hurt you."

"But you did. Again. Now go."

Jonathan didn't know what else he could possibly say, so he threw her one last apologetic look before grabbing his keys and walking out the front door. And as much as his heart ached from the pain he knew he had caused Angela, Jonathan couldn't help but feel the weight of the world had just been lifted off his shoulders.

33

David couldn't believe how nervous he felt. His mother didn't sound like herself when she'd called and asked him to come by and see her. She sounded strange, but refused to tell him what was on her mind, saying she wanted to talk to him in person.

Of course, David had tried to get out of going to his parents. He didn't want to risk bumping into his father.

"Ma, you in here?" David called out as he eased the door open.

"Back here, baby," Loretta called out from the den.

David nervously made his way to the back. He had a strange feeling in the pit of his stomach. Maybe it was just his nerves about being here and possibly running into his father.

"Why is the front door open? You don't need to be sitting up in here with the door unlocked," David asked.

"I left it open for you." Loretta smiled at David. He returned her smile, but it quickly faded once he walked in front of his mother. She looked pale, her eyes were beet red.

"Mama, are you okay?" David asked as he took her hand.

Loretta patted his hand. "Yeah, baby. Trying to fight off this bad cold."

"Are you sure that's all?"

"Boy, stop fussing over me. It's just a head cold."

David looked at his mother skeptically before easing down into the chair directly across from her. "Where's Dad?"

Loretta managed a small smile.

"Stupid question, huh?" David shrugged. "What time does church let out? I don't want to be here when he gets back."

"He'll be there pretty much all day. They have a deacon board meeting, then he has some paperwork he has to do." Loretta sighed, then smoothed out the afghan she had draped across her legs. "Baby, you know I hate the way things are between you and your father."

David bit down on his bottom lip. "I hate it, too, Mama. But it ain't all Daddy's fault."

"I know it ain't."

David shifted uncomfortably. "So what did you want to see me for?"

"How you doing? Really?" Loretta had a genuine look of concern across her face.

David contemplated lying, but as much as he tried to play her over the years, he knew his mother wasn't stupid. "It's a struggle."

"David, you are so smart, so handsome. Why are you throwing your life away for drugs?"

David shrugged again. He wondered, had his father told her about him almost killing himself? Tawny had told David how Simon had just walked out, leaving him there for dead. David probably should've been mad, but part of him couldn't blame his father. Part of him wished he had died.

"Is it Simon?" Loretta asked, interrupting David's thoughts.

"That may be part of it. But I just like the way they make me feel. Like I'm escaping." David felt himself tearing up and he couldn't understand why. Maybe because this was the first time he had even admitted to his mother that he had a problem.

"David." Loretta gently squeezed her son's hands. "I never ask you for much, do I?"

"No, Mama. You never do."

"Well, I'm asking. No, I'm begging. Please let the drugs go. I'll help you. I'll stay with you, or you can come here. I'll do whatever it takes. If I have to put my foot down with Simon so you can stay, I'll do it. It just breaks my heart to see you like this." She caressed his cheek as tears trickled down her face. "Where is that vibrant young man with the big dreams and even bigger heart? Where is that loving young man who would lay down his life for his family? I need him back. Please, David. I need him back before . . ." Loretta stopped abruptly.

David's heart was ripping apart. "Before . . . before I kill myself?"

Loretta softly nodded. "I can't bear the thought of that, baby."

David hadn't thought about death much, until he almost overdosed a few weeks ago. In the last year, he felt like he'd knocked on death's door several times, it just hadn't been opened yet. But he knew it was only just a matter of time if things kept up the way they were. That near-overdose was almost like a wake-up call.

But David also knew getting off drugs would be easier said than done. First, he'd definitely have to get rid of Tawny and that sort of pinched his heart. Because as much as she got on his nerves, he did care for her.

But even without Tawny, David simply didn't know if he could just walk away. After all, he'd tried and failed several times before.

"Can you give up the drugs? For me? I'm begging you," Loretta said. Her voice was raspy.

David wanted desperately just to say yes, but the way his mother was looking at him, he simply couldn't fix his mouth to lie. "I can try, Ma. I promise I'll really try."

Loretta wiped her face. "That's a start. I'll pray, baby. You'll do it. I know you will. Do you want to stay here?"

David cringed at that thought. Not just because of Simon, but because he really didn't know if he was going to be able to just walk away and he wouldn't be able to bear to see the disappointment in his mother's eyes again.

Loretta closed her eyes and leaned back in the chair. David watched as her chest slowly heaved up and down. "Mama, are you sure you okay?"

"What's going on?"

David looked up to see Jonathan standing in the doorway.

Loretta opened her eyes, stood up, and smiled. "I'm just visiting with your brother, that's all."

"Mama doesn't feel good," David said.

"I told him it's just a cold. Where's Rachel?"

"She went upstairs to lay the kids down, both of them were sleepy," Jonathan responded.

"Okay. I'm going to go lie down. You boys just make yourself comfortable. There's some meatloaf in the refrigerator." Loretta grimaced as she tried to walk toward the stairs.

"Mama, are you sure you're okay?" Jonathan asked.

"I'm all right," she struggled to say. "I just need my medicine. Would you mind running up to the pharmacy and picking it up for me? It's under my name and ready for pick-up."

"Of course." Jonathan walked toward the door. "I'm going to grab this money off the mantel," he called out. "I don't have any cash."

"That's fine. Just hurry."

David, worry etched across his face, repeated his mother, "Yeah, Jon, hurry."

34

"WHERE IS IT? I know you took it, you thievin' crack-head!" Rachel screamed.

David glared at his sister. "You best get out of my face with that mess. I told you, I didn't steal your money!" He threw his hand up to wave Rachel off.

"Where is it?" Rachel was missing her last twenty dollars. She had taken it out of her jacket and left it sitting with her keys on top of the mantel before going upstairs to use the phone and put the kids to sleep. When she returned twenty minutes later, the money was gone. "I know it was here. Don't sit here and act like you don't know what I'm talking about!"

"Maybe Jonathan took it," David nonchalantly replied. "You don't see him around, so maybe he took it and ran off."

Rachel glared at David. "There's only one thief in this family," Rachel countered. "Why are you even here? I thought Daddy banned you. And where's Mama?"

"Mama is upstairs lying down. And for your information,"

David said, "Mama asked me to come over so she could talk to me. So, I was invited, unlike your mooching ass. But don't worry, I'm leaving as soon as Jon gets back."

"Whatever. Where is my money?"

"Just leave me alone." David turned his eyes back to the television like something was weighing heavily on his mind.

"David, if you don't give me my money, I swear I'm—"

"You goin' what? Cut me? Like you tried to cut Bobby?" David laughed. "No wonder he left your crazy ass for that fat girl."

Rachel fumed. "I know you did not just go there." She was within striking distance of her brother and took advantage of it. She reached back and swung her hand right upside David's head.

David jumped up. "You stupid bitch!"

Oh, it was about to be on, Rachel thought. "Bitch? Fool, you must think I'm that crackhead girlfriend of yours. Don't nobody call me a bitch, especially a washed-up, junkie, brown-teeth-having, sorry motherfucker like you!" Rachel was in her brother's face, about to claw his eyes out.

"Stop it . . . just stop it! And stop all that foul language in my house!" Loretta snapped.

Neither of them had noticed their mother standing in the door. She was pale and clutching her chest. "Stop all this noise! Rachel, I took your money." Loretta looked at David. "Why didn't you tell her I took her money to send Jonathan to the store for my prescription?"

David shrugged and plopped back down in his seat. "She didn't ask. She just came in here and started hurling accusations at me. Now apologize!" David yelled at his sister.

"I'm not apologizing for anything!" Rachel snapped. "And you apologize for calling me out of my name."

"I ain't apologizing to your psycho behind."

"I said, stop it!" Loretta held on to the back of a chair, still clutching her chest. Her eyes started to water up. "I can't take all this bickering. I'm sick of you two acting like you're ten years old." Loretta just started shaking her head, her chest heaving up and down. "I'm tired of all this nonsense in this family. I'm sick of watching you kill yourself," she yelled, pointing at David. "I'm sick of your drama and you acting like the word revolves around you," she said, turning to Rachel. "And I'm sick of Jonathan walking around here acting like he's okay when I can see that he's not. I'm sick of the whispers at the church, the women who want my husband! I'm just sick of everything!" Loretta sat down, a look of utter exhaustion across her face. She buried her face in her hands and sobbed. "I'm just sick and tired!"

Rachel and David stared at each other in amazement. Their mouths hung open. They couldn't understand where this was coming from. They seldom saw their mother engage in such an outburst, let alone break down crying.

"Mama . . ." Rachel knelt below her mother. David continued to stare.

"I'm sick and tired," Loretta kept repeating, rocking back and forth. "I can't take it! I can't take . . ."

Loretta clutched her chest tightly as the veins in her neck tightened and her eyes grew wide. She opened her mouth, but nothing came out.

"Mama? Mama? Are you okay?" Rachel grabbed her mother's hand. It was ice cold. Rachel could feel the tension in Loretta's body. Loretta leaned over, then fell to the floor. "Mama! David, call an ambulance! Something's wrong with Mama!"

*　　*　　*

The ambulance seemed to take forever to arrive. Rachel had thought for sure her mother wouldn't make it, but she finally got to the hospital. As the doctors operated on Loretta, David stood with his sister in the waiting room, a stunned look across his face. "Jonathan should be here any minute now," he said. "I called him on his cell phone. I also called Mrs. Olie from next door. She said she'll stay with the kids for as long as we need her. You think we should call Dad?"

Rachel hadn't even thought about her father. He was at the church, as usual. "No, *you* should call him."

"Now you know we're not talking."

"Well, I'm not talking to him, either."

"Come on, Rachel, somebody needs to call him."

"Fine!" Rachel stomped over to the phone in the waiting room. She dialed the direct number to her father's office.

Rene, the new secretary, answered on the second ring. "Zion Hill, Pastor Jackson's office."

"Rene, where's my father?"

"Well hello, Rachel. Are you doing okay today?"

"Where's my father?" Rachel shouted.

Rene was silent for a few seconds. "Excuse me for trying to make small talk. Your father is in a meeting."

"Well, go get him. Tell him it's an emergency."

"Yes, ma'am." Rene threw down the phone, but Rachel couldn't be bothered with her attitude right now. She shifted back and forth on her feet while she waited for her father to answer.

The other end was silent for what seemed like an eternity. "Rachel?" It was Rene again. "Your father said to take a message. He's busy meeting with a newspaper reporter. They're doing a full-length feature story on him and the church."

Rachel wanted to scream. Here her mother was damn near

death, and her father was too busy being interviewed to pick up the damned line.

"Fine, Rene. When he gets done with his important interview, and if he can fit in time between the deacon board meeting and choir rehearsal, tell him to come down to Hermann Hospital, where his wife is dying from a heart attack!" Rachel slammed the phone down. If her mother died without seeing her father, Rachel would never forgive him. If her mother died period, Rachel didn't know how she'd be able to live herself.

35

SIMON HAD NEVER BEEN so scared in his life. When Rene returned to interrupt his meeting again, he immediately grew irritated. He was about to chew her out, when the look across her face stopped him. She'd leaned down and whispered the words that would haunt him for the rest of his life. "Loretta had a heart attack."

He had immediately cut his meeting short, apologized to the reporter, and raced out of the office. His heart pounded all the way to the hospital. This was one of those times he wished he had a cell phone. He would've given anything to have called the hospital on his way over.

It didn't take him long to get there. The nurse directed him to the waiting room where he saw Rachel grieving on David's shoulder. She wiped her eyes and looked up at him long enough to mutter, "Glad you could make it" before laying her head back on her brother's shoulder.

Simon didn't know what to say to his daughter. He knew

she was angry he hadn't taken her call. "How's Loretta?" he asked in a weak voice.

"How's church?" Rachel mumbled.

Simon ignored her and looked at Jonathan, who was sitting numbly in a corner.

"We don't know," he said. "I just got here myself. The doctors aren't telling us anything."

"Well, who do we need to talk to?" Simon was getting frantic now.

"I can try and answer your questions." Everyone turned toward the short, portly doctor who had just appeared. "I'm Dr. Kwan, your mother's cardiologist."

Rachel jumped up and raced toward him. She feverishly clutched her hands as if she was praying. "Please tell us she's going to be fine."

The doctor hesitated before saying, "I wish I could. Your mother has been really ill. Today, she suffered a massive heart attack."

Both Rachel and Jonathan gasped. David just buried his head in his hands. Simon felt his knees go weak.

"I can't tell you your mother is going to make it. Right now, she's very weak, but she is adamantly asking for her husband." The doctor turned toward Simon. "I would assume that's you?"

"Yes, that's me." Simon was shaking now. He had never thought about life without Loretta. Where did all of this come from? He hadn't even known Loretta was sick.

"Just take a few minutes. As I said, she's very weak."

"Doctor, can we see her?" Rachel cried.

"We'll have to see how she's holding up after she talks to Mr. Jackson."

Rachel glared at her father. "He didn't even want to come," she snapped.

"Rachel, stop it," Jonathan interrupted. "Mama doesn't need this!"

Rachel rolled her tear-filled eyes and returned to her chair.

Simon looked at his family before leaving the waiting room with the doctor.

Loretta's room was just down the hall. Simon eased the door open. The sight of his wife lying in that hospital bed, tubes coming out of every part of her body, was enough to break his heart. She looked so helpless. Simon gently walked over to her bed and lifted her hand. "Hey, honey," he whispered. "It's me."

Loretta struggled to turn her head to him. Her eyes lit up some at seeing his face. She struggled to speak.

Simon put his finger to Loretta's lips. "Sshhh. Don't talk. I just wanted to let you know I'm here."

"Si-mon, I'm sorry." Loretta's voice was just above a whisper.

"Now, you don't have anything to be sorry about."

Simon was trying his best to be strong. It felt like Loretta was slipping away from him. Her hands were cold and clammy.

"I love you," she managed to say.

"I love you, too," Simon responded. "Now, you just hush up and rest. I need you to get better. You know if you don't get better by Sunday, Sister Hicks goin' try and take over the fellowship dinner we planned."

Loretta managed a small smile.

"You're gonna be okay, baby," Simon said, stroking her hair.

Loretta shook her head, her eyes glistening with tears. "I'm going. Going home to God."

"Hush, Loretta. You ain't goin' nowhere. You know I can't make it without you. Besides, you know I have to have my collard greens every Sunday and they don't make them in the cans.

So you just be quiet with that nonsense, you understand?" Simon was on the verge of tears himself.

Loretta closed her eyes and inhaled deeply. "Get the kids."

"Loretta, you need to keep your strength up."

She opened her eyes. "Please?"

Simon stood straight to protest, but decided against it. "Okay, if you insist. But ain't goin' be no good-byes, because you ain't goin' nowhere."

He pushed open the door and made his way back down the hall to the waiting room. Rachel, David, and Jonathan jumped up when he walked in.

"How is she?" Rachel asked.

"She's gonna be fine," Simon confidently proclaimed. All three of his children looked relieved. "God is taking good care of her."

Rachel's expression turned skeptical. "I want to see her."

"As a matter of fact, she was just asking to see you." He motioned to all three. "All of you."

"But the doctor said she wasn't strong enough," David said.

Rachel started down the hall. "I don't care what the doctor said, I'm going to see my mama."

Jonathan, who looked like he had been crying himself, quickly followed. Simon turned his gaze toward David. They hadn't had two words to say to each other in months.

"You going?" Simon finally asked.

David leaned back against the wall, his hands nervously shaking, a look of terror across his face. "Nah," he said, shaking his head. "I'll just see her when she gets better."

Simon nodded, then turned to leave the room.

"Dad?" David called out.

Simon stopped and looked back at his son. "Yes?"

"She's gonna get better, isn't she?"

Simon smiled at his son for the first time in a long, long while. "Yes, she is. The Lord knows it's not time for her."

David nodded his head with relief. "Okay, okay. I'll just talk to her later then," he said, more to himself than his father.

Simon walked back to Loretta's room. He heard Rachel sobbing before he even entered. She was bending over the bed, her arms draped around her mother. For a minute, Simon feared that she was dead, but he then saw Loretta lift her hand and caress Rachel's hair.

"Sshhh," Loretta whispered to her daughter as Simon appeared inside. "Cut all that out. I got some things to say . . ." She paused and took a deep breath, like she was gathering all her energy, "and I ain't got much time to say them." Loretta looked around. "Where's David?"

"He—ummm, he said he'll just see you when you get out," Simon replied.

Loretta smiled again. "That boy. Never has liked to face adversity."

Rachel gripped her mother's hand. "Mama, Daddy said you're goin' be fine."

"Well, that's your daddy's wishful thinking. I have an appointment with Saint Peter." Loretta's voice was getting weaker and weaker. The quiet beeping on the machine next to her was slowing down.

"Mama, don't say that," Rachel cried.

"I love all of you. You got to stick together now." She looked around her bed at everyone. "Y'all all you got now."

Loretta started coughing violently, and everyone looked panicked. The coughing subsided, and a single tear trickled down Loretta's face. "I know . . ."

The machine's big red alarm went off, and Loretta's chest heaved as she began convulsing.

"Mama!" Rachel screamed.

Doctor Kwan and several nurses rushed into the room.

"Nurse, get them out!" Dr. Kwan yelled. He tore back Loretta's gown, grabbed some paddles, and tried feverishly to revive her.

Rachel violently sobbed as Jonathan pulled her out of the room. Simon stood in a corner, dazed.

"Mr. Jackson," the nurse said, "you'll have to leave, too."

Simon blankly nodded, then backed out of the room, staring at the doctor as he worked to save Loretta's life. It was a surreal scene. God had to be telling him to treat Loretta better, do more things with her. "As soon as she gets out of here, Lord, I'm goin' do just that," Simon said to himself.

36

THE DAY WAS OVERCAST and dreary. Funeral weather. Simon still couldn't believe his wife was dead. Rachel, who was dressed in all black, hadn't stopped crying for four days. The family was awaiting their ride to the church. David sat stoically in a corner. Jonathan paced back and forth. He seemed to be taking it the hardest. Simon guessed that it had to do with the fact that he and Angela seemed to be having problems already, then he had to deal with Loretta's death. No matter what kind of disagreement they had had, Simon felt Angela still should be here with Jonathan today. But anytime Simon tried to broach the subject, Jonathan got quiet and depressed.

As for the kids, they seemed oblivious to what was going on. Jordan was chasing Loretta's Yorkshire terrier. Nia sat in her playpen, throwing plastic blocks.

The doorbell rang. Simon glanced at the clock hanging in the entryway.

"That must be the limo driver. I'll get it."

He didn't know why he even bothered to say anything; no one else made a move to answer it.

Simon opened the door. The tall, slender young man standing there didn't look like a limo driver. He was dressed in a navy blue suit, gray shirt, and gray tie. "Hi," Simon said anyway. "We'll be ready in just a minute."

The man looked confused. "Excuse me?"

"Aren't you the limo driver?"

"Oh, no, I'm sorry. You must be Mr. Jackson."

"I am." Simon wasn't in the mood for visitors. It was bad enough having to deal with all those people after the funeral. Couldn't he at least have this time with his family?

"May I offer my condolences? I'm so sorry to hear about Mrs. Jackson," the man said.

Simon nodded. This was probably one of Loretta's old students. Simon thought maybe if he didn't engage in conversation, the young man would get the hint to leave. They stood in silence for a few seconds, but he didn't appear to get the picture.

"Well, what can I do for you?" Simon finally said.

"Umm, I'm a friend of Jonathan's," he nervously responded.

Simon perked up a little. "Oh, okay. Any friend of Jonathan's is a friend of the family. Come on in." In the months that Jonathan had been home, none of his friends, except Kevin, had dropped by or even called. Simon thought it might be good if Jon had someone here for support right now, although Simon had never seen the man standing on his front porch before today.

"Thank you, sir," the man said as he stepped into the living room.

"I didn't get your name," Simon said, closing the door.

The man stopped and turned to Simon. "It's Tracy."

"Well, Tracy, Jonathan should be right down that hall in the den." Simon pointed the way. Tracy nodded and walked down the hall.

Jonathan was gazing out the window, his back turned from the entrance.

"Jon," Tracy called.

Jonathan spun around. An astonished look crossed his face. "Tracy!"

The two stood silently before Jonathan ran into his arms. "What are you doing here?" he cried as he hugged Tracy tightly.

"Now, you know I couldn't let you go through this alone."

Simon watched as the two of them embraced. There was something strange about this whole scenario. Jonathan seemed to be grabbing on to him desperately, and the loving way Tracy was rubbing Jonathan's back had Simon feeling uneasy.

It suddenly dawned on the two of them that they weren't the only ones in the room. Jonathan quickly removed himself from Tracy's embrace. "Everybody, this is my friend Tracy."

David and Rachel smiled halfheartedly at Tracy and nodded hello.

"I'm glad you came," Jonathan said softly as he turned his attention back to Tracy.

"Did you ever think I wouldn't? When you called and told me about your mom, I knew you needed me. I just didn't know if you wanted me to come."

"I'm glad you did," Jonathan mumbled.

Simon was leaning against the den wall, taking this all in. He raised his eyebrows in confusion. Something wasn't right.

"Have you told them?" Tracy looked around the room at everyone staring at them. "I think you should tell them."

A terrified look crossed Jonathan's face. "No, not now."

"Yes. Now or never. This has gone way too far. I only came

to be here for you, but I need to be all the way here for you. I can't be putting on acts." Tracy looked determined and serious.

"But my mother just died. Maybe we should just wait until later."

"I know how much you're hurting and I want to be able to comfort you without any guises. This has been our problem from day one. And if we don't get it taken care of right now, I'm leaving. For good," Tracy said.

Jonathan looked like he wanted to protest but changed his mind. His shoulders dropped and he walked over to the sofa and sat down. Tracy followed.

"What about Martin?" Jonathan whispered to Tracy.

"Martin is not who I want. Now tell them." Tracy was adamant in his demand.

"Tell us what?" Rachel asked. She had stopped crying, but her eyes were still red. Nia was sitting in her lap gnawing on her pearl strands.

Simon still wasn't getting a good feeling, but now wasn't the time to figure out what was going on. They needed to get going to the funeral. "Son, whatever you need to tell us, can't it wait until after the service?"

Jonathan looked at Tracy, who softly shook his head. He slowly gazed around the room. Everyone was staring at him.

Just then David jumped up. "Holy crap! Little brother, is this dude saying what I think he's saying?"

Jonathan briefly looked down at the floor, before holding his head up high. "Yes, he is. Everybody, Tracy isn't just my friend . . . He's my . . . my partner."

David started howling with laughter. Rachel almost dropped Nia as she gasped.

Simon was still confused. "Your partner? What does that mean? Are y'all in some kind of business together?"

Suddenly, it dawned on Simon that he'd heard of Tracy's name before. That's who Jonathan was on the phone with that time. Tracy. Simon had just automatically assumed it was a girl. But now that he thought about it, Jonathan had never confirmed that.

"Come on, Dad, don't be so naïve," David chimed in. "Is that why Angela kicked you out? Because you're gay?"

"Sweet Jesus." Simon was about to pass out. He sat in his recliner in stunned silence.

David continued on. "Man, I cannot believe you're gay!"

Simon shook his head. "But Angela?"

Jonathan sadly looked at his father. "Angela was a mistake." He paused. Tracy squeezed his hand. "Dad, I know this is a lot to take in, but this is who I am."

Simon rubbed his head, took a deep breath, and stood up.

"I'm going to call the funeral home and see what's taking the driver so long." He started walking out the room. "When I return, I don't want to hear no more of this blasphemous talk!"

Simon left without looking back. A promiscuous daughter, he could deal with. A drug addict, he could even deal with. But never in a million years would he accept that his prodigal son was a homosexual.

37

THIS HAD TO BE the hardest day of Simon's life. He had done hundreds of funerals with no problem, but then he never dreamed he would be burying his wife.

The doctors were never able to revive Loretta. Simon had left the hospital numb. How could he have not known Loretta was sick? He racked his brain trying to recall some sign that she'd had a heart problem. Did he just not notice? He had to admit, he hadn't paid much attention to his wife lately, but surely if she had been sick, he would've known.

Simon had just returned from the home of his sister-in-law, Vera. All of the family had gathered there after the funeral instead of at his home. He preferred it that way; he just didn't want all of those people in his house.

It seemed like everybody who ever attended Zion Hill was at the funeral. It was standing room only. Loretta was loved by so many people.

Simon removed his jacket. He was anxious to get out of his church clothes and just relax. As he was about to hang his jacket in the hall closet, he felt the envelope in his pocket. Simon reached in and pulled out the folded manila envelope. Vera had given it to him right after the funeral. She said Loretta wanted him to have it if she died. Simon was a little taken aback that Loretta had prepared for this. He was even angrier that Vera knew about it and didn't say anything. Vera apologized, but said her loyalty was to her sister. Now, standing there clutching the letter tightly, Simon didn't know if he could bear to open it. Maybe he needed to wait until his wounds healed some.

Simon had always been one to follow his first mind, so he tore the envelope open and started reading.

My Dearest Simon,
First let me begin by saying, you are my heart, and I will love you forever.

If you are reading this then my worst fears have come true. I've known for a long time I've had a weak heart, but you know me, I never have been one to trouble my family and I knew when God was ready to call me home to glory, it wasn't nothing no one could do, so no need to fret over it.

I'm writing this letter after my second scare. Doctor Kwan suggested I tell you all, but I just couldn't. Please forgive me for that. Honestly, I prayed that God would heal me on His own, but since you're reading this, I guess that wasn't His will.

Simon, I'm writing not only to ask your forgiveness for not being completely honest about my illness but because I know things will be tough for you and the kids. I need you to be there for them. For years, we have taken a backseat to Zion Hill. I accepted that because I know you're a good man who was trying to do God's work. But the children have never understood it and even resented it. Now it's time for you to put them first. Forgive David, for starters. No, he hasn't made you proud, but he's still your son. If he's going to beat these drugs, he'll need your support. I believe he can do it with your help. He wants your love so bad. Also support Rachel. She has disappointed you, too, but she's still your daughter. You don't have to like the message, but you still need to love the messenger. Isn't that what you always used to say? Rachel is searching for love herself. Maybe if you show her some, she won't be so obsessive about finding it. And Jonathan, let Jonathan be Jonathan. Jon has an emptiness inside him. I thought his marriage to Angela would fill that void, but it hasn't. I don't know what it is, but I see pain in his eyes. I need you to try and reach him. Find out what he's harboring on his heart, then help him work through it.

You rest easy, keep watching Sanford and Son, *and working for the Lord. Know that I am watching over you, smiling because I'm finally at peace. I'll see you in Heaven.*

Love,

Loretta

Simon didn't realize he was crying until he saw the tears drop onto the paper gripped tightly in his hand. The aching in his heart hurt more than anything he'd ever experienced.

So many things were racing through his mind. He knew his children felt slighted by his commitment to the church, but he had no idea it was that bad. How could his children not think he loved them? Simon thought back. Honestly, he couldn't even remember the last time he said it, but he did love his children—all of them, from the bottom of his heart. He knew he could be hard sometimes, but it was because he wanted them to be successful in their lives.

Then Simon was dealing with some guilt himself. He felt like a complete failure as a father. He tried to give his children the world and he had let each one of them down. Maybe his children had turned to outside forces because they couldn't turn to him. David had turned to drugs. Rachel had turned to men. And Jon, well he'd turned to men, too. And that thought alone just absolutely sickened Simon.

"Where did I go wrong, Loretta?" Simon sniffed as he smoothed out the letter that had become crumpled in his grasp.

As much as he loved his son, Simon couldn't see himself accepting the fact that his pride and joy, the light of his life, was gay. How could Loretta see that something was wrong with Jonathan and he couldn't? He talked to Jon all the time. He thought Jon was happy with Angela, even telling himself that their separation was just postwedding problems. How could he not see this? Maybe Jon's just confused. Maybe that Tracy just got him up there at school and messed up his head. That has to be what happened, Simon concluded. He knew he shouldn't have let Jonathan go to an all-male school.

"No son of mine can possibly be gay!" Simon stared at the large picture of Jesus hanging on his living room wall. "Lord, this is another one of your tests, isn't it?"

Simon stopped mid-tirade and looked over to the kitchen entrance. Jonathan was standing there, his hands stuffed in his pockets, a look of defeat across his face.

Simon stared at his son. He didn't know what to say. Part of him wanted to run to him, hug him, and tell him everything would be all right, that they would work through his confusion. The other part wanted to beat him like he was a twelve-year-old thief stealing from a candy store.

"Can we talk?" Jonathan asked, never taking his eyes off the floor.

Simon eased into his chair. Without responding, he motioned for Jonathan to take the seat across from him.

"Dad, I don't know where to start," Jonathan said as he sat down.

"Try from the beginning." Simon didn't mean to sound so cold to his son, but burying Loretta was bad enough. Now, he had to face this.

"I love Tracy," Jonathan said, finally looking his father in the eye.

Simon stared at his son like he was trying to find the right response. "You said you loved Angela, too," he finally said.

"I did. I mean, I do. But not this way, not like I love Tracy."

Simon turned up his nose in disgust.

Jonathan continued. "I know you'll never understand that, but I do."

Simon felt like he could no longer hold it in. He leaned forward, a look of exasperation across his face. "How, Son? How can you love another man? Why? What did your mother and I do wrong?"

"You didn't do anything, Dad. I don't know; maybe I was just born this way."

"Don't hand me that cockamamie answer. Ain't nobody in my family funny. It ain't in your blood, so where did it come from?"

"I don't know."

Simon leaned back like he was considering some possible reasons. "Did somebody molest you when you were a little boy?"

Jonathan exhaled slowly. "No, Dad. No one has ever molested me."

Simon wrung his hands. "It's because your mama let you take them dang piano lessons, ain't it? Or because you were always drawing pictures and stuff, and never roughhousing it like the other boys?" Simon shook his head like he was talking to himself. "I knew I should've been harder on you. Should've made you be a man. You know, one time I caught you doing cheers. Cheers with that girl from down the street. What was her name?"

"Suzette?" Jonathan numbly responded.

"Yeah, the Watson kid. You and her were in the front yard just cheering away. *Sis boom bah!* You weren't but eight or nine. I should've tore your hide up. But no, Loretta thought it was cute. Maybe if I had beaten the crap outta you, you would've toughened up."

"Dad, me doing cheers did not turn me into a homosexual."

"Stop it! Stop saying that blasphemous word!"

Jonathan lowered his eyes again. "That's me. That's who I am."

Simon tried to calm himself down. "No, it's not, Son. You're confused, that's all. I mean, you've been with a lot of women. I know. I've heard the stories. They can't all be lies."

"They're not," Jonathan responded. "But I think I was doing that because I was running from who I really am. I thought if I could be with women, it would prove the feelings I had were just a fluke. That's why I married Angela. I was trying to prove to myself that I was a man, all man."

"Is that why you moved home? Does she know?"

Jonathan sadly nodded his head. "I never meant to hurt her. I thought I could do it, be a husband. She never deserved me and I feel terrible about hurting her."

Simon got up and went to his son. He sat next to him, taking his hands. "It's okay, Son. We'll get you some help. Put you in therapy or something. We can overcome this. We'll cure you."

Jonathan eased his hands out of his father's grasp. "Daddy, there is no overcoming, no cure. This is who I am. I can't pretend anymore." Jonathan got up and walked toward the front door. He stopped to face his father. "Unless you can accept that, then I guess I'm as dead to you as Mama."

Simon vigorously shook his head. "I can't accept that. I won't accept that."

A sad look crossed Jonathan's face, but he didn't respond.

"What about the Bible?" Simon shouted as Jonathan opened the front door to leave.

Jonathan paused, but didn't turn around.

Simon got up and approached his son. "It's wrong. In the eyes of God, it's wrong. Don't you care about that none? Can you be happy damned to hell?"

"So I should choose a lifetime of misery so that my soul can have eternal happiness?" Jonathan asked with his hand on the knob.

"You won't be miserable."

Jonathan took a deep breath. "God made me who I am. I didn't choose to be gay. Who would choose this?"

"God didn't do this to you. You did it to yourself!"

Jonathan hesitated, like he knew the conversation was useless. "Well, it's a good thing I got to say good-bye to Mama."

"What does that have to do with anything?" Simon asked.

"I know she's resting in Heaven, and since you say I'm going to hell, I'll never see her again, kinda like I guess I'll never see you again." Jonathan fought back tears as he slowly closed the door behind him.

38

SIMON SAT AT the head of the large mahogany table in the church conference room. Uneasiness swept his body. The church board, five men and one woman, had summoned him there. Usually it was Simon calling the meetings. Today, they were in charge.

Simon could feel the intensity in the room. Something told him he wasn't going to like what the board had to say.

The lone woman in the group, Addie Lee Shepard, a member of Zion Hill since it was founded in 1928, spoke first. "Reverend, the board has been discussing this and, well . . ." Addie Lee stopped talking and looked around the room like she wanted someone to take over.

Deacon Jacobs stepped in. "What she's trying to say, Simon, is that we've appreciated all that you've done for Zion Hill, but this stuff with your family is too distracting for the business of the church. We think it's time you stepped down."

Simon was dumbfounded. He couldn't believe they were sitting there saying this to him. Zion Hill had been his life. It still was his life. And the fact that they would even consider firing him as pastor, especially after burying his wife less than a month ago, was unbelievable.

"So, you're saying you want me out?" Simon looked around the room. No one responded. "Brother Baker, you can't support this foolishness?"

Deacon Baker looked down.

Simon turned toward another man he thought was his friend. "Percy?"

Percy just stared at Simon. His eyes had an apologetic look, but he too said nothing.

"I don't believe this! I have given everything to this church!" Simon roared. He needed to contain his temper. It seemed like he'd been blowing up a lot lately.

"We know that, Simon," Deacon Jacobs said. "That's why we're willing to give you a nice stipend and tell the church it was your decision. If you step down without a fight, that is."

Simon gazed around the room, waiting on someone to tell him this was all a cruel joke. The looks across the faces in that room told him they were dead serious. "You all better be glad I'm a God-fearing man or I would tell you what you could kiss. I'm not going anywhere without a fight! I *am* Zion Hill! I built this church into what it is." Simon pointed to the laminated newspaper articles hanging on the wall throughout the conference room. "I'm responsible for all of that. I'm responsible for getting a packed house here every Sunday. I've been a good, faithful, honest steward and this is the thanks I get?"

Percy spoke up. "Simon, it's nothing personal. It's just, well, how can you lead the church worth anything when you can't even lead your own family?"

Simon pounded on the table. "What is that supposed to mean?"

"It means," Deacon Jacobs said, with firmness in his voice, "that you have a teenage daughter who has not one, but two kids out of wedlock. She goes to sleep during church, comes late, talks, and won't even show you any respect during your own sermon. Then you have a son on drugs who stole money right off the collection plate. Then you just go and all but appoint your other son as associate pastor and he turns out to be gay. Something we all suspected months ago."

Simon looked confused.

"That's who we were talking about, the day you came into the conference room," Deacon Davis spoke up. "I saw Jonathan openly hugged up with another man at the airport. They even kissed. Then had a big fight like an old married couple, crying and all. Hidden off in a corner, thought nobody saw them. But I did! Nobody believed me, though." He turned to face everyone in the room. "But you believe me now! I told you this one good eye knew what it saw! I can spot one of them funnies a mile away! But y'all thought I was crazy! It was the same man he was all hugged up with at Loretta's funeral. Just shameful!"

"On top of that, what he did to poor sweet Angela is unforgivable," Addie Lee interjected. "The child hasn't been back to church in weeks, just too ashamed to show her face. Her mama told me she's about to move to Wisconsin with relatives. They say they goin' move their membership because they don't want to be around none of the Jacksons."

"Then Jonathan didn't have no shame," Deacon Jacobs added. "The ink wasn't even dry on his annulment papers and he's sitting up at the funeral carrying on with that boy, knowing Angela was there!"

Simon didn't know what to say. He had been thoroughly embarrassed at Loretta's funeral. So much so that he could hardly concentrate. Jonathan had sat in the front row, clutching Tracy's hand the entire time. Tracy rubbed his back, wiped away his tears and wrapped his arm tightly around Jonathan. People were staring and whispering. Angela had stood silently in the back of the church the whole time, but Simon saw the pain in her eyes as she looked at Jonathan and Tracy. Simon had to pray real hard and then just pretend Jonathan wasn't there so he could focus on the funeral proceedings.

"Why didn't someone tell me then? Why didn't someone say something at his wedding?" Simon asked.

"Would you have believed us without proof?" Deacon Baker asked. "We weren't even sure Brother Davis knew what he was talking about. Besides, that wasn't our place. And someone *had* seen David shoplifting, so we just decided to let you deal with that."

Simon was speechless. Everything they said about his children was true, but how was that his fault? "So you're going to hold the father responsible for the sins of his children?"

"It just ain't right, Simon," Percy said.

"Yeah, it makes us look bad," Addie Lee added. "People talking about it left and right."

"My kids are grown! I can't be held accountable for their actions."

"They ain't that grown. And they're still *your* kids," Deacon Jacobs said. "Besides, you've been in another world since Loretta passed. You even blew up at poor Percy here, right in front of the youth choir."

Simon looked at his friend. He had yelled at Percy, calling him stupid in front of the children during their choir practice. He hadn't meant to lose his cool, but Percy had forgotten to call the newspaper and tell them about the upcoming Women's Day. Simon hadn't bothered to apologize. He thought Percy was his friend and understood he was going through a lot.

"And then," Deacon Jacobs continued, "that awful sermon you preached this past Sunday had the whole church talking. Getting up there talking about Sodom and Gomorrah and the sinful nature of its people, damning gays to hell."

"I think that sermon was fine," Simon said. He knew the sermon was a little over the top, a diversion from his normal style, but the Lord had laid that message on his heart.

"Pastor, you said 'fag,'" Deacon Baker retorted. "You called the men who came to Lot's house fags. You can't do that in the middle of your sermon. Everybody knew that message wasn't for nobody but you and your son."

Simon worked to fight back the tears. No one in church had ever seen him cry. He had always been a strong man. He even held it together at Loretta's funeral, only shedding tears at home. But this was too much. They were taking away the only thing he had left in his life. "How can you do this to me, knowing I just lost Loretta?"

Deacon Baker looked Simon in the face. "That's part of why we also think it's time. Loretta, God rest her soul, was the glue that held your family together. We all know that. Now, with her gone, ain't no telling what's goin' happen and Zion Hill just can't stand to endure that."

"Simon, we think you've run your course here at Zion Hill," Deacon Jacobs added. "Maybe you should just go home, get your head together, and come back to Zion Hill in an advisory capacity on the board." He had a look of satisfaction on his face.

Simon could see it was useless to argue. He stood up. His heart was aching terribly, but he made sure to hold his head up in a dignified manner. He took a deep breath and said, "I will not submit my resignation. And you cannot just vote me out. This is a matter that has to go before the entire church."

Deacon Jacobs let out an exasperated sigh. "We figured you would feel that way. Simon, it would be so much easier for you to take us up on the offer to step down. Things could get pretty ugly. Zion Hill doesn't need any more bad publicity."

Simon started gathering up his things, including a notepad. He had thought this meeting was going to be about some church business, not his firing.

"I repeat, I will leave if and only if the congregation votes me out."

He tucked his belongings under his arm, raised his head high, and left the conference room, praying that somehow God would deliver him through this storm.

39

ALL THREE of his children sat in the living room. They looked so out of place, sitting awkwardly on the sofa. Nobody knew what to say. Rachel had a look of bitterness in her eyes, Jonathan a look of hurt, and David a look like he'd rather be anywhere else. Simon said a silent prayer. God, how he needed Loretta. She would rally them together. He didn't even know where to begin. These didn't even feel like his children.

"Well?" Rachel said sarcastically. "You summoned us here, so talk. And can we make this quick? I have to go pick up Nia and Jordan from Twyla's." Simon stared at his daughter. She really was a pretty young lady, but so bitter. Had he done that to her? He couldn't remember the last time they had had a civilized conversation.

"Yeah," David chimed in. "I know how you don't like having me in your house, so the sooner we get this over with, the better."

Simon felt a deep pain in his heart. It's like they both hated him. And Jonathan wouldn't even look at him. *Lord, where did I go wrong?* Simon wondered. He cleared his throat and said, nervously looking away, "I sure do miss your mother."

Rachel huffed and stood up. "I'm outta here. I didn't come over here for this." She grabbed her purse and headed toward the door.

"Rachel, wait," Simon called out after her. Rachel stopped, but only slightly turned her head.

"Why are we here?" she asked.

Simon walked up behind his daughter and eased her purse off her shoulder. "Sit down, please." Rachel let out a long sigh and returned to her seat. Simon looked at her with tears in his eyes. "Do you hate me that much?"

Rachel didn't respond. She crossed her arms and leaned back against the sofa. She started looking everywhere except at her father.

Simon dropped Rachel's purse on the table and turned to David. "What about you? Do you hate me?"

David glared at his father. He didn't respond either. Finally, Jonathan spoke up. "Daddy, I don't think any of us hate you. It's just we feel like you hate us."

"I could never hate you all. You're my flesh and blood."

"You could've fooled me," David mumbled.

"It's just that I want what's best for you all."

"Oh, save that for your loyal church members," Rachel interjected. "You want what's best for Reverend Simon Jackson."

Simon held his head down. He had no idea his children despised him this much. "All I ever wanted was to be a good father, a good preacher."

"No, Daddy. All you ever wanted was to be a good preacher. Forget being a good father," Rachel said. "Think back. My first steps, my first date, my first school play. Do you remember any of it? No, but I bet you can remember your first revival, your first Baptist conference. That's what's been important to you all your life, not us."

"I'm just trying to live my life for the Lord."

"What about living for your family sometimes? You think God wants you to create this perfect church but a messed-up family?"

Simon felt himself getting defensive. "I provided for you all your life. You never wanted for anything."

"We wanted for a father," Rachel said coldly.

David, who had the least to say, finally spoke up. "It's like we didn't live up to your expectations, so you wrote us off. Jonathan married Angela because it's what *you* wanted. Why do you think he was so scared to tell you he's gay?" Simon looked at Jonathan, who still looked away. "It's because he saw how you wrote me off," David continued. "I turned to drugs in the first place trying to seek solace after my football injury. I knew I wasn't going to amount to anything without football, and football was the only thing I had that could make you proud. So when I lost that, I was like, fu—, I mean, screw it. Now don't get me wrong, I take total responsibility for my drug problem, that's on me. But, it's like you said, you're still my flesh and blood, yet you turned your back on me."

David sat up. He was on a roll. "You know I got high, real high the night Mama died. I wanted to die, too. I almost did. Ironically, it was Tawny who saved me. Found me in the alley and got me to a hospital. I was there three days. The worst three days of my life. The second time in as many months that I cheated death. I haven't touched drugs since. I did that for Mama. And for me. Her dying wasn't in vain. It made me take a long, hard look at my life. The day she had her heart attack, she told me to stop worrying about making you proud and try to make myself proud. That's what I'm doing. And I've never been happier."

Simon was speechless. That had to be the most David had said to him in ten years.

"I'm sorry," he finally said.

All three of his kids looked at him like he was crazy. Simon had never apologized to any them about anything. "I'm trying to make an effort here. Hopefully, it's not too late and we can try to make things better between us." Simon's heart had never felt so heavy. Loretta was right on the money. His children were lost to him. He wondered if he'd ever be able to get them back.

No one said a word. Simon had initially summoned them to his place to talk about forming a united front at the church, but now, that just didn't seem so important. "I know things have been difficult for us, especially with your mama leaving us, but we're a strong family. We can get through this."

He saw a tear trickle down Rachel's face. Simon walked over to his daughter, took a deep breath, then pulled her into his embrace. Rachel was reluctant at first, but she gave in, sinking into his arms, sobbing uncontrollably.

Rachel cried for ten minutes straight. Simon just held her, like never before. Finally, she sat up, wiping away the few tears still trickling down her cheek.

"I better get going," she said. "Twyla has somewhere to be."

Simon debated whether he should even bring up the church. He decided to go ahead. "Look, I feel you all should know. The church board has voted to fire me."

"What?" Jonathan gasped. "Why?"

Simon stood up and began pacing. "They say I can't lead my own family, that you all have brought shame to Zion Hill so I should step down. But they can't just vote me out. It has to go before the entire church. We'll do that next Sunday, and I just thought, well, I thought, it would speak volumes if all of us showed up in force."

Rachel stood up, angry, any trace of tears completely gone. "So that's what this is about? You call us over here like you want to make things right, and this is all about Zion Hill! Ugghh! I am too through!" Rachel snatched her purse off the table. "The board is right. You can't lead your family. Even now, you only want to use us to put on a front. Like we're one big happy family. Well, count me out!" Rachel stormed out the front door, letting it slam as hard as she could.

David and Jonathan stared at their father while shaking their heads. Finally David got up and walked toward the door also. "Man, I thought you were serious, too. Ain't nothing changed." He shook his head one last time and headed out the door.

Simon stared at Jonathan. This had all gone so terribly wrong. Why couldn't his kids see they were important to him? It's just this was important, too. "Son, can I count on you? I really need for the church to see that the Jacksons are strong. That we can endure hardships and make it through."

Jonathan glared at his father, before standing up as well. "There's just one problem with that, Dad. I'm sure you wouldn't want us to get up in that church, stand before God, and lie. We can't endure hardships. You've seen to that." Jonathan made his way to the door as well. "Good luck, Daddy. I hope the vote turns out the way you want. I know how important holding on to your pastor title is. I'll say a prayer. That is, if God will even bother listening to a heathen like me." Jonathan opened the front door, stepped outside, and left his father standing in the middle of the living room, alone and in shock.

40

THE CHURCH WAS PACKED. It seemed everyone who had ever been a member of Zion Hill was there today—they all wanted to see how what one person had called "the hottest story of the year" would turn out.

Simon couldn't gauge the reaction of the members. Word had spread like wildfire that the deacons were trying to oust him. Several people had called him to express their condolences. He had also overheard some people saying he needed to just step down.

Simon focused his attention on Sister Hicks. Surely after all that he had put up with from her, her extensive testimony and unsolicited advice, she wouldn't turn her back on him. If she supported him, then he would get support from many other members because, as crazy as she was, many people respected her and her judgment. However, when Simon tried to make eye contact, Sister Hicks pretended that she was brushing lint from her skirt.

As the young adult choir began singing their first selection,

Simon's fingers tapped along but his eyes made their way to the back doors of the church. He was hoping and praying that at least one of his children would show up and support him, but an hour into service, none of them had. He thought he'd seen that Tracy character come in, but he didn't see him now.

"Pastor. Pastor."

Simon was jolted out of his thoughts by Percy whispering his name. Simon looked around. The choir had stopped singing and everyone was staring at him. It was time for him to get up and call for the offering. Simon stood up and made his way to the podium. He kept thinking how good a minister he'd been to this church. He didn't make people feel guilty for not giving enough during offering time. He didn't drive around in fancy cars and sport expensive clothes while his parishioners struggled just to support their families. He was a modest man who lived a modest life, a life devoted to Zion Hill. Yet here he was, on the verge of losing it all. Simon wanted desperately to say something on his own behalf, but he'd agreed with the board not to bring up the voting matter until the church business meeting, after the service.

Luckily, there was a guest minister today, otherwise Simon didn't think he would've made it through an entire sermon.

"It's offering time," Simon said. "Please bow your heads. Heavenly Father, please bless those who can give and those that can't. Amen."

Several people in the congregation looked at each other in amazement. Simon was never one to give a brief prayer. He could get very long-winded when it came to praying, but today he just wasn't feeling it. Not when everything that he'd worked to build was on the line, and it sure didn't look good not having his family there to support him.

Simon waited until the deacons had collected the offering,

then turned the microphone over to Reverend Ernest Callahan of Sweet Home Missionary Baptist Church in Sugarland, a suburb of Houston.

Simon didn't think he heard a word of Revered Callahan's sermon. He did throw in a couple of amens, but they were only for good measure. He just couldn't focus. All he could think of was that he'd lost Loretta. He had lost his children. Now he stood to lose the only thing left.

Simon was grateful when he saw Reverend Callahan wipe his brow and return to his seat. The church was really jumping. Several people were up shouting and praising God. Suddenly, it dawned on Simon that maybe having a guest preacher today was a bad idea. It would let the church see how well someone else could do in his place.

Simon went back to the podium, thanked Reverend Callahan, then proceeded with his usual invitation to discipleship, followed by the benediction. He tried to make everything go as quickly as possible without trying to seem rushed. He wanted everyone to think he was in control.

Simon stood at the door, putting on a good front, greeting members as they exited the church. He kept his conversations brief. Afterward, Simon reached over to Reverend Callahan. "Thank you for coming out and sharing with us today. Your message was mighty powerful."

"Oh, really?" Reverend Callahan smiled slightly. "I didn't think you noticed."

"Pardon me?"

"It just seemed like you weren't here with us today, Pastor."

Simon looked down. "I'm sorry."

Reverend Callahan patted him on the shoulder. "Hey, don't worry. I've heard about what's going on. I totally understand and I want you to know I'll be praying for you."

"Thank you." Simon looked relieved that the reverend understood. The last thing he wanted was to appear unappreciative about Reverend Callahan sharing with them today.

Simon noticed a flurry of activity as the deacons went around trying to make sure everyone still inside was indeed a member.

After they were satisfied, they closed the back doors. Deacon Jacobs went in front of the congregation. "Church, as you know, we have some issues at hand. As difficult as it has been for us, the board has decided to call for the resignation of Reverend Jackson. We feel that he does not serve in the best interests of Zion Hill and that the church needs to go in a different direction. We also feel that the emotional strain of losing his wife, the numerous problems with his family, and the adverse publicity is keeping him from being an effective leader of our beloved church. Our founder," Deacon Jacobs pointed to the huge oil painting of an elderly white-haired man hanging on the wall over the choir stand, "Reverend Virgil Hicks, would not have been pleased with the direction our church is taking. Other churches are talking about us. I was in the barbershop the other day, and Zion Hill was the topic of discussion. We're talking about it amongst each other, and it's just not productive. We can't get to the business of praising the Lord effectively and carrying out His mission, because there are too many outside things going on. I think we need to start fresh."

Simon looked on in utter amazement, silently praying that he would wake up from this nightmare.

Deacon Jacobs continued. "And we don't think things will get any better. Reverend Jackson doesn't even have his own family here to support him. That is not how an upstanding pastor should lead. We would ask that you vote with the board in calling for the resignation of Reverend Simon Jackson."

Simon cast his eyes downward. He had never felt so alone in all his life. He hadn't planned a speech. He hadn't been able to, even though he stayed up all night trying. Every time he tried to write something down, he would end up balling up the paper and throwing it away.

Simon took a deep breath, rose, and made his way to the front of the church. He decided to let God lead him in what he should say. Simon made eye contact with Deacon Jacobs, then turned to the congregation. "As I'm sure any of you can imagine," Simon began, "this is difficult for everyone involved, especially me." Simon softly laughed. "I'll be the first to admit, I haven't been the best father, but I have been the best pastor I can be. I'm proud of my accomplishments at Zion Hill. Since I've taken over, membership has risen; we've gotten the attention we deserve; and I just feel that I've been a good, honest, faithful servant. I hope that it is the Lord's will that I stay on. But if it's not, then I will accept it. If you vote in favor of keeping me on at Zion Hill, I do want you to know that this will not adversely affect my relationship with the board. In fact, I will work to try and overcome the differences and the concerns of the board. I will continue to work for you. If you choose to vote in favor of the board, then I will understand and respect your decision and step down as pastor of Zion Hill." Simon returned to his seat.

A couple of people looked like they had questions and Simon wished he were able to address them. However, no questions were allowed.

Addie Lee made her way to the front. "At this time, the ushers are passing out ballot sheets. On them are two boxes: Yes, I vote in favor of the board's decision to call for Reverend Jackson's resignation or No, I vote to keep Reverend Jackson as pastor of Zion Hill. We'll ask that you check one, list your name, and turn it in. Your votes will be kept confidential."

The ushers handed out the slips of paper. There was a lot of whispering and murmuring among the congregation. Simon felt his heart pounding with anticipation.

Voting took only ten minutes. After all the ballots were collected, Addie Lee, the church treasurer, the secretary, and other selected members went to the back to tally them. Both Simon and the board had agreed on who would be present during the counting so that there would be no discrepancies.

Simon returned to his office, where he sat nervously awaiting the outcome. He couldn't bear to wait in the sanctuary with the other members. Some had left, saying they'd just find out the vote later, but many remained.

Simon rubbed his temples as he rocked back and forth in his chair. He simply could not believe how much of a disarray his life had become. The ringing of the telephone interrupted his thoughts. Simon picked it up, bypassing his usual moniker. "Hello." Simon sat for a second waiting on a response. "Hello," he repeated.

"Mr. Jackson."

"Yes?" Simon wasn't much in a talkative mood. He wished he hadn't even answered the phone.

"This is Tracy, Jon's friend."

Simon sat in stunned disbelief. "What do you want?"

"Can I come talk to you?"

"There is nothing you need to talk to me about. Unless it's to tell me you're sorry for corrupting my son and you're leaving him alone."

Tracy sighed. "Even if he isn't with me, he'll find another man," Tracy softly said. "You have to accept that."

Simon slammed the phone down. He couldn't bear to listen to that madness.

It seemed like an eternity before Deacon Baker finally knocked on the door. "They're done," he said.

Simon nodded, pushed back from his desk, stood up, and raised his arms skyward. "Lord, give me the strength to accept whatever Your will may be." He unzipped his robe to get some air, then pulled it back up, making his way out.

At the front of the congregation, Simon scanned the crowd. Several members looked uneasy, while some smiled confidently at him. Simon tried not to look at any of them too long because he didn't want to read anything into their faces.

Addie Lee was in the back corner whispering to the church treasurer. The look on her face was blank, so Simon couldn't tell how the vote had gone. She finally made her way back to the front and the crowd immediately settled down. "Well, church, you made your decision." She looked back at Simon, who was sitting nervously in the pulpit. She then turned to the board sitting in the first row, followed by the congregation, before finally pulling out the slip of paper. "By a vote of 170 to 134, Reverend Simon Jackson will stay on as minister of Zion Hill." Addie Lee tried to appear indifferent, but the way her shoulders sank told Simon she was disappointed.

Several people clapped, others groaned. Simon's shoulders dropped with bittersweet relief. He was happy to have won, but 134 people wanted him gone. That was disheartening. Even so, he pulled himself together, smiled, and stretched out both of his hands. "Thank you, Jesus."

Simon glanced at the deacons who were whispering among themselves. Many wore scowls. Simon told himself he'd deal with them later; they were going to have to overcome their differences. Several people raced to the front to offer Simon their congratulations. He thanked people for voting for him, promising to make Zion Hill proud.

Slowly, the people began making their way out of the

church until Simon was the last person left. He walked back into his office and returned to his desk. "God is definitely good," he said, leaning back with a smile. "He didn't take away what I needed most." His smile faded as he glanced at the family picture on his desk. Then he heard a little voice say, "No, but you did."

41

SIMON REMOVED the turkey pot pie from the oven. This is what his Sunday dinners had been reduced to.

Some of the church members invited him over regularly, and one time Simon actually took Wanda Gilmore up on her offer. But that evening had been a disaster. She drilled him with all kinds of questions about Jonathan. Then she'd made innuendos about him finding a new woman. Simon knew she was talking about herself. He'd been so uncomfortable that he swore he'd rather just sit at home alone.

After eating, Simon would go back to church or handle some other church business, or spend the evening in front of the TV. He'd turned down offers to visit other churches, sometimes telling outright lies so he didn't have to attend.

Simon was depressed. He hadn't seen Nia and Jordan since the funeral. Even Loretta's dog, Brandy, had sunk into a deep depression. She was no longer the frisky, annoying terrier who got in everyone's way. She would stay in the corner, sulking.

The house was empty, cold, and quiet. Simon had never been more miserable.

That's why when he heard the doorbell ring, Simon was nearly startled out his chair. No one, not even a church member, had been by the house since the vote a month ago. Simon eased back from the table, walked to the front door, and pushed back the window curtain. He didn't know what to say or do when he saw who was on the other side.

"Hello, Mr. Jackson." Tracy waved.

What is he doing here? And what gives him the gall to think he can set foot on my doorstep? Simon debated whether he should open the door, but he had not been able to get in touch with any of his children. They wouldn't return his phone calls and he longed to know how they were doing. Simon decided the only way to find out would be to let Tracy in.

Simon opened the door, stood back, and watched the feminine way Tracy sauntered into the room. *I must be real desperate for conversation,* Simon thought as he closed the door.

Tracy turned to face Simon. "Thank you for letting me in. I was worried you wouldn't."

"I almost didn't." Simon surveyed Tracy, who bore a look of confidence.

"I'm glad you did." Tracy looked around. "Are you alone?"

I'm always alone, Simon wanted to say. "Yes."

"Good. Can we talk?" Tracy motioned toward the sofa.

Simon wanted to throw this man out on his behind. Instead, Simon simply nodded, then walked over and sat down. "Talk."

Tracy took a deep breath, then sat down in the Victorian high back across from Simon. "I've been trying to get up the nerve to do this since the funeral." Tracy waited for Simon to respond. When he didn't, Tracy kept talking. "Mr. Jackson, or can I call you Simon?"

"You can call me Mr. Jackson," Simon sternly said.

Tracy tried not to smile. "Mr. Jackson, I know you'll never understand my relationship with your son."

"You're right about that," Simon said.

Tracy continued, unfazed. "And I know you can never understand this, but I love Jon. And Jon loves me."

Simon felt like he wanted to throw up. Tracy seemed almost arrogant in his confidence, but there was something genuine about his words.

"Jon also loves you," Tracy said.

Simon shook his head again. "I just can't accept that my son is gay. It's wrong. It's in the Bible."

"A Bible written by men."

"Who were led by God." Simon prepared for the defensive. He knew this man wasn't about to try to take him and the Word of God on.

"Look, I didn't come here to get into a religious debate on homosexuality," Tracy said. "Nothing I say is going to get you to agree with my lifestyle, and nothing you say is going to make me think how I'm living is wrong. So can we just agree to disagree?"

Simon thought about it. "Fine. We'll agree to disagree."

"Good." Tracy slapped his hands on his legs. "Can we talk about Jon?"

That's a conversation Simon didn't mind having, even if he did have to have it with Tracy. "How is he?"

"He's happy. Really and truly happy."

Simon nodded. He still longed to hear more news about his son. "So, he's doing okay?"

Tracy nodded. "He was unhappy for so long because he couldn't be honest with you. I think it was eating him alive. Although he's much better now, a piece of him is still missing. You."

Simon knew exactly what Tracy was talking about. He felt empty also. Jonathan had been his joy for so long, it pained him to be estranged from the one child who had made him so proud.

"How did you two meet? I mean, did you approach him? I mean . . ."

Tracy laughed. "You mean, did I approach your son and make him gay? No, Jon was gay long before I entered the picture. He just wouldn't admit it."

"But he dated girls and everything. And Angela," Simon stammered.

"Call him bisexual, then."

Simon cringed.

"I actually think he was trying desperately to make himself believe he was straight. Angela was just the icing on the cake. I'm sure you've heard about his exploits with women."

Simon had heard the rumors that Jon was just as promiscuous as Rachel, if not more so. But he had blown it off because one, he took it as just idle gossip and two, it wasn't that big of a deal since he was a boy.

Tracy continued talking. "Jon told me all about his wild ways, but he was like that because he was running."

Simon couldn't stop shaking his head in disbelief. None of this was making any sense. He couldn't understand how something like this could have happened. How could his son, his flesh and blood, be into something so wrong, so vile?

"Judging from the look on your face, you think being gay is as low as a person can sink, right?" Tracy asked.

Simon stared at the man sitting in front of him. This had to be all his fault. Jonathan was fine until he went away to college. "So, I guess you're going to tell me you were born this way, too?"

"Honestly, I don't know why I'm gay. I can tell you with all we have to endure, it's definitely not a choice I made." Tracy mockingly put his index finger to his temple and tilted his head like he was thinking. "Let's see, should I like men and be ridiculed all my life? Or, fly through women and be called a stud?" He removed his finger, his expression turning serious. "Trust me, if I had to choose, I'd choose the latter. But this is just who I am. Much like it's who Jonathan is. The only difference is, I've accepted it. Jonathan, on the other hand, had not. Until these last few weeks."

As much as Simon missed his son, he didn't know how much longer he could stomach this conversation. "What did you come here for?" Simon asked.

Tracy lowered his eyes. "I love Jonathan."

"You said that already."

"And because I love him, I want him to be happy, completely happy." Tracy lifted his head and looked Simon in the face. "Why can't he have both of us?"

Simon didn't know how to respond. He desperately wanted to see Jonathan, to make things right. He actually wanted to make things right with all his children. But he honestly didn't know if he could ever accept Jonathan's lifestyle. "Where is Jonathan now?"

"He's at home. We got an apartment by Reliant Stadium."

"We? So you live here now?"

"Yes, I moved here to be with Jonathan. It was a deviation from our plans, but it's what we both want."

Simon wanted to ask him a lot more questions, like what kind of job did Tracy have that he could just up and move hundreds of miles away in a matter of weeks. But right now, his mind was focused on his younger son.

"Jonathan is cooking dinner next Friday. David, Rachel, and

the kids will be there. I was hoping you would come. I was praying you would come." Tracy smiled. "Believe it or not, I do pray."

Simon leaned back on the sofa and closed his eyes. He would love to see his kids. All of them. He reflected on Loretta's letter. *Show them you love them.* Tracy was silent, letting Simon simmer in his thoughts.

"Let me pray on it," Simon finally said, opening his eyes. "Call me on Friday morning and I'll let you know." Simon couldn't believe he was saying this, but it was time, even if it took Tracy to make it happen.

Tracy beamed. "Friday morning it is, then." He stood up. "I'll see myself out." Tracy made his way to the front door, stopped just before opening it, then confidently turned toward Simon. "Jon needs you. So do Rachel and David, even if they won't admit it." Tracy walked out, gently closing the door behind him.

42

"So how do y'all do it?"

"What?"

"How do y'all do it?" Rachel was stretched out across the sofa at her brother's new apartment. "I mean do you do it like normal people?" She had been trying to get up the nerve to talk to Jonathan about this. She'd never been one to mince words, but this was one topic she felt funny raising with her brother.

"Rachel, don't be silly." Jonathan was leaning over the stove, stirring a big pot of gumbo he had spent all day cooking. He'd learned how to make it from his mother.

Jonathan loved cooking. Rachel and David's only interest in food was eating it, so, growing up, he became his mother's apprentice. Loretta would mix, broil, bake, and he'd be right there soaking up all her tricks of the trade. It became their bonding ritual together; he loved the holidays because he and his mother would spend all day in the kitchen.

Jonathan's eyes got glossy at the thought of his mother. Then he smiled when he imagined his father saying his spending all that time in the kitchen was probably why he was gay.

"Are you listening to me?" Rachel had walked into the kitchen and now stood behind Jonathan with her arms folded.

"Actually, I'm not." Jonathan reached in the cabinet and grabbed some oregano. He sprinkled a little in the pot, then stirred the gumbo.

"For real. I wanna know. Do you really have sex with him? How can two grown men get turned on sweating and bumping booties and stuff?" Rachel turned up her nose at the thought.

"Rachel, you're being ridiculous," Jonathan responded.

"Just answer the question. I thought you said you were going to be open about who you are."

"I am. That doesn't mean I'm going to share intimate details about my sex life with my little sister." Jonathan lifted the ladle out of the pot, blew on it, and sipped the gumbo. "Perfect."

"So you *do* do it with him? Ewww. Do y'all kiss and stuff? Like with your tongues? And are you the woman or is Tracy?"

"Enough, Rachel!" Jonathan snapped. He placed the lid back on the gumbo, dropped the ladle in the sink, then turned back toward his sister. "Those stupid stereotypes are why people don't come out of the closet. We kiss just like you kiss. Now leave it alone!" He walked out of the kitchen.

Rachel followed close behind. "I was just asking!"

Jonathan ignored her, checking the apartment for the twentieth time that day, making sure it was immaculate. Tracy had left his furniture in storage in Atlanta until they found a house, so the furnishings in the one-bedroom were sparse; only a sofa, loveseat, and coffee table. A nineteen-inch television sat on a TV stand, a radio/CD player on the floor next to it. A dining table that Jonathan had bought at a garage sale was centered in the small dining room just off the kitchen. Jonathan had hung one African print, but other than that, the walls were bare. Still, the place was sparkling clean and he had never felt more at home.

"What time did David say he'd be here?" Jonathan asked.

"I don't know. Do I look like my brother's keeper?" Rachel asked as she plopped down on the sofa. She picked up the remote and flipped the TV on. "Cable! Yes. That's what I'm talking about." She started flipping through the channels until she found BET. They were playing a Ludacris video. "That's my next baby's daddy," Rachel said, pointing to the television.

"That's ludicrous," Jonathan responded.

"Duh . . . I know who that is. Everyone knows who that is."

"No, I mean that idea is ludicrous, as in absolutely crazy. And your next baby's daddy needs to be your husband."

"Oh, he's gonna be my husband, too. At least my first husband." Rachel bounced to the rap music.

Jonathan shook his head. "I can't believe you even watch that garbage." He glanced at the clock on the dining room wall. It was six-thirty. He had told David to be there by six. "So David hasn't called?" Jonathan asked.

"Did you hear any phone ring?" Rachel responded.

"Tracy should be home any minute now. I told David to be here on time. It's our first dinner together and I don't want anything to go wrong." Jonathan cut his eyes at his sister. "And that means no stupid, smart-aleck comments from you."

Rachel looked up. "What? You know me."

"Exactly. So could you for once be on your best behavior?"

"Yeah, yeah, yeah." Rachel turned her attention back to the TV.

There was banging on the front door.

"What's up, bro?" David said, after Jonathan opened the door.

"Nothing much. It's about time you got here. Come on in."

David walked inside and threw his car keys on the end table. "Better late than never. Where's your boyfriend?"

"Don't you start." Jonathan shut the door.

David laughed. "Man, I'm just messing with you. Do yo' thang. I ain't got no problem with you or your man. Hell, I got enough issues of my own. Tawny slashed my tires. That's why I'm late. I never have understood why women do stupid stuff like that."

Rachel heard his remark, but kept her attention focused on the television.

Jonathan sighed as he said to his brother, "The last thing I need is you and Rachel giving me a hard time all evening."

"You know," David continued, "I do think it's so funny that I'm the one that Dad was so disappointed in, then here you come with this bombshell. Boy, the irony of that!"

Jonathan glared at his brother. It had been five weeks and he hadn't talked to his father. He'd heard that the church had voted to keep him, so he was probably floating on cloud nine, not giving any of them a second thought. Jonathan tried his best not to think about his father.

Anyway, these last few weeks had been wonderful; he loved having Tracy here with him. It was how he made it through his mother's death and the ordeal with his father. Tracy was right. It made a world of difference having his support. Open support. Oh, they'd garnered strange looks and whispers and, at first, Jonathan was very uneasy, but Tracy stood with his head held high, giving Jonathan a shoulder to lean on. Jonathan realized having Tracy's support was how it should be. He kicked himself at the thought of almost letting Tracy slip away, just because he was worried about what people would think.

The part that pained him most was Angela. She didn't

deserve what he had done to her. He tried to call her several times to apologize, but she refused to talk to him. Her father brought over the annulment papers, telling Jonathan he should rip his heart out with his bare hands. Jonathan had only mumbled an apology, signed the papers, and let Mr. Brooks go on his way. Their anger was understandable. But at the time, Jonathan really thought he could make it work with Angela.

They had yet to make any decisions about the baby. He hated that he wouldn't be there for his child's birth, but with Angela refusing to talk to him, he couldn't discuss anything about the baby. He decided to give her time. He was hopeful that eventually she would allow him to have a relationship with their child. Gay or not, Jonathan felt he could make a positive impact on his child's life.

Kevin had almost as hard a time dealing with the news as his father. He looked genuinely hurt, saying he felt like he'd been lied to all these years. While he eventually said it wouldn't change anything, Jonathan could tell their friendship would never be the same.

"So, can we eat?" David said. "I'm hungry."

"Not until Tracy gets here. He's on his way."

David grunted, then sat down next to Rachel. "You ain't goin' speak?"

"Hello, David."

"What, no hug? You can't hug your brother?"

Rachel looked at David like he had lost his mind.

"Maybe that's what's wrong with our family. We don't show each other enough love!" David pounced on his sister.

"Get off of me! You stink!" Rachel wiggled from under her brother and hit him in the shoulder.

Jonathan laughed. That's the David he remembered. The playful, sober David.

"So, David, are you still clean?"

David leaned back, grinning widely. "Yeah, man, can you believe it? It was one of the last conversations me and Mama had. That's what she called me over for the day she had the heart attack. She asked me to let the drugs go. At the time I thought she was crazy and I promised her just to make her happy, but when she died, it caused me to reevaluate my life. You know I told Daddy I was hospitalized after almost overdosing. Well, I tried to take a hit the night I left the hospital. I felt like Mama was haunting me or something. It was just weird. So, for once I wanted to keep my word to her. I went cold turkey and haven't touched drugs since. I had to get out from under Tawny, though. She ain't about to give the stuff up and being around all that ain't good for me. She swears I left her for another woman. That's why she cut my tires. Right now, I'm staying at a halfway house until I get myself together."

"Wow, I'm impressed," Jonathan said.

"Don't be," Rachel muttered. "Just see how long it lasts. You know, once a dope fiend, always a dope fiend."

David threw a pillow at his sister. "Shut up. You don't have to have any faith in me. I got faith in myself."

"Whatever you say," Rachel responded.

"You seem to forget that once upon a time, I did have it together. Back before the drugs. That's what I'm shooting for again."

Jonathan knew David was right about once having it together. He was a C student in high school, but only because he was too mischievous to take his studies seriously. When he put his mind to something, he accomplished it with no problem. Since he was determined to go to a big-name school, he studied for the SAT and scored a 1200. He figured being smart, as well as an all-star football player, would guarantee his admission. And it did. He got a scholarship to the University of Nebraska. He probably would've graduated if he hadn't gotten hurt and dropped out.

"I'm happy for you, David," Jonathan said. "And I know Mama would be, too."

David smiled broadly. "Might as well make somebody proud."

"Hmmph," Rachel muttered, as she flipped the channel to MTV.

"What about you, Miss Two Babies and no baby daddy?" David said.

"What about me?"

"What are you gonna do? Are you going to let Bobby and his wife have Jordan?"

"You must still be smoking that crack." Rachel frowned. "But the judge says I gotta let them see him. That's where Jordan is now. Nia's in the back asleep."

"Rachel's all right with that, though," Jonathan said, "because she's been spending her time with her new beau."

"What new beau?" David asked.

"Lester Willis."

"Pimply faced Lester Willis?" David laughed.

"He's been seeing a dermatologist, for your information," Rachel responded. "It's a skin condition."

"Oh, now he's Michael Jackson. And she's taking up for him," David said, pointing to Rachel.

"For your information, Lester is a good man. And we're just friends."

"That's who you need to marry," Jonathan said.

"What part of friends are you not getting?" Rachel snapped.

Jonathan smirked. They were just friends now, but he knew

that would change. Lester was persistent and obviously loved Rachel. Jonathan could see it in Lester's eyes at the custody hearing. Anybody could see it. Jonathan was confident that sooner or later, Rachel would give in.

"Lester and Rachel sitting in a tree," David sang.

Rachel rolled her eyes. "Oh, grow up."

"K-I-S-S-I-N-G."

"How old are you again?"

"First comes love, then comes marriage."

"Would you tell him to stop?" Rachel yelled to Jonathan, who was laughing.

None of them heard the front door open. "Some things never change."

"Dad?" Jonathan said. Simon was standing in the door with Tracy behind him. "What are you doing here?"

Tracy stepped forward. "I asked him to come."

The laughter and kidding had stopped. Rachel turned her focus back to the television. No one said anything.

Tracy finally spoke up. "I thought it would be good for him to come. You guys have some family issues and you really need to work this out."

"He's right, you know," Simon said. Jonathan looked on in amazement. Was his father agreeing with Tracy?

"What do you need us for?" Rachel snapped, without taking her eyes off the TV. "You won even without us showing up. You got to keep your pastorship. So why do you need us?"

"I'm your father."

"For real?" Rachel acted surprised.

"Okay," Tracy stepped in, clapping his hands together. "I'm going to play interventionist. In order to make any progress, we have to get past the bitterness."

Rachel looked at Tracy like he was crazy. "Didn't we just

meet you? So why do you think you have the right to psycho-analyze our family?"

Jonathan jumped in to protect Tracy from the family drama. "Tracy is just trying to help."

"Well, didn't nobody ask for his help." Rachel rolled her eyes and turned back to the TV.

Simon turned to her. "Baby girl, I've made a lot of mistakes. When they announced that vote, I didn't feel like I thought I'd feel. I was happy, relieved, ecstatic, and alone. I realized none of that means anything without someone to share it with. Just give me another chance to prove to you I can be a good father."

"So, does that mean you're going to let Zion Hill go?" Rachel asked.

Simon sighed. "I can't do that. I have a mission to serve the Lord. But I'm not going to let you go, either. I want to start over."

"It's a little late to start over," Rachel replied.

"Can we try? I love you kids, all of you. And I need you in my life." Tears formed in his eyes as everyone sat in silence.

"Aw, dang," David spoke up. "Can we cut all this mushy talk? I'm hungry."

Jonathan ignored his brother. "Dad, can you accept me for who I am?"

Simon looked his son straight in the eyes. "I can't do anything but tell you I'll try. That's all I can promise you."

Jonathan smiled tentatively. That was better than nothing. He loved and respected his father so he desperately wanted to have a relationship with him.

"When Tracy showed up on my doorstep last Sunday night, my first inclination was to throw him out, but I couldn't bring myself to do it because it seemed to be the only way I could reach you. I can't say I'm welcoming him with open arms."

Tracy walked over and draped his arms through Jonathan's. "Oh, you'll get there, Dad."

Simon glared at Tracy. "I can say, I won't ever be comfortable with him calling me 'Dad'." Everyone chuckled. Even Rachel let out a small laugh. "But, considering everything else, I'll try to accept. If you're a package deal, I don't have a choice."

"Oh, we're a package," Tracy said, grinning like a Cheshire cat.

Simon smiled, then turned toward his daughter. "Rachel, what do you say?"

Rachel still wasn't totally responsive, but her harsh look had softened. She shrugged her shoulder. "Whatever."

"That's a start. I know Loretta won't be able to rest in peace until we make up. What about you, David?" Everyone turned toward David but he was gone. "David?" Simon called. They all looked toward the kitchen. David was leaning over the stove with a bowl in one hand and the ladle in the other. He looked up when he noticed everyone staring at him.

"I told y'all I'm hungry."

"At least let me set the table." Jonathan laughed. Five minutes later, they were sitting at the small glass table in the dining room. Simon sat at the head. Tracy and Jonathan on one side. Rachel and David on the other. "Dad, will you bless the food?" Jonathan asked.

"Oh, no," David mumbled. "Let me say the grace. It'll be another hour before we eat if we let Dad do it."

Simon laughed. "I would be proud to hear you pray . . . Son."

David smiled at his father. That was the first time he'd called him Son in years. "Bow your heads, please," David began. "Dear God, thank you for the food. Amen."

David ignored the laughter as he reached for the crackers and dug in.

43

SIMON STOOD at the podium. This had to be the best Sunday he'd had in all of his time at Zion Hill. The choir had been great and his sermon seemed to be received just as well. He had preached about judge not, lest ye be judged. For once, he admitted this sermon was directed at him and his family, but he was sure there were others in the congregation who would benefit from the message.

Simon swayed from side to side, letting the soft sounds of the organ fill the air. For some weeks after the church vote, he'd delivered rousing sermons, but knew he was just going through the motions. Now his spirit was lifted again. He asked everyone to join him in a silent prayer. He wanted people to take a few minutes and talk one-on-one with God.

Simon looked at his children in the front row. This was the first time all three of them had been to church together since they were little. His grandkids were both fast asleep, Nia lying across Rachel's lap, Jordan across David's. Simon was surprised Tracy wasn't there, but when he'd asked Jonathan about it during their mix-and-mingle fellowship, Jonathan said Tracy stayed at home because he wanted this to be the family's day.

Both Jonathan and David were silently praying, rocking side to side with the music. Rachel was adjusting Nia's barrettes, an "I wish they'd hurry up" look across her face. Simon smiled. Oh well, he couldn't ask for everything. He was just grateful she'd made it to church on time.

Simon hadn't asked them to come that day. They came because they wanted to. It had been a huge surprise to him.

After dinner Friday night, the four of them sat around and talked about growing up, future plans, and, most of all, missing Loretta. Tracy, intrigued, took it all in. Simon had felt like they were a family again.

He thanked God for leading him to make the right decision and go to Jonathan's. He had prayed all week on what to do. He asked God for a sign to point him in the right direction. He got nothing until Thursday evening when he was leaving the office and accidentally knocked the family portrait off his desk. It fell to the ground and the glass shattered into several little pieces. He had stared at that picture, realizing that was indicative of what had happened to his family.

That's when he decided he was going. He had to glue his family back together. He not only wanted to honor Loretta's wishes but he desperately wanted it for himself.

Simon motioned for the organist to begin winding down. He took a deep breath and said, "Church, I know now is the time I usually call for testimony, but if you don't mind, I'm going to deviate from that a little today because God has placed a testimony on *my* heart."

There were several "Go on, Preacher" and "You release it" comments made from the congregation.

"Y'all know I been through some family drama."

"Boy, do we know that," Sister Hicks loudly proclaimed.

Rachel rolled her eyes. Several people laughed.

"But what family hasn't?" Simon continued, ignoring Sister Hicks again. "How many of you in here can say you're proud of every single thing your child has ever done?"

Many members shook their heads. "I know I can't," one lady shouted.

"Amen to that," another man said.

"But I'm here to tell you, put your faith in God and he'll deliver you and your family through troubled waters."

"Tell it!" someone shouted.

Simon made his way down to the front row where his children sat. "Church, if you will excuse me for just a moment. This here is for my kids." He focused all his attention on Rachel, Jonathan, and David. "I take the blame for some of what you've become. Some, not all," he said smiling, before becoming serious again. "I wanted to build Zion Hill up so bad that I didn't realize I was tearing you down in the process, David," he said, facing his eldest son. "The devil was at work on you and instead of forming an army to battle him, I left you out there alone. For that I'm sorry. I know you said you're clean now, but I want to help you stay that way. I want to show you that I'm proud of you no matter what."

Simon turned to Jonathan. "And you know the issues I have with you. But I'll pray for myself, that I will be strong enough to accept your choice. I want to let my love overpower any negativity I may feel about your lifestyle. I hope that you will be patient with me while I work through that.

"And Rachel," he said, turning to her. "You are a beautiful young woman who has made some mistakes. But we all have and I'm sorry that I withdrew my love as a punishment."

Rachel started tearing up.

"I know repairing our family won't be easy, but I want to try," Simon continued. "I love you all and I can only ask that you forgive me. Can you do that?"

He looked at each one. All three hesitated, then nodded their heads simultaneously. Rachel lifted Nia's head and gently laid it on the pew as she stood up. She took a couple of steps, then threw her arms around her father's neck. David and Jonathan followed suit. All four of them began crying as the church loudly clapped.

Simon eased away from his children's grip, still holding on to their hands. He looked at his congregation. Several members were in tears. "Praise the Lord. I got my family back." He lifted his arms, still grasping Rachel's hand on one side and David's on the other. "Let the church say amen!"